Praise for Jeanette Grey's *Get What You Need*

"I enjoyed the writing style and I liked Marsh and Greg—separately and together."

~ *Dear Author*

"I just love this endearing and lovely story, and I highly recommend that you read it as well!"

~ *Prism Book Alliance*

"I am always looking out for good college-age stories, and this one just hit all my sweet spots. And there may have been some absolutely hot dirty talk going on...just in case you like your sweet with a little kick. "

~ *Love Bytes*

"*Get What You Need* was fun, angsty, sweet and down right sexy! Good lord was it sexy. If you are into the sexy geek and hot joke trope, you don't want to miss this."

~ *Boys in Our Books*

"What a gift this woman has for telling you a story that could be so true. It comes off so real that it feels like you are at the house with them living throughout their craziness."

~ *MM Good Book Reviews*

"New Adult fans should absolutely read this erotic romance."

~ *The Book Vixen*

Look for these titles by

Jeanette Grey

Now Available:

Unacceptable Risk

Take What You Want

When It's Right

Get What You Need

Through the Static

Get What You Need

Jeanette Grey

SAMHAIN
PUBLISHING

Samhain Publishing, Ltd.
11821 Mason Montgomery Road, 4B
Cincinnati, OH 45249
www.samhainpublishing.com

Get What You Need

Print ISBN: 978-1-61922-603-6
Digital ISBN: 978-1-61922-228-1

Editing by Jennifer Miller
Cover by Lou Harper

First Samhain Publishing, Ltd. electronic publication: July 2014
First Samhain Publishing, Ltd. print publication: July 2015

Dedication

Dedicated to the overworked graduate student of my heart, Scott.

With additional special thanks to Brighton Walsh and Heather McGovern, as well as all of the ladies of Bad Girlz Write and the Capital Region RWA.

Chapter One

"You're seriously staying in tonight?"

Greg looked up from his computer screen, peering over the rims of his glasses. Ronnie was going through Greg's closet. Again. With a sigh, Greg shook his head and turned back to the data he'd been trying to make sense of all night. "Yeah. Too much to do."

One of the peaks on the graph just didn't make any sense. Biting the inside of his cheek, he reached for the notebook propped up on his desk. He opened it and scowled. Damn it, he was sure he'd brought home those printouts.

"Hey, Ronnie? You didn't happen to grab my stuff off the printer, did you?" He took another glance up, only to frown even harder at the shirt Ronnie was holding against his chest. "That one? Really?" It was Greg's favorite.

Ronnie turned, grinning broadly. "I think it'd look good on me. Brings out my skin tone, right?"

He'd made up his mind, then. Greg sighed. "I actually need that one back this time."

One of these days, he was going to take his own turn rummaging through Ronnie's closet, only it wouldn't be to borrow Ronnie's stuff. He just wanted his own crap back.

Taking that for the assent it was, Ronnie said, "Thanks. You're the best."

Ronnie tugged at the hem of the shirt he was wearing, and there was a flash of bare, dark skin. The rise of a hipbone cresting over the waistband of his jeans. Greg looked away before he could take in any more. He worried the corner of his notebook between his fingers and shifted his feet against the base of his chair. The back of his neck felt warm.

Christ, maybe he should go out. If he was looking at his officemate-slash-housemate-slash-best-friend like that, it had *really* been too long since he'd gotten laid. Way, way too long. He huffed out a deep breath and punched the side of his thigh. No. He didn't have time for that, and one-night stands never worked out for him, anyway. Not that relationships did, either, if his last disaster of a breakup was anything to go by.

No, he was better off here. Alone.

"Whaddaya think?"

The rust color did look good on Ronnie's complexion. Probably better than it ever had against Greg's paler one, and it fit him better, too. Greg was a little too broad in the shoulders for it, really. He smiled less than enthusiastically and gave a vague thumbs-up. "Looks like it was made for you."

"Right?" Ronnie preened in front of the mirror for a minute.

Greg rolled his eyes. "You know, I could take you clothes shopping sometime." It wasn't something he offered to do very often. As the resident queer in their department, he didn't like reinforcing that kind of stereotype. His sense of style wasn't even all that good, relatively speaking. His mom always told him his engineer genes must have overpowered his gay ones. Really, the only thing he had to recommend him in that area was that he did his laundry about twice as often as Ronnie did.

"Nah, I'm broke. And anyway, this is more fun." Turning back toward Greg, Ronnie smoothed a hand over his chest. "You sure you don't want to come with us?"

"Maybe next time." Grimacing, Greg gestured at all the work spread out across his desk.

"Suit yourself." Ronnie smacked the top of the doorframe on his way through, then stopped short, twisting to poke his head back in. "Oh! Almost forgot. Your printouts are in my bag." He jerked a thumb down the hall. "Left it on my desk."

Oh, thank God. Greg really didn't have time to run to campus tonight, and he needed to finish crunching these numbers this weekend if he was going to get his proposal for the symposium done on time. "I'd say I owe you, but I did just give you the shirt off my back."

Ronnie laughed. "Dude, your closet is not your back. You totally still owe me one." He made the shape of a gun with his hand and pointed it at Greg before cocking it and firing. "You're slipping."

There was a little twinge in the base of Greg's gut. He *was* letting things slip. Too many things. Still, he waved it off. "Whatever. Go. Have fun. Wash my shirt before you give it back."

"Don't I always? Don't answer that." Ronnie grinned. "See you tomorrow."

"Sure, sure." Greg shook his head as the sound of Ronnie thundering down the stairs echoed through the house. He stared after him wistfully for a second, then mentally slapped himself. Next weekend, if the guys from the engineering department went out again, he'd go. He'd definitely be caught up by then. Just to prove it to himself, he pulled up his calendar program, but one glance at all those angry blocks of color had him wincing and X'ing out before he could linger too long.

Maybe next weekend he'd be free. He just had to work his ass off every minute between now and then. He blew out a deep breath. The house would be quiet tonight, at least. Nodding to himself, he refocused on the numbers and graphs in front of him.

Almost an hour crept by before he reached absently for his notebook again. He blinked. Oh, right. Those graphs he needed were still in Ronnie's room. His spine made a couple of ominous, creaking cracks as he leaned back in his chair and stretched his arms up over his head. Setting his glasses aside, he dug the heels of his hands into his eyes. They were gritty and dry. Probably time for a break anyway.

He climbed out of his chair and shoved his feet into his shoes, taking a quick glance around as he did. Crap, his room was a mess. Not as bad as the other guys he shared this house with, but still. Not how he liked it. Grimacing at the piles of books and papers everywhere, he at least picked up the couple of plates and mugs he'd accumulated over the past few days.

Arms full of dirty dishes, he picked his way across the room and went out into the hall. Someone had left the light on. Typical. He took the stairs two at a time down to the shared living area. Out of instinct, he peeked his head around the corner. Nobody on the couch. He got to the kitchen to find it deserted, too. He heaved out a sigh. This had been what he'd wanted—a quiet, productive night in with no distractions, but one of the perks of living with a bunch of other grad students was always being able to find somebody to talk to when you needed to unwind for a minute. His shoulders sagged. Oh, well.

He put his dishes down in the sink, hesitating there for a second. Things were piling up on the counter, but no. Not his job this weekend. He grabbed a Coke from the fridge and switched off the light before turning to head back up to his room to slog through a few more hours of data tables and graphs.

Only... No. He shouldn't. On the threshold between the kitchen and the hallway, he paused, rocking on his heels. He should just go straight upstairs, he shouldn't stop and...it wasn't like his housemate, Marsh, was even going to be there or anything. So it wouldn't do any harm to check real quick. No. Yes. No.

Oh, who was he kidding? His breathing picked up as he diverted from his intended path, down the little hallway and around the corner.

Only to find the last little bedroom tucked under the stairs just as empty as the rest of the house.

Talk about pathetic. His stomach curled just a little with disappointment. It was stupid, really. He leaned against the doorway and rubbed his hand over his face, then cupped the back of his neck. Hell, it was probably a good thing Marsh wasn't there. Greg didn't exactly have an excuse to be stopping by. They didn't have anything in common, and every time Greg had tried to make small talk this past month, he'd crashed and burned. God forbid he actually managed to carry on a real conversation with a hot guy, and worse, one who didn't speak engineer.

Grumbling to himself, Greg stretched his neck from side to side. It had been a fluke that Marsh had even ended up living there. He was an undergrad, though at least he was a senior. A history major. And a jock. He'd been a last-minute addition to their lease when their other housemate had had to withdraw at the last minute to deal with a family crisis. Facing down the prospect of each having to chip in an extra share of the rent, Greg and the guys had posted an ad on Craigslist, given a little prayer, and the next day, Marshall Sulkowski had shown up with two duffel bags and a rumpled check.

And Greg had been finding reasons to loiter around the entrance to his room ever since.

He popped the top of his soda and took a long gulp of it. Rubbed the back of his wrist over his mouth.

Marsh's room hadn't really changed much since he'd moved in. The walls were still mostly bare, the closet open and half empty. The only things that marked it as lived-in at all were the unmade bed, the short stack of books beside it, and the baseball jersey and glove on the dresser.

"You looking for Marsh?"

Greg just about went out of his skin. He caught his Coke before he could drop it and managed not to actually jump as he twisted around to see his other housemate, Jason, standing in the hall.

"Oh. Um. Hey. No." Could Greg sound any less smooth? He pushed off the wall, fidgeting with the can in his hand as he did. He held it up. "Just needed a caffeine break. Thought I'd see if anyone else was home."

"Think it's just you and me."

Greg took a better look at Jason. He was dressed casually, if not as scrubby as Greg was in his T-shirt and sweats. "Thought you were heading out with Ronnie and the other guys?"

Jason shrugged. "I stopped by but didn't stay." He motioned toward the stairs. "Early night for me. Group meeting at eight tomorrow."

Poor bastard. "That sucks."

"Tell me about it." Jason was in one of the largest research groups at the university. It was prestigious, and it would be great for his career when he graduated, but in the meantime it meant putting up with an inattentive advisor and meetings at god-awful hours on Saturdays. He turned and gave a little wave over his shoulder. "Good night."

"Night."

Jason headed up the stairs, leaving Greg alone. He took one last glance at Marsh's room. Nothing like getting caught hovering like that to make a guy feel like a creep. He knocked the side of his fist against the wall, then made his way toward the stairs himself, turning off lights as he went.

One quick stop at Ronnie's room for his printouts, and then he holed himself up in his own again, the door ajar and loud rock pounding through his headphones. He resettled his glasses on his nose and cracked his knuckles. He looked at all the books strewn out across his desk. This was his life. And that was fine.

And with that he dug back in.

Apparently, he dug in deeply enough that he wasn't sure if hours or minutes had passed when something rose above the sounds of drums and guitars and the sight of numbers on his screen. At first, he thought he was just hearing part of the bassline, but then he turned the volume down and looked up, and—

"Shit." He put one hand to his heart while with the other he scrambled to pull his headphones off his ears. "You. Um."

Because that was Marsh standing at Greg's door. Marsh, with his sandy hair all mussed to look like sex, his blue eyes and his *arms*. Christ, the veins standing out on his forearms, the thick muscle under golden skin, the bulges of his biceps beneath the rolled-up sleeves of that tight black button-down.

That was *Marsh* standing at his door.

And Greg was cool. He was totally cool as he set his headphones aside and pawed at his glasses to get them off his face, because, no. Marsh did not need to see those. "Um," Greg said again. "What?"

Marsh flashed an easy grin, just a glimpse of perfect, white teeth between plush lips. "You okay?"

"Yeah. Of course. Yes." Did Greg not look okay? He ruffled a hand through his hair, then rubbed at his eyes. He gestured futilely at his monitor. "Just. Working."

He winced at himself. Working at—he glanced at the clock—midnight on a Friday night. Sure, he was cool.

"Yeah?"

There was something to the way Marsh spoke. Something tired. Greg didn't quite know what to do with that. So he just tilted his head to the side. "Yeah." And cool or not, Greg should be able to be a little bit smoother than this, but it was midnight on a Friday and he'd been working all night, and Marsh didn't ever seek Greg out. Greg scrunched up his brow. "Are you… Can I… Did you need something?"

There was no other reason he'd be here, right? No other reason that wasn't the prelude to some sort of really cheesy porn. Not that Greg had ever entertained fantasies about just that kind of thing. Nope, not at all. He swallowed hard and shifted to rest his arm across his lap.

"I—" Marsh scratched at the back of his neck, crossing one ankle over the other. He glanced behind himself toward the hall. "Er, Jason said you were looking for me?"

Shit. "No," Greg said, too fast, and did Marsh just frown a little? No, he couldn't have. "I mean. I was, earlier. I was taking a break. From all of this." He pointed at the papers strewn across his desk. "And I was seeing if anyone else was home."

"And you checked in my room?"

"Well, you're someone aren't you?" Then it occurred to Greg, "I thought Jason crashed out a couple of hours ago."

Marsh shrugged. "Ran into him when he was coming out of the bathroom. He looked half asleep."

"Oh."

"Yeah."

"Well." Greg gave himself a little bit of credit. This was one of the longest conversations he'd had with Marsh. That was worth something, right?

But not as much as Marsh shifting his weight, looking around...and then walking right through Greg's door to plop himself down on Greg's bed. "So, you ready to take another break?"

Oh God. Maybe this was a cheesy porn. Greg pinched his elbow as hard as he could, but nothing happened. Because this was real.

Cool, he reminded himself. *You're cool.* He glanced back at his computer screen. He still had a million things to do, but it wasn't like he was going to accomplish any more of them tonight, not after this. Turning off the monitor, he nodded. After another deep breath, he swiveled in his seat until he was facing

Marsh. Marsh on his bed. “Sure,” he said, voice way more level than he felt.

As easy as it had appeared when he’d shown up, something in Marsh’s posture seemed to relax. “Awesome.” He shoved himself to the end of Greg’s bed and bent over, one finger extending out as he looked over the portion of Greg’s movie collection that hadn’t managed to migrate to the living room yet. Greg chewed on the inside of his cheek and was about to suggest that there was more of a selection downstairs when Marsh’s gaze caught. His hand darted out, and he pulled the case for the Abrams *Star Trek* reboot, holding it up as he twisted. “This any good?”

“Well,” Greg started, then stopped himself. Marsh didn’t care that the purists thought it was a travesty, or that the Spock-Uhura romance didn’t make any sense. He *definitely* didn’t care what the slash community thought of it. He lifted one shoulder, as nonchalant as he could be. “I like it.”

“Do you mind?” Marsh was already reaching to pop the tray on the Blu-Ray player.

Of course Greg didn’t mind. A movie would sure be easier than trying to carry out a conversation or whatever else Marsh might want to do. In the set of all possible options for spending time together, watching a geeky sci-fi movie was probably the least threatening one Greg could imagine.

But even that didn’t make any sense. Part of him wanted to just go with it, but his thirteen-year-old spidey sense was tingling too hotly to ignore. The last time a popular kid had tried to spend time with Greg, he’d been looking for homework to copy. There wasn’t any homework here, wasn’t anything Marsh could possibly be trying to use Greg for, but still. The whole idea made his stomach roil.

He must have hesitated too long, because even as he was opening the case, Marsh looked back at him, his brow furrowed. “We could do something else if you don’t wanna.”

"No." The response came automatically enough, but Greg didn't feel quite so confident about it. He hesitated. "I mean, no, but..."

"But?"

"But..." Fuck it. "What are you doing here? You just, what, want to hang out?"

And was that—it couldn't be. Was that *hurt* in Marsh's expression? "Is that so weird?"

Greg bit off a raw little hint of a laugh. "Yeah. I mean, we've been living together for, what? A month now? And when have you ever just stopped by to say hi?"

Marsh winced, and yeah, maybe that wasn't fair. There was something else going on, though, too, Greg could see it. Part of him wanted to take it all back, but the bigger part wanted the answer.

"Look." Marsh set the movie case down on the bed beside him with force, like the sound of the impact should have resounded in the room. The mattress was too soft to make a thud, but there was gravity there, and his arm looked achingly heavy as he braced his elbow on his knee. "I had a really shitty night. And a shitty day."

He looked up, and any second-guessing went out the window. That self-assured smile was gone, and the dullness in his eyes made him look more tired than Greg had really realized a happy, popular, good-looking guy could be. For just an instant, it all slipped, and Marsh seemed ready to break. Greg had been nursing a bit of a crush on the guy for a while now, but that split second of vulnerability made it feel like Greg's chest was about to crack open, too. Marsh ground his teeth and grated out, all in one breath, "And I don't want to be alone."

The crack split wider. It wasn't homework Marsh was looking for, or anything else he could use Greg for. It was just company. Greg could empathize with that. It was all Greg had wanted himself.

But Marsh was shaking his head, pushing off the bed. "Or not. Whatever."

Greg moved before he could stop himself, stepping right into Marsh's space, blocking his way and standing over him, his throat dry. Marsh looked up and sat back down. Leaning forward, Greg picked up the movie case and pulled the disc out. When he squatted down in front of Marsh, it put them so close that Greg could feel the warmth of Marsh's big, lean body through the air. He chanced one glance up at Marsh before looking to slot the disc into the player. "It's a good movie," was all he said.

One second's pause, and the whirring of the Blu-Ray was the only sound in the room. Then Marsh breathed out hard. "Yeah?"

"I own it, don't I?" As if Marsh had been asking if it was really a good movie—like he hadn't been actually asking if he could stay.

"Yeah. Good point." And apparently that was that. Marsh kicked off his shoes and pushed himself up the bed, stretching out all along one side of it, propping himself against Greg's pillow.

Somehow in the process, his shirt had bunched up underneath him, and there was a thin, tan line of flesh exposed above the waistband of his jeans, a hint of a trail of dusky hair. Shadows hinting at the dips and crests of abdominals and hip.

Greg licked his lips, then forced his gaze away. There was nowhere to sit in his room except this bed and his office chair, and fuck if he was going to spend another minute there after hunching in front of his computer screen all night. He eyed the space beside Marsh. It looked so inviting.

Marsh had found the remote sitting on Greg's nightstand, and he turned on the TV. The room filled with sound, but Greg didn't even have to ask before Marsh was turning it down.

"Okay?" Marsh asked.

And, yeah, it was. Loud enough to enjoy but not so loud that sleeping housemates down the hall would be upset. But Greg wasn't okay. Not by a long shot.

Nodding, he stood, tugging the hem of his own shirt down. His ancient, oversized T-shirt. Even if he'd known this was going to happen, he couldn't have planned to look any worse. Not that it mattered. Shit, he needed to relax.

His gaze hit on the Coke can next to his computer. "I'm, uh, gonna grab something to drink. You want anything?"

Marsh nodded without taking his eyes off the screen. "Sure. Beer would be good." His eyes darted toward Greg. "Or whiskey if you're feeling really crazy."

"That's me," Greg said drily. He traced a little circle in the air with his finger. "Life of the party."

Fortunately, Marsh was kind enough to only dignify that with a grunt of a laugh. Greg pushed out of the room and down the stairs, where it was all dark and deserted. He opened the fridge and peered inside. The whole top shelf was beer, and Greg had to think for a second. He'd seen Marsh with a beer at some point, and it hadn't been the piss Ronnie liked. He took his best guess and grabbed two Sam Adamses, then shut the door. He hesitated for just a second.

"Fuck it," he mumbled to himself and threw open the liquor cabinet and grabbed the bottle of Jack he'd put there just the weekend before.

Thus armed, he made his way upstairs. At the threshold to his room, he had to do another double take. Yup, that really was one of the star members of the baseball team laid out on his bed. His knees went a little weak, but he had it together. He was fine. Cool.

"Grab the lights?" Marsh asked.

Oh God. "Right." With an elbow, he hit the switch, leaving the room in darkness but for the blue glow from the screen. He wavered, then went ahead and closed the door, too. For the noise.

Marsh didn't comment on it. He just held his hand out for his beer, and Greg passed it over. He set the whiskey down on the shelf above their heads without comment and twisted the top off his own beer. And then there was nothing left to do but go for it. Sucking in a deep breath, he sat on the bed beside Marsh. He did it gingerly, probably way too carefully, so the mattress hardly rocked. Wadding up the other pillow, he wedged it behind his back so he could sit up against the headboard.

It was only a double bed, so he was inches from Marsh, his shin so close to his knee, their elbows almost touching. It sent electricity through Greg's body, and he pulled at the hem of his T-shirt, suddenly grateful for the darkness and for his decision to wear briefs beneath his sweats. He took a big gulp of his beer and tried to focus on the screen as the ads and previews finally gave way to the opening of the film.

Warmth brushing his side made him startle. Marsh was holding out the cap of the bottle of Jack, the inside dark with liquid. He was propped up on his side, free hand touching Greg's arm. "You look like you need this more than I do."

What? Oh. "Sorry." He willed his body to just *relax*, but he couldn't help it. All that stress and work, and now this—this proximity and this man on his bed. He was just a ball of tension. He eyed the whiskey.

"Just one. I'm not trying to get you drunk."

Pity, that. It would probably do Greg good. Resolved, he took the cap and threw it back, grimacing at the burn before he passed it to Marsh who refilled it and downed it with practiced ease. He paused, then took a second shot. Before he closed the bottle, he glanced at Greg, giving him a chance to ask for another shot before twisting the cap on tight and setting it aside.

And the booze couldn't possibly be affecting Greg, but there was something about the heat of it, still echoing in his throat. It made him feel like he could let go a little. Like he didn't have to hold himself quite so carefully. He kicked his legs out and rolled his neck. His spine was all kinked. He glanced at Marsh.

Marsh hadn't hesitated to make himself comfortable. He looked as easy as could be, and maybe Greg knew part of it was an act. Maybe he'd seen beneath that disaffectedness, if only for a moment. It still didn't make it any less difficult for Greg to be so calm.

Finally, he pulled the pillow out from behind his back and lay down. Marsh didn't react, and it was fine. Just two men lying beside each other on a small bed, watching a movie.

He looked at the screen, but he didn't see a thing.

Not the fight in the bar or the first time Spock was a dick at the Academy, not the freaking sword fight on the drilling platform in the middle of the sky. All he could focus on was the heat of the body beside him and the ripples of warmth and want winding their way through his skin. He licked his lips and shifted and kept to his own damn side of the bed.

And then Marsh kicked his leg out, and that was his knee against Greg's. Marsh had to realize they were touching, and he was a sports guy. That couldn't be okay. He probably knew Greg was gay, and what about this could possibly be okay? But he didn't move, and the heat in Greg's spine was ready to boil over. He was so keyed in on this one bright point of awareness, of contact.

Marsh shuffled again, and his arm hit Greg's. And Greg was going to explode. It had been so long, and Marsh smelled so good, like amber and pine and something clean. Something that seared right through Greg and left him ready to go out of his skin. He was aching and hard and he wanted...

Something that was never going to happen.

It was just a crush. With the pretext of picking up the beer he'd left on the floor beside the bed, Greg rolled over, carefully disengaging himself from the places where their bodies had been touching. He instantly felt cold. After taking a long drink, he set the beer down and resettled on his back. There was space between them again, and that was good. For the sake of Greg's sanity, that was *necessary.*

Marsh didn't make any further overtures, and bit by bit, Greg started to relax. He'd seen the movie enough times that he was able to figure out where they were, and maybe he was a little hyperaware of Marsh and where he was on the bed, but there wasn't any harm in that. Other than the twinge of disappointment in his gut each moment Marsh didn't choose to close the gap between them again, it wasn't hurting anyone.

Toward the end of the movie, he was actually pretty engrossed, his heart rising through the victory lap, and he knew full well that the end was coming. He was still surprised, though, when the credits starts to roll. Marsh fumbled over their heads and found the right remote from the pile and pressed a button.

The room went dark and quiet all at once. There was just the faint glow of the still-powered-up TV, thin lines of light from the slats in the blinds. There was just silence.

Just the sound of breathing.

And that was all it took. Suddenly, although they weren't touching, they were entirely too close. Greg could feel the static, could feel the inches between their bodies.

His swallow was an audible gulp in the quiet and the dark. He turned his neck, only to find eyes staring back at him. Marsh's gaze was a buzz of electricity, something that had Greg lighting up from the inside out. Everything blurred except those twin points, and beneath them the curl of Marsh's lips.

Marsh closed his eyes and shook his head. Beneath his breath, he muttered, "This is such a bad idea."

Greg didn't have time to ask what he was talking about, because then Marsh was opening his eyes and propping himself up on his elbow, twisting and leaning forward, and putting his hand on Greg's face. Greg sucked in a breath, all harshness and too loud in the space.

"What are you—"

It was confusion and want and disbelief, a complete short-circuiting of his brain at the first press of lips, and he froze. His hand stuttered in the air, and his eyes were wide, everything cracking. Because never, not through the month of stilted not-quite conversation, not through the sudden appearance of this man in his door or the way they'd almost touched...*never* had it occurred to Greg that he might not be the only one to feel this way.

Air rushed into his lungs, realization dawning, and it was too impossible a thing. But the second kiss was a question, and the answer was yes, of course it was yes, if Greg could only get it out. He scrabbled at the sheets, wanting to haul Marsh closer. But Marsh was drawing away, dragging his fingers down Greg's cheek, breathing out a laugh that sounded like an apology, and Greg made a choked little noise. He surged forward. In a blur, he latched on to the collar of Marsh's shirt and reeled him in, closed his eyes and pressed his mouth to Marsh's and licked the surprise from his lips.

And it was...perfect, really. Marsh tasted warm and real, a tang of hops on his tongue as he opened up and let Greg suck at his bottom lip. All the curled-up energy from lying beside Marsh leapt from Greg's skin, electricity crackling through the wet push and pull and the grip of Marsh's hands on Greg's hips. Greg groaned into the kiss, because he'd been wanting this for so long, had been starved for someone to touch him and to let him touch, and Marsh was gorgeous. Was so out of his league, but he was here. Greg got his hand up under Marsh's shirt and pressed his palm to smooth skin. Marsh's stomach was all muscle, the trace of hair down the middle so sensitive as

Marsh shuddered and pulled Greg closer. Rising up, Greg pushed Marsh back and climbed into his lap, straddling him, and maybe this was too fast, but it felt so good.

"Yeah," Marsh said, one big hand coming up to cup Greg's neck, holding his mouth there, and a thrill went through Greg. Being held in place like that made him harder, made him want nothing more than to rub himself off against Marsh's thigh. Maybe, someday, Marsh would really pin him down and take him apart, put all those muscles to the task of turning Greg to liquid, but tonight he wanted something different.

He ground his hips into Marsh's, shivering when Marsh grabbed his ass and thrust up. Heat pooled deep in Greg's belly at the answering hardness against his own, and he wanted skin, wanted the musk of arousal and the taste of pre-come and the fullness of hot flesh in his mouth.

"Wanna suck you," he mumbled into Marsh's mouth, and Marsh gave a pained little grunt that seared Greg to his bones.

There was a hand on Greg's shoulder, the one on his ass coming to rest on his hip, and both urged him down. "Yeah, that sounds so good."

Greg scrambled, crawling down Marsh's body and taking needy bites at him, getting damp fabric between his teeth. At his navel, Greg pushed Marsh's shirt up to run his tongue along the ridges and dips of his abdomen, to taste the salt from his skin. Marsh's hand pressed into the space between them, tugging at the fasteners of his pants, and Greg nosed down into the gaps, pushing fingers out of the way to part his lips around the clothed head of Marsh's cock.

Marsh groaned and shoved at the waistband of his underwear, and Greg loved this. It had him aching and desperate, the way Marsh arched and the push at the back of his neck. The long, flushed line of Marsh's dick, the tip slick, and the neat thatch of gold-brown hair, the scent of male wanting. Greg flicked his gaze up Marsh's body, and his own dick throbbed inside his briefs.

Oh God. Marsh was a wet dream. His eyes were locked on Greg, his chin tilted back, and Greg loved the sharp point of his jaw, the shadow of his stubble in the dim light. His abdomen gleamed, and he wrapped a hand around himself and tilted it toward Greg's lips.

Greg didn't hesitate. There was the low frisson of shame, because he shouldn't love this so much, but he did. He loved a good mouthful of cock and the way the head shoved up against his throat; he loved letting go like this. He pushed himself farther than he could take, only letting himself up when he choked, and then he bobbed, up and down. What he couldn't fit in his mouth, he stroked with his hand. He sucked and licked, and he *loved* this. He ground himself into the mattress, making his lips nice and soft, slurping and working at the underside with his tongue. Marsh was all little gasping sounds, threading his fingers through Greg's hair and whispering, "Yes," and "Oh," and "Like that."

Marsh rocked up into Greg's mouth. His thigh was tense beneath Greg's palm, the muscles of his abdomen rigid. Greg bobbed faster, tightening his fist.

Marsh keened, fingers tugging hard at Greg's hair, and Greg had to shut his eyes, because that felt so good. He gave his own little whine, cock kicking, balls going tight. And he wouldn't move, he'd take it all, drink it down, and then it was pouring in. Marsh bowed off the bed as he rasped Greg's name. Salty come slicked Greg's throat, and he swallowed and chased every shudder, every spasm until Marsh let go. His hips sank back down, and he gave a little nudge at Greg's shoulder that Greg ignored. He laved Marsh clean and sucked at the tip until the sounds spilling out of Marsh turned from wrung-out pleasure to the faintest lick of distress.

He let Marsh slip, softening, from his tongue and flexed his jaw as he rose up onto his knees. Holding Marsh's gaze, he dragged the back of his wrist over his lips. They were swollen, probably looked red and used. Marsh reached for him, and he came readily, tugging at the drawstring of his sweats, and then they were pushing them down together. Marsh got a hand around Greg's aching dick and stroked it, fast and punishing as Greg panted and fell into his mouth. It was less a kiss and more a sharing of air, more just a place to rest and connect and feel. Marsh's other hand was on Greg's cheek, holding him and grounding him, and Greg pressed his forehead hard against Marsh's brow.

Pulling away, panting for breath, Marsh swiped his thumb through the slick at the tip of Greg's cock and twisted his wrist. "Fucking loved your mouth, so filthy, you felt so—"

Greg didn't hear the rest. He shook his head and buried his face against the hot, damp skin of Marsh's neck as he shot across his naked hip. Shaking pleasure made his vision go blank.

And he was laughing and pulsing and convulsing, because, God, he'd needed that.

When he started to come back to himself, Marsh was easing him down onto his side. He rolled easily enough, sliding off onto his back, and he flung his arm across his eyes as he let out a deep, long sigh. The thrumming beneath his skin was something good now, something sated and satisfied, and he hadn't felt this easy and pliant in months. Rubbing his hand over his face, he looked down at himself. He was still fully clothed except that his pants were around his thighs, his cock lying half-hard and wet against his stomach.

The mattress shifted beneath him. Marsh was tucking himself away and refastening his jeans, dragging a hand through his hair as he sat up against the headboard. Somehow, he managed to look composed enough. Greg gave a little groan as he tugged his own sweats to rest on his hips and pulled his shirt down.

Without a word, Marsh reached for the bottle of Jack on the shelf. He uncapped it and took a big swig straight from the bottle before passing it over. Greg almost didn't take it, but the lingering taste of come wouldn't stay sexy for long. He paused as he grabbed the bottle. It was lighter than it had been.

His gaze darted to Marsh's face, looking deeper, and it was dark, but his cheeks were flushed. Maybe with more than just the sex. Greg had been so aware of him all through the movie, but he'd been paying attention to his closeness. Not to what he'd been doing. The hazy afterglow started to fade, and a pit opened up in Greg's stomach. He sipped at the whiskey before handing it back. Marsh capped it and set it aside.

Marsh pulled a face as he sat up higher and rose. He stumbled a little on his way to Greg's desk. He yanked a couple tissues from the box there and hiked up his shirt to dab at the mess Greg had left on his skin.

"Sorry," Greg started.

Marsh shook his head, a lazy grin curving parted lips. "No apologizing." He came over to the bed and bent down, bracing himself with an arm against the mattress as he ducked to press a slow, filthy kiss to Greg's mouth. "You were so good at that."

It was a compliment, but it left Greg cold. Marsh was gorgeous and popular. He probably had a lot of mouths to compare Greg's to. The pit in Greg's stomach deepened into something gaping. He'd asked Marsh why he was here—he'd been so sure there'd had to be a reason.

Maybe this had been it. Maybe he'd known Greg was a repressed little queer who'd suck anything if he could just get up the courage to let himself go. The shutters fell, all the tension seeping right back in.

He forced a smile, touching Marsh's neck for just a second before letting his hand fall away. "It was good." He steadied himself and leaned back.

It had been *so* good, but that didn't mean anything. Especially if Marsh had been drunk. If Marsh had been drunk, Greg shouldn't even have touched him, but he hadn't been thinking beyond the heat and the press and the pleasure of being kissed. Of having all that attention on him. It had made him feel...special.

He shook his head at himself as Marsh stood. Steeling himself, Greg looked up at him and tried for nonchalance. "You going to be okay getting back to your room by yourself?"

Something strange passed across Marsh's face. But then it was gone. Maybe it hadn't been there in the first place, just a trick of the shadows in the dimness. Marsh straightened his shoulders and gave a little laugh as he crossed his arms over his chest. "Yeah. Pretty sure I'll be fine."

Marsh unfurled his arms, and his hand twitched at his side. He stuck his hands in his pockets and turned away. Pulling the door open, he poked his toe at the jamb. "Thanks," he said, not looking up. "For the movie. And everything."

"Anytime." And shit, Greg shouldn't have said that. He'd do it again, but Marsh didn't need to know that.

"Great," Marsh said, and it sounded like relief. He met Greg's eyes and nodded. "Good night." His voice was warmer now, and yeah. Greg would do it again.

"Good night."

Marsh let himself out and closed the door behind him. The instant he heard the click, Greg dropped to lie flat on his back and pulled a pillow over his face, breathing into it to try to calm his heart. He'd made a dent in all the work he had to do, and he'd sort of gotten laid. He'd gotten everything he wanted, and yet he felt just as frustrated as he had when the night had begun.

He shoved the pillow away and lifted his head to glance at the piles of papers that still needed his attention, then down the length of his body. At the spatters of white drying on his shirt. He might have gotten what he wanted, but it hadn't been the plan.

A quiet, productive night in, his ass.

Dropping his head, he ran his hand through his hair. Somehow, things had gotten completely out of control.

He didn't know what he was going to do about it.

Chapter Two

There were days Marshall Sulkowski really, really, really didn't want to get out of bed.

Shit, how long had he been dozing now? He dragged his head up and off his pillow to glance at the clock. At the sight of double digits, he groaned and face-planted again, pulling the covers up over his head. Not that it did any good. It was too fucking bright in his room. Maybe Yulia could use her ninja-girl skills and make him some curtains or something. Someday. Then again, that would mean he'd have to ask her to make some, and she and he both knew that wasn't going to happen. One more thing to add to his list of stuff to see if he could find at the thrift store.

He rolled over and punched his pillow down, but it wasn't any use. Giving up, he tossed the covers off and stretched his arms over his head, then scrubbed his hand across his face, rubbing at the crud in his eyes. For a long minute, he stared up at the ceiling without really seeing anything.

This wasn't where he'd been planning to wake up. He was supposed to—

—Fuck, fuck, *fuck*, he wasn't going there. Because, sure, maybe he'd finally made a move, and maybe he'd even gotten what he wanted, and maybe he'd gotten kicked out on his ass before he could even get up the guts to ask if he could stay, but whatever. It was done. He'd gotten laid. He knew what was between Greg London's legs now, and it had been awesome, and he wasn't going to sit here stewing and feeling like shit about it all day.

Who was he kidding? Of course he was.

He groaned into his arm. That was it. He had to get out of here.

Decided, he rolled his carcass out of bed and stomped over to his closet. He found a pair of jeans and a sweatshirt that didn't look too bad and crammed a fresh-ish undershirt and boxers into his backpack, shoving down whatever papers and books he'd hauled home from campus the day before. Everything he needed for practice later that afternoon was already in his locker at school. Shoes and a baseball cap, and he figured he was good to go.

Before opening his bedroom door, he checked himself, though, listening with one ear to the wood. It didn't sound like there was anyone out there, but you never knew. He really didn't need to run into anyone right now. Preferably not Jason—who knew what he'd heard last night. *Definitely* not Greg.

"Goddammit," he swore at himself. He might prefer to avoid things that were destined to put him in a shitty mood, but he wasn't a coward. He pulled the door open and stole out.

No point chancing the kitchen. He'd just pick something up on the way.

As it turned out, all his concern was for nothing, anyway. There wasn't anyone in the hall or in the living room. Half a dozen strides and he was out the door and off the porch and onto the sidewalk. Just that had him feeling easier. Head down, he made it to the corner without looking up at Greg's bedroom window and without looking to see if his car was parked in its usual spot at the end of the block.

One quick stop at the bodega on the corner for coffee and a packet of crappy donuts. He even got lucky, and the number twelve bus was coming down the street just as he was coming out. He flagged it down, flashed his student ID and climbed inside, then threw himself down in a seat.

Christ, Marsh hated buses. Finally, twenty dull, jerky minutes later, he pulled the cord to signal his stop. When the bus lurched to a halt, he hopped up and pushed out the rear door, then humped it the half-block down the street.

Yulia's apartment was in the back corner of a crumbling three-story walk-up with a broken front door that never managed to latch right. He pushed through it with his usual grumble of annoyance at the shitty job it was doing keeping creepers out, then made his way down the hall. At her door, he knocked out three short raps before fumbling for his keys. He'd just gotten them out when the door swung open in front of him, the chain going taut.

"What happened to you?" Yulia asked, standing there in a tank top and baggy flannel pants.

Marsh scrunched up his nose. "What happened to your hair?"

Running her hand through the tangled now-blue strands, she rolled her eyes and closed the door. The chain made a scraping sound as she slid it aside. He pushed the door open and strode on through.

"You don't like it?" she asked to his back.

He set his bag down on the floor beside her couch and dug out the spare shirt and boxers. "Gonna borrow a towel."

"You know where they are." She followed him through the space, leaning up against the wall as he dug through the closet next to her bathroom. "Really, though."

He stood, terry balled up in his hand. Tilting his head to the side, he took a better look. Blue. What the hell was he supposed to say about that? "It's okay. I liked the red better."

"Red is so pedestrian. It could almost be mistaken for something natural."

"Not that shade of red."

"Whatever. You're just envious."

"If you say so."

With that, he locked himself in her bathroom and started up the water before stripping out of his clothes. He winced at the feeling of the dried come on his skin. Never a good thing. Except when it was.

Shaking his head at himself, he stepped under the spray. It wasn't fully warm yet—the pipes in this tenement took forever to get going, but he didn't care. He braced himself against the chill and ducked his head into the stream, scrubbing at his hair.

I'm gonna wash that man right outta my hair. He wished it were really that easy. The memory of Greg on top of him was burned into him, that warm, wet mouth surrounding him, the nice hard dick inside his hand, and the pulse, the way he'd arched when he came...

Marsh cursed and reached for Yulia's shampoo. The water was warm now, and he relaxed into it the best he could as he cleaned the shitty day and the shitty night away. He rubbed soap over his dick with disinterest, unwilling to do anything about it, even though he was half-hard. Stupid dick.

By the time he was done, he was feeling a little more human, and his erection had mostly gone down. He shut off the water and grabbed the scratchy towel from where he'd left it on the counter, dragging it over his skin with as much efficiency as he could muster, considering how crummy and tired and disappointed he felt. He pulled on his fresh underclothes and the same hoodie and jeans. Bundling his dirty clothes under his arm, he left the warm solitude of the bathroom and braced himself for whatever was coming next.

Only Yulia was apparently not in a ball-busting mood. She was sitting on the end of the sofa, a book in her lap, bright blue curls tied up with an elastic. There was cup of real, strong coffee at her elbow and another on the coffee table, and his vision got a little blurry for a second. He plopped down next to her and reached for the second mug. Sure enough, it was doctored up with just the right amount of cream and sugar, and it was the best thing he'd tasted all week. He hummed and sipped until it was about half gone, then set it aside.

He lay down next to her and put his head in her lap.

"We're not having sex," she said quietly, not looking up from her book even as she ran her fingers through his hair.

"Thank God."

It had happened a few times since he'd met her during orientation their freshman year. Once that very day, and again the day after, and then not again for a year—not until she'd let herself into his room the morning after something she still hadn't explained to him had rattled her to her bones. Once his junior year when a recruiting scout had passed him over.

Sex with Yulia was dangerous and athletic, and it always left him panting and empty and happy that, in the end, they were really just friends.

She sat in silence for a minute, petting his hair, not turning pages in her book. She didn't ask again what was wrong, and he loved her so fiercely in that moment that he wanted to shake with it. Instead, he squeezed her thigh and pressed his face against her abdomen.

"I fucked up," he whispered.

The gentle motions of her fingertips against his scalp stuttered, but she picked up her rhythm soon enough. "Oh?"

And it was too much to explain. There were the conversations he'd had the day before, first with the bursar's office and then with his coach. The call he'd tried to make home to his brother was definitely off limits. Then there'd been the fruitless outing to the bar with the team that he *knew* he shouldn't have gone on, but fuck. He'd wanted to drink and he'd wanted to get laid, and he'd wanted to feel like *someone*, but nothing had worked.

He'd gone back to the house he shared with a bunch of guys who were so much smarter than him it made him want to break something, and when everyone else had been either asleep or out on the town, he'd gone to the one place he never should have.

"I slept with him," he admitted, quiet, eyes closed.

"Marsh..."

"And it was good. Fuck, you should have seen him. He was so good." Greg had sucked dick like he lived for it, like he was dying for it, like beneath that genius scientist exterior, he was a cock-slut of the most epic proportions, and worse... "He looked at me like, like..."

Like Marsh was somebody he wanted.

Marsh curled up tighter and dug his nails into his palm. "Whatever. As soon as he got off, he kicked me out."

"Are you sure that's what happened?"

Laughter bubbled up, dry in the back of his throat. It hurt. "Pretty hard to miss the signs. He was considerate, too. Asked if I could make it to my room myself or if I needed help."

He chanced a glance up, only to close his eyes right back down. The expression on Yulia's face was downright dangerous. "He's an idiot, then."

Marsh snorted. "He's the smartest guy I've ever met. Hell, he'd have to be. Sure wised up fast to the fact that he was wasting his time with me if I wasn't actively touching his dick."

"That's bullshit and you know it."

He shrugged. Nonchalance didn't cover up the way he felt cold inside. And it was the worst kind of self-pitying, whiny crap, but that was why he came to Yulia. She might kick his ass as often as not, but he could say anything to her. Turning farther into her warmth, he mumbled, "What would he want with me anyway? Dumb jock..."

In the span of a breath, her gentle stroking turned into a sharp tug, and he had to fight to keep from showing how much that hurt. "That's your father talking."

His shoulders shook, and he hid his face. “Maybe. Still.” He bit his tongue, but it didn’t help. Fisting his hand into the space between his body and the couch, he mumbled, “Doesn’t mean it isn’t true.”

Chapter Three

Good Lord but cold coffee was disgusting. Greg pulled a face as he slugged back the last little bit left at the bottom of his travel mug. Sliding the lid shut, he grabbed a mint from the container of them he kept in his other cup holder and popped it in his mouth. There wasn't much chance of anyone getting close enough to really appreciate his coffee breath, but still. He had some standards left.

Not that it was easy to tell, looking around his car. It was a ten-year-old beater he'd picked up used, sure, but he could do better than this. Sighing, he took a minute to ball up the couple of protein bar wrappers and napkins from the seat well of the passenger's side and jam them in an old fast food bag. Trash and coffee mug in one hand, he jimmied the door handle with the other and let himself out.

He hit the lock and slammed the door shut behind him, then rounded to the trunk to get his bag. Damn, it was heavy. He slung it over his shoulder and headed toward the house, ticking off the items on his to-do list in time with his steps. Finish analyzing that data for his advisor, proof his proposal for the symposium, come up with some kind of plan for the class he had to TA tomorrow.

His stomach let out a distressed, rumbling growl, and he rolled his eyes at himself. Food first, then coffee, then work.

Well, at least he had his agenda set for the evening. And the night. And the late night. Sighing, he dragged himself up the steps and pushed open the door no one ever seemed to remember to lock, only to be assaulted by the sounds of gunfire. Nonplussed, he dropped his bag and shrugged off his jacket, slinging it over the other dozen or so of them hung up on the hooks in the entryway, then peered around the corner.

"Hey," Jason said, not looking away from the screen, thumbs flying over the controller.

"Hey." Greg looked on for a minute. "That the new *Call of Duty*?"

"Yup. Totally awesome." He listed to the side, tongue sticking out from between his lips. For a fraction of a second, he darted his gaze Greg's way. "You want dibs?"

Hell yeah, Greg did. He shook his head, though. "Maybe tomorrow." Ha. Hahahahahahaha. Ha. And maybe he'd also decide to give up on a PhD and get a job at McDonald's instead.

"Suit yourself."

Greg pointed toward the kitchen with his thumb. "There any of my Chinese left from last night?" If anybody had eaten the last of his sweet and sour, they were going to get a talking to.

"Should be."

Better be. And if Greg were a better person, he'd offer to share, but then dinner would turn into dinner and conversation, which would turn into dinner and conversation and a drink or two, and maybe just one quick game, and no. There wasn't time for that. Besides, he wasn't sure he had enough to go around, and he was starving.

Greg watched for another minute, then shook his head and meandered down the hall. He barely hesitated at the offshoot that led toward the little bedroom under the stairs. And he was going to resist. He really was.

Fuck it, who was he kidding? He put his hand to the wall and swung around the corner toward Marsh's room. His heart dropped the second he saw the empty door and the total lack of a muscle-bound blond anywhere within.

He cursed himself in his head for getting his hopes up. Sliding his hand down the wall, he pushed off it.

The day after he and Marsh had...done what they'd done, he'd woken up and stumbled down the stairs, feeling hopeful and anxious and ready to be crushed by disappointment all at once. He'd made up so many possible scenarios for how things could go down, but the only one he hadn't been prepared for was to not see Marsh at all—to get no reaction from him.

An empty room Saturday morning had been par for the course. Marsh had a lot of friends and a lot of obligations with his team. By Saturday night it had been distressing. By Sunday, disheartening, and Monday Greg had started to feel sick.

Now it was Tuesday evening, and he was edging toward resigned and numb.

He shouldn't have done it. Shouldn't have taken what Marsh offered. A taste of cock and flesh and touch—touch he'd been wanting for so long—had made all the months of repression fade away. It had made resuming his sexless, solitary life unbearable.

But he'd bear it, all right. It was what he was good at, pushing away the things he wanted. He was goal-oriented and addicted to his work.

And he was lonely and horny, goddammit.

Grumbling to himself, he turned, only to slam right into a damp, bare, rippling chest.

"Jesus Christ."

Greg couldn't have said it better himself. He reared back, one hand coming up, and— Oh. Oh, he'd just walked into Marsh. Half-naked Marsh, fresh from the shower, wrapped in a towel and dripping, and repression was a lost cause, was stupid, was the most pointless thing Greg had ever heard of in his life. God, Marsh smelled good.

Dropping his hand, Greg blinked hard and tried to get a grip on himself. "Um—"

"Hey."

"Hi. I—" What the hell was he supposed to say? "You're here."

Marsh tipped his head to the side, one eyebrow rising. "I do live here."

"Right. Sure." *Then why haven't I seen you in four days?*

Marsh chuckled and pushed past him, body brushing all along Greg's, and Marsh wasn't clumsy. He exuded grace and strength, and before Greg could stop himself, he was grabbing Marsh's wrist.

Marsh rounded, still all up in Greg's space, eyes dark. "Yeah?"

"I—" Greg had to get his feet under him. He had to take control.

Because that had been the whole problem the other night, hadn't it? He'd let Marsh invade his space and kiss him and take what he wanted from him. He'd been the same lonely, desperate, sad sack he always was, and he'd had enough of that with the last asshole he'd dated. He'd let Marsh walk in and walk out and he'd been left feeling like shit about it in the aftermath, and that wasn't how it was going to go down this time.

Because something was about to go down. Goddamn it all, it was.

Dominant. In control. Greg could do this. Grounding himself, he twisted to intertwine his fingers with Marsh's, and he slid his other hand up the hot, damp skin of Marsh's side. He lifted his chin and looked him straight in the eyes.

And his voice didn't crack. It came out all husky and low, and nothing like him, but exactly like how he felt, deep in the parts of him that were starved for contact. "I'm glad I ran into you. You were going to show me that thing. In your room."

Marsh's pupils were dilated, and his breath caught. It made Greg want to lean in closer. *God, please invite me to your room.* Still, there was mischief in Marsh's smile. "Was I?"

"Yes."

A breath and then another, and the cacophony of noise from the video game in the living room was bleeding into the hall. There were people home. Any one of them could stumble onto this scene and think all kinds of things that were way too close to the truth, and Greg didn't care.

He gave in to instinct and pushed himself closer into Marsh's space. This was putting himself out there, but that was what take-charge kinds of guys did. Right?

Lips close to Marsh's ear, he said, voice rumbling, "I've been dreaming about sucking you again for days."

And that was all he had to say. The next thing he knew, he was being tugged into Marsh's room, the door closing behind them, and then his back was against the door. Marsh turned the lock and stood before him, one thigh between his, hands braced to either side of his face. Upward pressure forced Greg to spread his legs.

Oh God. And Greg could have gone for that. He hadn't been fucked in years, and he'd never been fucked up against a door, not by someone strong enough to hold him up. To make him take it. Just like that, he was hard and aching and ready to go.

But that wasn't how this was supposed to happen. With one swift move, he flipped them, crashing Marsh against the wall and pressing his own body into his. They were about the same height, for all that Greg felt smaller, and they were eye to eye, mouth to mouth and cock to cock. He slid a hand up under Marsh's towel. Cupped his palm around that thick, firm thigh.

Marsh's breath hitched. "So what were you wanting me to show you?"

"I think I can find it. Just needed you to let me in."

"Door's open."

Greg looked down to watch the path he was tracing out over that golden skin, pushing back sparse, coarse hair. He nudged the sides of the towel aside, and it was all he could think about, getting his hands between Marsh's legs. Fitting his mouth to every part of him there, where he was all musk and man and sex, and he wanted this. Needed it.

"Door's always open," Greg said, breathy and dry. "Doesn't mean anybody's home."

And there was a moment. Greg's words hung in the air, thoughtless and stupid, and he hadn't meant to call Marsh on the disappearing act he'd pulled these past few days, but there was no pulling it back now.

"Hey," Marsh said. It was too serious.

Greg shook his head. "Sorry." This wasn't how this was supposed to go. He was ready to sink to his knees and start exploring with tongue and lips, but strong hands curled around his upper arms.

"Hey."

Greg looked up and connected with probing, blue-grey eyes. Everything went still, the heat dissipating for all that the two of them were pressed against each other and hard. And he couldn't keep it in, his annoyance and his fear. "You were avoiding me."

Marsh didn't flinch. "Maybe."

"Don't." It was too honest, too honest by half, but there it was.

"No?"

"No." Greg dropped his gaze and looked down. He pressed his palm over the center of Marsh's ribs. "If you don't want—" *Me.* "Just don't—" *Let me drive you from your own home.*

And now he couldn't say the things that mattered?

He cursed himself, ready to push away, but Marsh wasn't letting go. Instead, he was pulling Greg in even closer, mouth right there, and he breathed, "Okay."

And then it was all the slow, deep heat of his kiss and the taste of his mouth, and yes, yes. Fuck, please. A needy sound passed Greg's lips, and he opened wider, pressing forward with his tongue, nipping at the fullness of Marsh's bottom lip.

Marsh clutched him closer, then got a hand between them to cup Greg through his jeans. He moved to bite at the skin beside Greg's ear. "Been thinking about this, too."

Damn if that wasn't a whole new rush. Greg was so forgettable, so easy to put out of mind, and the idea that Marsh had been remembering how they'd touched and tumbled and made each other come was almost too much. "Yeah?"

"*Ngh*, yeah." His palm stroked up and down. "Barely got to meet it last time. Didn't get to taste you or anything."

It was too much too soon, and Greg had to *control* this, this time. The noise in his throat was almost a growl as he pushed off, and he could do this, could do anything he wanted, and what he wanted was to take Marsh to pieces. He sank to his knees and tore the towel off, leaving Marsh naked and so fucking beautiful, hard and flushed, and Greg could really see him now. No half-blind fumbling in the dark, this was messing around in full daylight, with people in the house and awake, and he wanted so much.

He slid his hand up over perfect flesh, took a second to roll the soft skin of Marsh's sac in his palm, then pressed his hand against the base of his cock, holding it against Marsh's abdomen. He nosed all around the hot length of him, breathing it in before sweeping his tongue over the crown, and it tasted so good. Power rushed through him. He shook his head as he nuzzled and licked, drinking in Marsh's groans and pants and the feeling of blunt nails against his scalp and carding through his hair.

People always made it out as if sucking dick made you the submissive one, but there wasn't a better rush in the world. There was nothing like having all that room to move, to be the one giving pleasure, to hold an orgasm at bay, edging until a guy was ready to lose his mind.

Humming loud, he tipped Marsh's cock forward and took it in until it nudged against his throat, and Marsh's fist hit the wall behind him. Greg popped off and looked up, and God, Marsh looked wrecked and perfect. "Quiet," Greg admonished, then took another mouthful, wrapped his lips into a tight ring and hollowed his cheeks.

"Shit. *Shit.*"

Greg bobbed and stroked, fist moving with his mouth, and Marsh's thighs were corded with strain, his grip tight and perfect and almost too much.

Greg pulled off, dropping one hand to press against himself, need sharp and almost painful in his gut. Marsh's cock stood tall and proud in the space between them, little spasms in the muscles just behind it making it jerk, leaving slick, shiny fluid glistening at the tip.

"Greg." Marsh's voice was almost a whine, and Greg loved hearing his name on his lips.

He took another swipe of his tongue over the sensitive skin just beneath the glans and put his hands between Marsh's thighs. Farther and farther, until his fingertips brushed the cleft, and Marsh curled in on himself, his hand a fist at his side.

Oh, and that was good. It'd be even better if it were Greg's tongue making Marsh writhe. The very thought of it made him throb. He glanced up without moving his head. The skin behind Marsh's balls was still damp from the shower, everything Greg touched warm and water-soft. Stroking higher, he nudged against Marsh's hole. "You wash all your nooks and crannies?"

Now that was *definitely* a whine falling out of Marsh's throat, and Greg didn't need any other sign. He leaned back and pushed at Marsh's hip. Marsh turned around willingly enough. Shaky with how much he wanted this, Greg mumbled, "Spread," teasing apart the firm cheeks of his ass with his thumbs.

Marsh's head thumped against the wall at the first long stripe Greg licked up through that valley, tasting earth and salt and soap, wanting deeper and closer. Marsh was starting up a litany of "Yes," and "Christ," and "Fuck," and "Please." Greg got a hand up between Marsh's legs, touching balls and cock and abdomen as he laved and probed and licked circles around that tight little opening.

"Like being opened up?" he panted into Marsh's skin. "Gonna get you all soft and loose." He pushed the point of his tongue just inside, and the pressure of his own dick inside his jeans pinched and made him gasp. "Wanna fuck you so bad. You want that?"

"Yeah, yeah, anything, just—"

"Next time." If there was a next time. Greg didn't do this with just anyone. A furtive handjob or a blowjob in a corner on a lonely night with a stranger? Sometimes. But getting up inside someone, or letting someone come inside him, that was another thing entirely.

Panting, he closed his eyes for a second and pressed his brow to the firm swell of Marsh's ass. Not this time, no, but soon. For Marsh...for Marsh, and the way he made him feel free and unhinged like this...he would.

He forced his eyes open and bit down on the flesh against his face. For now, he'd settle for this, settle for the taste of him and the sound of his breath, and fuck, it wasn't settling at all. Licking harder at his opening, he reached around and grasped Marsh's cock in the circle of his fist, and Marsh keened, shoving into it, fucking Greg's hand and pushing back against his tongue. His hole was all nice and wet now, and Greg pulled away to press a kiss to the red mark where he'd bitten him before. Got a finger in.

Marsh choked Greg's name out, clenching down. He rocked twice before going still as he pulsed, hot, all over the wall and all over Greg's fist, and God, God, fuck, Greg was going to—he had to—

Then Marsh was twisting, was shoving Greg down and climbing over him. He kissed Greg full on the mouth, and it was filthy and delicious. Almost as good as the way he slid down Greg's body, tearing at the buttons of his shirt to kiss his bare chest and opening his pants.

Greg's toes curled at the squeeze of fingers around his cock, pulling him out. At the feeling of Marsh's soft, wet mouth around him, he almost lost it.

"Oh God," he moaned, fighting to keep his hips still, to not fuck up into all that perfect heat, to not come the first instant he bumped up against an open throat, and— "Fuck!"

He put his own wrist in his mouth because that was Marsh's *throat*. "So good, so good," he chanted. Marsh was deep-throating him, and Greg wanted to find whoever had taught him to do that and kiss him and kill him, and he wanted Marsh to never stop, and he wanted to come.

He didn't even know what he was saying anymore as the pressure built and his balls tightened. The noises being forced out of him were too loud, and he sank his teeth harder into his wrist until it hurt. When a hand touched the inside of his thigh, he didn't hesitate at all to open up.

The first press of a fingertip against his hole, and everything went dark and blurry and too much. Screaming into the skin between his teeth, he shoved at Marsh's head. Marsh just pushed deeper, just kept his perfect mouth right there, though, and Greg gave over to it, to the fantasy of Marsh spreading him wide and fucking him into the floor. One more pump and he spilled into the tight stricture of Marsh's throat as he came and came and came.

Jesus.

The first sound to break through the fog was a quiet chuckle from above Greg. He blinked his eyes open to find Marsh kneeling naked between his legs. As he watched, Marsh's chuckle became a laugh, became something on the edge of hysteria, and a hard knot of ice took up residence inside Greg's chest. He started to curl his knees in, but then Marsh was leaning forward, still shaking as he pressed a kiss to Greg's bare hip before tugging his boxers to cover him up.

"Didn't think that would happen again." Marsh's voice was low, his gaze down.

Greg's head was still a jumble. "Of course it did," he mumbled, reaching, wanting to touch some part of Marsh.

Marsh shook his head and hopped over Greg's leg to sprawl out on his back at Greg's side. He ran a hand through his hair, breath still coming fast although the laughter had subsided. Turning his head to look at Greg, he asked, "So is this a thing now?"

The question was simple enough, but there was a little twitch to Marsh's eye. As if he didn't realize how sure a thing Greg was—how sure a thing Greg had been from the instant Marsh had first leaned over and kissed him.

Greg hesitated. The chance to keep doing this was so tempting. Greg didn't have time for a real relationship right now. Other men had given up on him in the past because he was so damn busy with all of his work. But he'd been losing his mind without anything to distract him, without any relief and without contact. Without Marsh lying beside him and making him feel easy and loose when usually he was so tightly wound.

Greg needed the outlet. The sex was amazing, the company just as good, and Marsh was so beautiful.

And there lay the problem. Marsh was beautiful, and fun, and popular. Greg couldn't possibly keep up with everything else Marsh had in his life, and he knew himself. His chances of staying detached over the long term were somewhere between slim and none.

Could he really turn this down, though? If he got attached—*when* he got attached, he could deal with it then. Maybe Marsh would laugh for real, but Greg would get the chance to touch and be touched until then, and when his feelings did change, he'd be able to walk away before things got too messy. He'd get to have this for now.

Greg blew out a long breath and turned his gaze toward the ceiling. "Do you want it to be a thing?"

Marsh shrugged. "I could do a thing."

That should have been enough of an agreement. Only Greg had to know. Twisting his neck around, he edged his hand toward Marsh. Bumped the back of his knuckles against his thigh. "Casual, right?"

"Sure." Marsh's eyes pinched.

Greg could do casual. "Okay." The words were hardly shaky at all.

"Okay." The grin that lit Marsh's face thrummed all the way through Greg, better than the afterglow. Brighter than the sun. Marsh rolled to the side and lifted his arm, like he was going to throw it over Greg's chest.

And Greg could go for that. The sex was so much of what he missed about trying to do the relationship thing, but he missed the affection and the talking and the other, simpler touches. He missed holding and being held. His hand twitched at his side.

Marsh dropped his arm. He shook his head, and another little snicker left his lips. In a sharp, abrupt motion, he rolled to seated. He dug the heels of his hands into his eyes for a second, then he stood and strolled over to his closet.

Greg's vision narrowed to the twin globes of Marsh's ass and the long line of his spine. Damn, his shoulders were broad.

And, shit, Marsh was talking to him. Greg snapped his gaze up to Marsh's face. His eyebrows were cocked, his mouth twisted in a smirk.

"Huh?"

"Nothing." Marsh stepped into a pair of sweatpants, and Greg just about lost the power of speech all over again, knowing there wasn't any underwear underneath Marsh's sweats. Did Marsh do that often? Greg would never be able to concentrate again, wondering.

Then again, this was a thing now. He didn't have to wonder. Any time he wasn't certain, he could ask to see something in Marsh's room. If nobody was looking, he could slide a hand beneath the waistband of those pants.

But Greg was getting distracted again. With a little groan, he got his arms braced and levered himself up. For a few seconds, he sat there on Marsh's floor, watching all that gorgeous skin disappear beneath a T-shirt. Pity.

Oh, well. One hunger satisfied, Greg's stomach gave another growl. Sighing, he rose the rest of the way to standing. "I'm going to go try to find some food." He hesitated, but then asked, "You want anything? I think there's some sweet and sour chicken left from last night."

Crap, maybe he had it bad already, if he was offering to share.

Marsh shook his head. "Nah. Meeting the team for pizza before weight training."

Right. "Okay," Greg said, as if he wasn't irrationally disappointed by that. It was probably for the best anyway. Two guys who were just fucking didn't need to hang out. "So I guess I'll..."

"...see you around," Marsh finished for him. He was standing in front of his closet still, half-turned toward Greg.

And guys who were just fucking didn't necessarily touch or interact once their clothes were back on, but Greg couldn't resist. He took the couple of steps over to where Marsh was standing. He transcribed his movements, waiting for the brush-off, but it didn't come. Damn it, what did he have to be scared of?

Channeling all the attitude that had let him proposition a half-naked Marsh in the hall, and pin him against the wall, and lick him out, Greg put a hand to the side of Marsh's face.

It was a quick kiss. Light and chaste, without any tongue or anything at all, but it still lit a fire in Greg's chest. A fire that didn't have anything to do with sex, and he was going to be in *so much trouble.*

But Marsh was smiling as Greg pulled away. "Catch you later."

"Yeah." Greg dropped his hand.

Then he walked away without looking back.

Chapter Four

"Hey! Sulkowski!"

Marsh whipped his head around, scanning the crowd until— He nodded at Ben over the sea of heads. It was a wonder he'd heard him at all over the noise, but Ben always did have a set of lungs on him. Taking a good slug off his beer so he wouldn't spill it, Marsh turned away from the keg set up in the corner and started across the room.

The Delta Upsilon guys had really outdone themselves this year. Their parties were never lacking, but from the looks of it, they'd gotten every undergrad with two legs and two tits to come this year.

One of said pairs of tits brushed up against him as he pressed forward. Marsh paused, looking over. Very nice. He glanced higher to find the rack also had some serious come-hither eyes, and he smirked out of instinct as he did another quick up-and-down. But it was an idle appreciation. Two years ago—hell, two *weeks* ago, that kind of thing would have done it for him, but tonight his interest was lukewarm.

Because it wasn't exactly horniness driving him tonight. He didn't know what it was, only that it was itching under his skin, making him restless and uptight. He gave Cute, Blonde and Perky a wink, then tilted his head toward the other side of the room, communicating as best he could over the crush that he had to keep moving. It was a brush-off, but not a personal one.

Not like the one he felt like he got every time he'd finished letting Greg come down his throat.

And he really didn't need to be thinking about that right now. Yeah, maybe he could appease the itchy feeling in his palms with a quick suck-and-duck up in Greg's room, but he'd already given that a couple of goes since he and Greg had decided to make whatever they were doing a regular thing. It had made him feel better, but only for a little while. Every time, after, he'd been left just as twitchy, just as wanting for something more. So, yeah. Not something he wanted to revisit tonight.

No, tonight he was here, at a party with half the campus, and the better-looking half, at that. His too-smart housemates and his frustratingly perfect fuckbuddy were far away. Out of sight and out of mind, and there were a lot of other distractions here to push it all even further still. Mind made up, he weaved around another tight cluster of kids.

It was a little less crowded over on the other side of the room where Ben and the other guys from the team were set up. As soon as Marsh got close, Ben held out a hand, and they clasped, pulling each other in for just a second. Ben clapped Marsh on the back before letting go.

"Glad you could make it, man." Ben held out a silver flask, and Marsh took it and downed a swig. Nice and smooth. Ben always brought the good stuff.

Marsh passed the flask back and wiped his mouth with his wrist. "Wouldn't miss it."

He exchanged similar greetings with the other guys, but before he could get pulled into whatever they were talking about, Ben grabbed his attention again. Ben was leaning against the wall as he quirked an eyebrow up. "So, what's this I hear about you living over on the west side this year?"

Oh. Right. A knot formed in Marsh's stomach, and suddenly he remembered why he'd been a little scarce at team social things for the past month. He covered up his discomfort with a one-shouldered shrug as he took a pull from his beer. Christ, that tasted like piss after Ben's bourbon. "Just how it worked out."

"Is that right?" Ben's skepticism was clear.

Marsh gave another shrug. "More or less."

Who knew what Ben had heard about the whole situation. Chances were, the other guys involved hadn't painted Marsh in the best of lights. They still thought he'd screwed them over, after all.

From Marsh's point of view, though, it had been exactly the opposite. He'd been excited as hell when the other guys from the team had invited him to go in on an apartment with them last spring. Told them how much he could swing and what he was looking for in terms of space. Figuring it was all in good hands, he'd gone off to do his training camp thing over the summer, leaving them to sort out the details. Come fall, he'd headed back into town only to discover the place they'd picked had been about double what he could afford, after everything had changed.

And that didn't stick in his craw. Not at all. He downed some more beer to try to wash down the bitterness that was even sharper than whatever crap they were serving at this thing, striving all the while for the casual nonchalance that had always carried him through.

Whatever problems he was having with his housemates and his team both now, he'd been damn lucky the geek squad had put that ad up on Craigslist. Even the room he was letting from them was at the edge of what he could swing with his budget the way it was, but he was managing.

And he didn't need to take any shit for it.

Before Ben could ask any follow-up questions, Marsh caught the eye of the girl from before. She was looking at him like he was something to eat. Like he was exactly what she wanted, and like he wasn't lacking, and yeah. Forget two years ago or two weeks ago. He could go for that.

"Excuse me." Marsh downed what little was left of his beer and shoved the empty cup at Ben as he stalked away. The girl's sly smile was a full-on sultry grin now. When he was just a few feet away from her, he keyed in on the music playing, matching his stride to it. He stopped way too close to her, right in her space. She was dancing, and her tits were perfect even if she wasn't what he really wanted. It was probably just as well, because at least he wouldn't have to feel like shit when *she* hightailed it out of there as soon as they were done.

Moving his hips in time with hers, he leaned in close, lips brushing the shell of her ear and asked, "What's your name?"

"You gonna remember it tomorrow?"

"Depends. Don't you want me to scream it tonight?"

"Just call me 'baby'," she murmured, and her mouth was hot and wet against his throat. She danced in closer, pressing the tight-wrapped denim of her thigh against his dick. He wasn't hard, but that was fine. He would be soon enough.

"Wanna get out of here, baby?"

She pulled back long enough to catch his eye, and then her mouth was on his. She tasted like lipstick and blueberry punch, and it was awful, but when she grabbed his wrist and pulled him toward the stairs, he followed.

Up the stairs and past the pile of people smoking in the loft and down the hall. She must have known someone, because she slipped a key into a lock and opened a door.

She didn't turn on the lights and neither did he. He slept with girls from time to time. They did it for him well enough, but as he ran his hands over her curves, he was thinking about sharper angles. About stubble and dick and thrusting hard into a nice, tight ass. Or giving in. Opening his legs for it and letting someone take him.

Just like Greg had promised, right after he'd given Marsh the rimming of his life. Marsh groaned into a different mouth, and in his head he was up against the wall, hands braced on plaster, soft tongue loosening him up while he bucked forward into Greg's fist, drowning in all his filthy talk about how next time he'd open Marsh up and fuck him.

That was all Marsh needed. In the span of a breath he went dizzyingly, achingly hard, and he whirled Whatshername around to press her into a wall, because that was what he really wanted.

He wanted to go back in time and make Greg take it, but that wasn't what their non-relationship was about.

Self-loathing burned his throat. Oh, no. His and Greg's thing, it was about getting off and getting back to their rooms, and Marsh was just a stop-gap. Greg hadn't said it, but Marsh could tell. Greg was the guy who was looking for forever, and Marsh was for just right now, and that was fine. Even if he wished...

Even if he wished someone wanted to keep him.

Tiny hands palmed his ass, big breasts pushed up against his chest, and fuck, this girl didn't want him either. Not really. Marsh bit down on her lip and tried to blank it all out, but he couldn't. He gave one more rough push against the wrong-shaped hips, and actually growled in frustration.

He couldn't do this. He wrapped his hands around her wrists and pushed even as he was pulling away, licking his own bottom lip where it was raw. Arcing against his grip, she gave a little shimmy. She flexed her wrists inside his grip. "Oh, yeah," she moaned, like she liked that kind of thing, and he was going to be sick.

Yanking his hands back, he took two fast steps away, dodging when she moved to reel him in again. "Sorry," he mumbled. "Sorry." He readjusted himself in his jeans and tugged the door open, throwing light from the hallway into the darkness.

"What the fuck?" she called after him, but all he could do was shake his head as he stumbled out and rushed toward the stairs.

Because maybe he couldn't get what he really wanted, but he didn't want this. This wasn't helping him forget anything.

Deep inside, he burned. He knew where he could get at least a bit of what he wanted, and if it wasn't real and wasn't all of it, well... You took what you could get sometimes. And when your ass hit the curb, after, at least you got to remember it.

Marsh had a moment as he climbed the stairs. A bad moment. Sure, Greg's car had been parked exactly where it was supposed to be, and the light in his room was on, but that didn't mean anything on a Saturday night. He could be out, or he could have taken a cab, or he could have just forgotten to turn off the light. He could have someone in there with him right now.

The cup of punch Marsh had slammed back on his way out of the party was sitting in his gut all wrong, making his head feel like it sat half an inch off his neck, but whatever. He'd done stupider things while drunker. He touched his fingertip to his nose just to check, and yeah. He was fine.

His gait was heavy as he trudged up the last few steps. He turned the corner and steeled himself. He'd said he still had his pride, but he didn't have anything, not if he was really going through with this, but goddamn it. The itch under his skin was deeper now, and he couldn't reach it by himself.

Greg's door was cracked open. Marsh had his hand on the knob, was poised to knock when he stopped cold. Voices. There were voices. Shit. Cold sweat broke out on the back of his neck, and how could he have been so stupid?

He turned away, but then there was the quiet call of, "Marsh?"

Busted. Marsh twisted around and put his hand to the molding. Through the gap in the door, those gorgeous eyes were staring at him from behind thick-framed glasses, and Marsh pushed the door a little wider. Flash and dazzle, and never let them see you sweat. He leaned against the doorframe, and his heart skipped a beat when he saw Ronnie standing next to Greg's desk. They were both fully dressed, and there were graphs and notebooks spread out all over the place.

Because they were *working* on a Saturday night at midnight. Who did that?

Marsh wanted to sag with his relief, but he kept up the nonchalance he was so good at. He glanced between Ronnie and Greg. "Hey. I was just..."

What *was* he doing here? Ronnie was looking at him like he knew exactly how weird it was for Marsh to be seeking Greg out. Marsh swallowed hard.

"Hey," Greg answered, then he flinched and reached for his face, pulling his glasses off and folding them up. Clearing his throat, he turned to Ronnie. "Can we finish this up tomorrow?"

"Um. Sure." Ronnie retreated a step, grabbing one of the notebooks and a small pile of printouts. His expression was still all confusion, but he wasn't going to question this out loud, at least.

Who knew what kinds of questions he might ask tomorrow. Marsh shouldn't have come. "If you're working, you don't have to—"

"No," Greg said, "it's fine." He tipped his head up to look at Marsh, and there was something in the set of his jaw and in the depths of his eyes. "I thought you'd gone out."

"I did. But I came back." His voice was too thick by half. *I came back because I tried to get laid and I couldn't stop thinking about you, and it's better for you to use me than for me to get used by anybody else.*

The furrows on Greg's brow eased, just fractionally, and maybe Marsh had done the right thing. Maybe Greg was as happy to see Marsh as Marsh was to see him.

Then Greg twisted to look at Ronnie. "I've been tutoring Marsh on some..." His voice was tight and all wrong, and he trailed off.

The coldness crept back in. "Statistics," Marsh supplied. Because he could lie like nobody's business, had been lying all his life.

"Oh. Sure." Ronnie looked between the two of them again, and Marsh wanted to throw one of their giant engineering textbooks at his face, because Lord knew he couldn't read one of them, and all he was good for was throwing things.

He certainly wasn't good enough for a guy to fess up to fucking around with in front of his friends.

Marsh's mouth hurt from the ugly smile he plastered on as he crossed his arms and stepped into the room. Greg and Ronnie exchanged a couple more words, making plans to finish their work tomorrow.

Ronnie nodded at Marsh as he pushed past. Marsh gave an answering one, then stood there, silent and waiting in the stifling air as the sound of footsteps rang out down the hall. After a minute of waiting and staring at Greg, Marsh turned, ducking his head out into the corridor to check that Ronnie was really gone. He pulled the door closed, holding the knob so it wouldn't make a sound as it shut, then flipped the lock.

If the room had been stifling a second ago, it was positively oppressive now. Greg was sitting in his chair still, legs spread, wiping his hands on his pants, like they were sweating the way Marsh's whole body felt like it was.

"Did you have a good night?" Greg asked.

Marsh gave a wry little laugh at that. "Good enough that I came back here at the end of it." He crossed the space over to Greg and stood before him, but he didn't touch, not yet. He was cemented in place, wanting and uncertain beneath the weight of Greg's darkened stare. "You?"

Greg's reply was just as wry. "Thrilling. Didn't you notice?"

The guy was wound so tight, like there was something in him just dying to break free, and in that moment, Marsh wanted nothing more than to shake him up a little, to peel away everything that was keeping him hemmed in. Just like that, he was in motion. He was too damn big to be straddling people in desk chairs, but he made it work, climbing onto Greg to kneel over him, one leg bent up against the seat of the chair, thigh pressed to thigh, hips grazing, his other leg straight behind him so his foot anchored him to the floor. Greg's breath caught, and Marsh leaned in, nudged his nose up against Greg's cheek.

"I don't know." He slid a finger from Greg's ear, down his throat, and lower to dip under the collar of his shirt, tracing a slow circle in the patch of hair there. Keeping his voice seductive, he murmured, "The giant, throbbing...vein in your temple might have been a clue."

He smiled against Greg's mouth as Greg let out a chuckle, and then another. The sound of his laughter was almost as good as the way his shoulders dropped an inch, his jaw unclenching. Voice more open than Marsh had really heard it before, Greg sighed and put a hand at the base of his spine. "How do you always make me feel better?"

That hit Marsh square in the chest, making him feel things he shouldn't, not with someone like Greg. "I don't know," he said, struggling to put them back on solid ground. Back in the place where they always ended up, even though that wasn't necessarily where he wanted to go. He purred and licked a stripe up the side of Greg's neck. "Must be my charm."

"Right." Greg's throat bobbed, a little of that tension returning, but he cupped Marsh's ass and gripped the back of his neck, and yes, that was what Marsh had wanted earlier. This was what they were supposed to do.

Marsh let himself sink into the masculine body beneath his. Rubbed his hard dick up against the answering bulge in Greg's jeans. He dragged his lips over stubble, and it felt so fucking good. "Sure you wouldn't rather be working on..." he twisted until he could spot the title on one of those books, "...finite element analysis?" Whatever the fuck that was.

"Tempting." Greg turned Marsh's head back toward him, angling him for a kiss they were still hovering on the edge of, so close and not nearly close enough. "Didn't think you'd come by tonight," he grated out, and was that a flare of jealousy in his eyes?

Oh, Marsh could so get into that. Could take Greg being possessive and rough, had always wanted just that.

Greg's hand tightened on Marsh's neck and his voice went dark. "You smell like a bottle of perfume tried to make out with you."

Fuck, Marsh did not want to think about that. "Maybe it did." Marsh ground down on him, one quick press of his hips before he lifted up again, a hot pit of desire unfurling in him at the way Greg arched up into it. "But I'm here with you now, aren't I?"

"Yeah, you are." Greg touched his face, and it was so incongruous, the heat in his eyes and the brush of fingertips, so gentle they burned.

There were so many layers tucked up inside whatever Greg was trying to communicate, and Marsh didn't come here for layers. He came here for something simple. He was good at simple. So he made it about sex again, about things he knew how to get as he pulled Greg's hand from his face and put it with his other one, firmly on Marsh's ass. Marsh pushed into that, mouthing his way to Greg's ear.

"Wanna make sure I remember it?" He moved Greg's arm so his fingers grazed the seam of his jeans, right over his crack. "Wanna fuck me so I never forget it?"

Greg let out a sound that was anything but complicated as he squeezed and pulled Marsh down.

Marsh sucked on the lobe of Greg's ear. "You said you would, remember? When you licked me open? Said you'd fuck me, and I've been waiting."

He hadn't had that specifically in mind when he'd made his way over here, but at the push of fingertips over the fabric covering his hole, at the way Greg groaned and shoved his hips forward, it was all he could think about. Getting all of that inside of him, being claimed, even if only for a little while.

"You like that?" Greg ground out. "Like getting fucked?"

"I'm flexible." Really, Marsh very rarely did it like this, he usually liked to be the one on top. It was safer that way. But he didn't have any of the power here; he was just the poor dumb kid asking the guy who had his life together to take pity on him and make him come. It felt right to open up and take it. "But right now?" He bit down hard on the cord of tendon beneath Greg's jaw. "I'm gagging for it. Want it so bad."

Greg clutched Marsh close and buried his face against Marsh's neck with a low groan that went straight to his cock. Greg's arms were a crushing pressure against Marsh's ribs. Then he rose, pushing Marsh out of his lap, standing him up before shoving him down onto the bed. Marsh went in a pile of willing limbs. Scrambling for the hem of his shirt, he kicked his shoes off. Greg was tearing at his own clothes, too, and by the time he climbed on top of Marsh, he was naked to his waist as well. Marsh just about choked at the feeling of the coarse hair on Greg's chest and the weight of him. He spread his legs and lifted his knees, dumping Greg forward so he was sitting right on Marsh's hips.

Only Greg didn't go straight for the kill. Hardly even ground his hard cock into Marsh's abdomen. Instead, he put one hand flush over Marsh's ribs, thumb tweaking at a nipple, and he put his other palm to Marsh's face, fingers digging into his jaw.

And, oh, this was the kiss Marsh had been waiting for. It was all teeth and tongues and the rub of a rough chin, the heat of breath and the way Greg smelled like lightning and lust. The way that bristling exterior stripped away to leave this needy, possessive, sexy-as-fuck man leaning over him.

"So good," Marsh said into his mouth. He grabbed Greg's ass, trying to get him to thrust a little. Greg let him, making low noises against his breath, and then he was reaching up, past Marsh's head. There was the sound of a drawer sliding open, and jostling, and yeah.

The lube and condom hit the bed, and then Greg's hands were back on Marsh's body. Marsh fumbled to the side until he touched the hard plastic of the bottle.

"C'mon," he urged, working at the cap and— Huh. New bottle. There was something about popping the seal on it that just turned him on even more.

But Greg was still kissing Marsh like he was dying for every touch, kissing him like he didn't care when they got to the main event.

Something twisted in Marsh. He wished. Ready to hurry things along, wanting that burn out of his chest and down in his ass where it belonged, he pushed at Greg's shoulders, leering as Greg pulled away, face flushed and lips kiss-swollen, and fuck. Marsh could get used to this. So easily.

He swallowed, his throat thick. Changing tactics again, he reeled Greg in and kissed him hard, until there wasn't any room left to breathe or think or want. With a growl in his throat, he pressed the bottle against Greg's chest. Made his voice deep as he spread his legs. "You wanna open me up? Get me all ready for your cock? Or you wanna watch?"

A flicker of something shadowed Greg's eyes, and he shifted, putting his brow against Marsh's. He closed his eyes for a second, then opened them again, taking the bottle and flipping the cap. Grabbing Marsh's hand and holding it between them to drizzle the slick across his fingers.

Clear enough. Greg kissed down Marsh's chest, face hidden as he angled his neck and worked at Marsh's fly. He tugged down pants and boxers, then knelt between Marsh's legs, chest heaving and looking so good. The only thing that would make it better would be if he'd lose his damn jeans already.

Marsh had never taken the time to ask before, but tonight, with his ass on the offer, maybe it was time to press his luck.

Marsh slid a hand over his cock, thrusting into the tight clutch of his own fist, then reached lower to circle around his hole. He glanced at Greg. "You gonna?" With his free hand, he gestured toward Greg's pants.

It took Greg a second for his eyes to focus, his gaze on the place where Marsh was slipping slick fingers over himself. He jerked his head up. "Huh?"

And Marsh had been naked in front of Greg before, but he'd never managed to get Greg out of all of his clothes. Maybe that was a thing of his. A way of keeping distance or power or fuck if Marsh knew. But he wanted it gone. All of it, until it was just skin and need and that long, smooth glide. He wanted to curl his legs around naked ones, wanted to palm the bare flesh of Greg's thighs as Greg fucked into him.

With the tip of his finger, Marsh breached himself, and wow, yeah, it'd been a while. It felt good, though, and he played it up, writhing into it as he pressed deeper. He stroked his cock with his other hand and let his mouth fall open. "Take off your clothes," he said on an exhale.

Maybe it wasn't a game after all. Greg looked down as if surprised to see he was still wearing anything at all, as if he'd been so consumed by watching Marsh that he'd lost track of himself. Marsh gave a little whine as he pressed a second finger in beside the first and Greg slid his thumb into the waistband of his jeans.

He popped the button and Marsh bottomed out to the knuckle. Undid the zipper, and Marsh grazed his prostate, and damn, damn, damn. It was too early, Marsh still too tight, but when Greg pushed his pants and boxer-briefs off and knelt before Marsh naked, Marsh forced the third finger in because he couldn't wait.

"C'mere," Marsh groaned, and oh God, all that naked flesh pressed against him. Marsh let go of his cock and grunted at the solid heat of Greg's erection sliding alongside his. His hand was all slick and gross with lube, but he palmed Greg's ass all the same and pulled him into the deepest, wettest kiss, and he could come from just this.

Greg slowed them down before he could, though. He slid a fingertip around where Marsh was stretched tight around his own digits, and it was like all the air left Marsh's body.

"Keep going," Greg urged. He caressed all around the taut rim, and Marsh keened as he pressed deeper into himself, catching on his gland and having to close his eyes before he gave it up without even getting Greg inside him.

"Need you." He winced. "It." And he was a bumbling mess, shaking his head. "Need it, now."

"Just a little more." Greg took Marsh's palm in hand and guided him. "Won't hurt you."

God, Marsh wished that were true. He shook his head harder. "I'm ready."

Greg gave his wrist a twist. "Don't stop," he rasped into Marsh's ear, and then he rose onto his knees, pulling his hand away. He reached over onto the bed where the condom had fallen, and the ache in Marsh's abdomen and behind his balls flared even hotter.

With the promise of finally getting fucked, he went at himself with purpose, making it just that little extra bit raw, biting the inside of his cheek.

There was the sound of crinkling, and then a low huff, and a warm hand pulling at Marsh's arm. Marsh opened his eyes and let Greg pull his hand from his body, choking at the sudden ache of emptiness. "Gentle," Greg murmured, and he pushed Marsh's fingers back into himself once, painfully slow.

"C'mon, please—"

And Marsh didn't beg. Didn't beg for anything or anyone, not out loud.

Greg brushed soft lips over Marsh's, a too-gentle press of tongue. "Shh," he said, touching Marsh's face. "I'll give you what you need."

With that, he pulled Marsh's hand free again, and this time it wasn't a tease. It was to press his cock into Marsh's palm. Marsh stifled a shudder and grasped that flesh, spreading the lube around. Cool liquid poured over the whole affair, and everything went perfect and easy. Greg took his own wet fingers to Marsh's opening, and that shouldn't feel so much better, but it did. He took two quick strokes, dipping in and out of Marsh's body, as he kissed him full and smooth, making throaty noises as he sucked on Marsh's tongue.

Seeming satisfied Marsh hadn't been lying about being stretched and slick, Greg pulled his hand away. Pulled his cock from Marsh's grip.

And it didn't make any sense how Greg entwined their fingers, giving Marsh something to hold on to as he settled himself between his legs. He lined himself up, lips hovering just above Marsh's, breath a warm wash of air. Marsh stared up into gorgeous eyes, and maybe he did beg. If it was this good, he'd beg all day.

"Greg. Please."

Greg's throat clicked, and without another moment's hesitation, he pressed forward.

Marsh's toes curled, his whole body going rigid at that pressure. His body opened for it, though. He squeezed hard at Greg's knuckles, and with his other hand, scrambled for purchase, tugged at hip and arm and shoulder, grasped at anything he could hold on to.

When Greg was all the way inside, he pressed his forehead to Marsh's temple, and made a sound that was so sexy Marsh almost lost it right there. "So... God, Marsh..."

"Yeah," Marsh managed to grunt out. Fuck, he felt full—bright and needy and perfect and *full*.

And he might not ever get what he wanted, but this was something.

Greg leaned back, bracing himself with one arm and moving their joined hands so they rested on the mattress beside Marsh's head. He took a deep breath like asking for permission and drew back. The second thrust inside was faster and rougher and so fucking fantastic. Marsh's whole abdomen was tight, and Greg was this straining line of muscle, his jaw flexing with every new push in.

He looked gorgeous and perfect and like he was really here. Really present and unleashed. And that was almost better than the fuck, getting to see all those inhibitions stripped away, just like Marsh had wanted. Marsh reached up to put his palm to the shivering line of Greg's pulse, thumb scraping below his ear. "That's it," he murmured. "Let go. Give it to me."

"*Ngh.*" Greg pushed even harder, even deeper. He finally pulled his hand free, leaving Marsh ungrounded and floating, and it was fine. More than fine.

Greg fit his palm to the underside of Marsh's thigh, moving him how he wanted him. He lifted up and touched inside Marsh's knee, and the angle was too good, sparks shooting off with every press against Marsh's prostate.

And Marsh had to. He had to.

He snuck a hand between their bodies and wrapped it around his cock and almost screamed.

"Yeah, that's it," Greg echoed. He leaned in closer, near enough that Marsh could taste the sweat from his skin. "Wanna feel you come."

"Fuck—" And Marsh rode that edge for so long he thought he'd lose his mind. Everything else disappeared, leaving just the slap of bodies and the smell of sex and being fucked open. The slick touch of his own hand on his cock, and Greg.

Greg staring at him and not closing his eyes, and Greg seeing him, and Greg looking like he wanted him—

The orgasm pulled itself out of Marsh's toes. He curled in on himself, digging nails hard into Greg's back and dragging them down as he pulsed. His vision swam with the force of it, come spattering his chest, and it was a mess, and it was maybe the best sex he'd had in his life, and he was so glad. So glad he'd waited and come home, here, to have it with Greg.

Greg fucked him through it. The instant Marsh started to get his hearing and his sight back, Greg gave another few unsteady pumps of his hips, and then his eyes, open right up until that moment, clenched tight. He pushed deep, abdomen flexing, and then there was just the groan and Marsh's name.

And Greg collapsing onto Marsh's chest, spent.

Forgetting himself, still catching his breath, Marsh encircled Greg in his arms, making long, slow strokes over his spine and eating up his shivers. Marsh's body was thrumming, everything feeling loose and good.

Until Greg stiffened and pulled away. Marsh winced when he slipped free. He slung an arm over his face and breathed into the darkness.

Fuck. Fuck. He'd known this was what he was getting himself into, but that didn't make it suck any less. He couldn't have the good feeling without the aftermath, so after a few deep lungfuls, he fixed his expression and dropped his arm, moving to sit. Greg had shifted to the end of the bed, his body twisting away as he dealt with the condom, and maybe it was better that way. It was easier if Greg didn't have to look at him.

Marsh swiped his pants off the floor and stuck his legs through. He hiked them up as he stood. Draping the sheet over his lap, Greg sat back against the wall, and Marsh could feel his gaze on him.

"You taking off then?"

Marsh couldn't quite make out Greg's tone, and Greg's face was as unreadable as ever. Marsh looked down at the ground and picked up his shirt. "Yeah." And he had to tack on, "Don't wanna overstay my welcome."

"You're not. Overstaying. You can stick around, if you want."

What Marsh wouldn't give if he thought Greg really meant that. All he could hear, though, was the lie about the tutoring from before as he looked at the papers still strewn across Greg's desk. "Nah." He flashed a smile that tasted bitter on his tongue. "Besides, your study buddy'll be back in the morning, right? I don't think I need that much help with my stats homework."

Greg's face turned guilty, and fuck, why couldn't they just go back to five minutes ago, when everything had been perfect? "I didn't know if you'd want..."

"Want people to know?"

"Well, yeah."

"He's your friend," Marsh said, like he didn't care. "It's your business."

"You live here, too. It's your business."

"No skin off my back." Marsh wasn't the one with anything to be ashamed of. "Did you want him to know?"

When Greg hesitated, Marsh's stomach dipped. Was there anything else he needed to hear? He cleared his throat and looked away. "I don't know."

"Well, when you do, let me know." Marsh pulled his shirt on and stepped into his shoes. He didn't waste any time getting to the door. "Until then, I'm out."

Stupidly, he had to go and take a glance over his shoulder before he walked out. Greg was sitting against the wall, looking way more conflicted than Marsh knew what to do with, his cheek sucked in like he was biting the inside of his mouth. And damn it all, Marsh was trying to keep things simple, but with Greg looking like that it was almost impossible to go.

There was more to say. Lots more. But this thing they had would never hold up to scrutiny, and he wasn't ready to lose it yet.

Greg lifted his head and offered up a smile that looked as forced as Marsh's had been. "Okay." He raised his hand weakly. "Good night."

"Night."

No more looks back. Marsh pulled the door wide and walked out into the silent house they shared, alone.

Chapter Five

It always started with the aura. Greg blinked hard and dug the heels of his hands into his eye sockets. When he looked at the screen again, it was still there, though, that shining rainbow haze. He groaned. Now? Really?

Hardly glancing away, he tugged at his desk drawer and grabbed the ibuprofen to shake two out into his palm. He really, really didn't want to need his script tonight. It left him useless and groggy. Less useless than he would be if this turned into one of those dry-heaving sorts of nights.

The migraines had been coming since he was a kid, but they hadn't been this bad since he was a senior in high school. Funny, that. Almost like stress was a trigger. Washing the tablets down with a swig of Coke, he looked over his to-do list. Maybe he could just get this one last thing done before he had to turn off the lights and wish he'd never been born.

He slid his glasses on and refocused on the screen. His proposal for the symposium the department was hosting later this fall had been accepted, which was great, which was *awesome*, but now he had to get this presentation put together by the end of the month, on top of everything else. Just another three slides...

Somehow, he got through it. By the time he finished the last piece, though, it was an hour later, and his skull felt like it was pressing in. Tugging his glasses off, he saved the file and backed it up to the server, then lurched out of his chair. As soon as the light was off, he felt a hundred times better, which was saying a lot, considering he still felt like his head had been run over.

Nothing for it.

Fumbling in the dimness, he got the little orange bottle out and fished around for a single pill. He swallowed it down and stumbled toward his bed. And this was the worst. He'd maybe fall asleep once the meds kicked in, but for now all he could do was curl up in a ball and shake and try to keep his dinner down.

He closed his eyes and floated for a while. Thoughts of all the work he had to do kept creeping up, but that way led to a trip to the emergency room for a shot of Demerol in his thigh, and, yeah, no. He should go grab his phone or something and put on some music, something quiet to drift along to, but just the thought of getting up made his stomach turn. And so it was darkness and silence and shifting to try to keep the cool part of his pillow against his face without actually *moving* and setting himself off again.

He was finally edging in and out when a series of quick knocks on his door exploded across his brain. He swore and forced an eye open, and that hurt, but it didn't hurt quite as much as it had—he did the math in his head—an hour and a half ago. Thank you, Maxalt.

Another sharp rapping sound rang out, and crap, he didn't remember scheduling anything with Ronnie or any of the other guys tonight, but who knew? Burying his head in the pillow, he mumbled, "Go away, I'm dead."

There was just a beat of hesitation, and then a voice that was not Ronnie's saying, "Oh. Um. Sorry."

Greg snapped his head up and then cursed out loud, because, fuck. He dropped his head and rubbed his temple. That was Marsh at the door. He didn't want to be a dick to him.

His throat tore and his head ached as he called out, wincing, "Wait."

And it didn't make any sense. Greg had been working so hard to seem cool, and to keep himself together in front of

Marsh. Marsh had kept coming back, again and again, so it must have been working. It would be sheer idiocy to let Marsh see him now, when he was ready to pass out or puke from the pain. But he...wanted Marsh. He was hurting, and he wouldn't want any kind of human contact, normally, but the idea of Marsh coming in here was different, somehow.

Greg swallowed hard. The last time he'd had a regular boyfriend, two or three years ago, sometimes, when the migraines had come, the guy had let Greg lie there with his head in his lap in the dark. He'd rubbed Greg's shoulders and combed his fingers through his hair and told him quietly about his day. He'd told Greg it would all be okay, and it had felt so good.

And Greg wanted that, so badly it competed with the throbbing in his skull and the squeezing of his heart, the fear there.

The door eased open, shining a line of light into the darkness, and Greg squinted. A shower of firecrackers went off in Greg's skull, but he could make out Marsh's face through the gap. Marsh's gaze darted around the room before settling on Greg, and he frowned. "Sorry, were you asleep?"

"I wish." Greg shaded his eyes with his hand against the brightness. Haloes still ringed his vision, but the auras weren't dancing quite so sickeningly. He waved his other hand toward his head. "Just...migraine."

"Ouch." Marsh made a sympathetic face.

"Yeah."

And there was a moment, awkward and stretching as Marsh hovered in the door. Greg's stomach, already unsettled, sank a little. Except for that first time, Marsh had only ever come to Greg for sex. He hadn't come here to watch Greg be a shivering mess or to rub warmth into his skin or comfort him with mumbled reassurances.

Marsh's uncertainty was written into every line of him as he hovered. He jerked a thumb to point behind him. "I'll come back later, I guess?"

"Do you wanna come in?" And it was stupid. So dumb.

"Um..."

"You don't have to," Greg backtracked, and he closed his eyes. "I mean, I'm not up for...what we usually do." Sex was beyond off the table right now. "But you could hang out for a bit. If you wanted to."

Marsh laughed, a little uncertainty clinging to the edges, but the sound was rich and warm. "Yeah, I can stay a little while." Did he sound...relieved?

Marsh slipped inside and closed the door, leaving the room comfortingly dim again. The scuffing sounds of his feet on the carpet paused, and Greg could almost see Marsh looking between the chair and the bed. With a groan, Greg shoved himself over, leaving room. *Just take the invitation.*

There was another moment's hesitation when Greg scarcely breathed, then movement again, coming closer to the bed, and Greg melted into the mattress.

"Can I?"

"Yeah," Greg said. *Please.*

The mattress shifted as Marsh sat where Greg had been lying, his back against the headboard. It was probably pathetic to be so comforted just by having Marsh close. He wanted to shift even farther over and settle his head in Marsh's lap. Reach out and place Marsh's hand on the base of his neck. Instead, he slid his arm forward to rest his own hand on Marsh's thigh. The muscle there was solid and warm through a layer of denim, and it was enough.

Except then Marsh brushed Greg's hair from his face. A broad palm settled, light as can be, on the back of Greg's head, thumb stroking gently at his temple, and Greg let out a little noise, it felt so good.

"Sorry—"

"No." Greg grabbed at Marsh's wrist when he made as if to pull away. No. Please. "Just—" He didn't have words for what he wanted, but Marsh seemed to hear them all the same. The tension went out of his body, as fingers resumed massaging gently against Greg's scalp, and it was soothing and perfect and made the pain simmer down just a little. Just enough to be okay.

"I'm not hurting you?"

"No." Greg let go of Marsh's wrist and put his hand on Marsh's thigh again, relaxing into the simple pleasure of touching and being touched and not being alone.

For a few blissful minutes, he soaked it up in silence, but the motion of the fingers in his hair wasn't as easy as he would have liked. The muscles beneath his hand weren't lax and soft, and then all Greg could hear was the beating of his own heart, and it echoed, guilty and hollow. He looked up to find Marsh staring into space. Greg swallowed and closed his eyes. "Sorry," he mumbled. "This probably isn't what you wanted."

"It's fine," Marsh's hand stuttered against Greg's scalp. "Do you want—do you want to talk? Or is quiet better?"

It was actually a relief to have that warm, smooth voice to focus on. It pushed the pressure behind his eyes further into the background. "Talking is good." He reconsidered. "Just not about math."

Marsh chuckled, the sound darker than made any sense. "Definitely not something you have to worry about." He shrugged, fingers drifting lower, toward the base of Greg's skull, and Greg could have purred. "Guess that's one of the benefits of hanging out with a dumb jock."

What? Greg would have shaken his head, and only just stopped himself from furrowing his brow. "You're not a dumb jock."

"Sure, if you say so."

"You *could* be into math." Anybody could be, jock or no.

"Not my speed." And Marsh's voice got a little rougher. "Sorry to disappoint."

Where was this coming from? Greg wanted to lift his head, to look into Marsh's eyes and try to see if he really believed any of this stuff. As it was, all he could do was mumble, "Not a disappointment." Because it wasn't. He lifted his shoulder a fraction. "Everybody's into something different. Besides, bet you're good at baseball stats. Those are harder than some of the stuff I do."

Marsh practically dripped with derision. "Those are easy."

"Anything's easy if you're really into it."

All he got for that was a quiet hum, like an agreement to disagree, and they were going to have to talk about this more, someday. Preferably when Greg's brain wasn't mush and everything didn't ache. He stroked his thumb over Marsh's knee, but the gesture didn't say everything he wanted it to.

After a minute of uneasy silence, Marsh made a little clicking sound with his tongue as he skated his hand up the side of Greg's face. "So...migraines?"

"Yeah." Greg gestured in the general vicinity of his head. "Come on every now and then. More when I'm stressed."

"Are you ever not stressed?"

"They didn't start 'til I was five," he said drily, then admitted, "They've been worse than usual recently. This is my third this month."

"Ouch."

Greg rolled over onto his back, and things felt better, now, more comfortable. When his head butted up against Marsh's leg, he didn't move it. Just stayed there and let the contact wash over him. With a little groan, he said, "Still not as bad as my senior year of high school."

"I can imagine." Marsh had both hands on Greg's face now, rubbing so softly at his temples, and it was perfect. "Let me guess—you were that asshole who actually studied for his SATs. Oh hell, you didn't take a class, did you?"

"No, but I may or may not have used up a highlighter on my prep book. Add four AP classes to that, and..." Looking up at the ceiling, he thought back on that year, and maybe it wasn't really the time to bring it up. But maybe it was. "And driving myself crazy trying to get up the guts to come out."

God, that had been a rough year. Studying and working and losing his virginity to the gorgeous tight end from the next town over. Then freaking out the next day when Mr. Tall, Dark and Closeted threatened to punch him in the face if he didn't get out of his bed.

Marsh's fingertips made a detour to ease around behind Greg's ear. "You're gay, right?"

"A Kinsey six," Greg agreed.

A second of hesitation. "Out of six, right?"

"Yup." Stupid. Not everyone read books about human sexuality in their spare time. Greg was such a nerd. He waved his hand to try to show it didn't matter. "Girls do nothing for me." He darted his gaze to Marsh. "You?"

"Bi-ish."

"Ish?"

"Girls are fine. Guys are better?"

"Gotcha." That was kind of a surprise, actually. Left to his own devices, Greg would have figured it was the other way around. Sure, Marsh seemed to be into it when Greg was going down on him, and he certainly hadn't had any objections to bottoming. But Greg had seen him around campus with girls hanging off his arm enough times. Not so much with men.

"So..." Marsh swallowed and traced a line over Greg's brow that had him closing his eyes again and tilting his head up into the touch. "Coming out?"

Greg shifted and turned his face farther into Marsh's leg. Usually, scents made his headache even worse, but Marsh always smelled so good, and Greg breathed him in.

"It's funny, to think about it now. I got myself so worked up about it, you know?" The whole thing was burned into Greg's sense-memory, and he could taste the rain, could feel the soreness as he'd walked away from that house. He'd felt so good, had loved giving in and letting himself be taken like that. He'd woken up after having sex for the first time feeling like he was on top of the world, and then, ten minutes later, he'd been cringing against the pain in his ass and realizing he'd just gotten fucked, in every sense of the word.

"I went back and forth about it," he continued. "Then I had, um, a bad date. A really bad date." And wasn't that the understatement of the century? The thing was, he should have known. A gorgeous guy, an athlete, and Greg this weedy little geek, and how could he have thought anyone would want him that way? "The guy was...not out. Really not out. And I got home after..." And his mother had been standing in the kitchen, and she'd taken one look at him, and said, "Oh, honey," and he'd lost it.

"I told my mom as soon as I got home, and I was so scared." Greg chanced a glance up, but Marsh's gaze was shuttered, his expression unreadable in the dimness, and Greg closed his eyes. "I was ready for her to kick me out, but she gave me just about the biggest hug I think she ever had."

"Your father and I love you," she'd said. "No matter what."

Greg's breath shook as he let it out. "They were fine with it. They weren't even surprised. I basically walked in there feeling more alone than I had in my entire life, and then..." He'd walked out knowing he had two people at his back. And because of that he could walk any road, even if it was on his own. "They were just *awesome* about it."

Marsh's fingers resumed their stroking through Greg's hair—when had they stopped?—and Greg felt the knot in his chest easing.

Silence settled over them, and for a while Greg drifted, the migraine fading to something low and manageable in the back of his head so long as Marsh just stayed there, touching him and petting him.

Then Marsh scratched a little harder at the space behind Greg's jawbone. "My dad saw me with a guy. This summer."

Greg opened his eyes. This didn't sound like a good story. "Oh?"

The bed shifted as Marsh redistributed his weight. "I always knew he'd be an asshole about it. Bastard was never exactly subtle. Until..."

Greg waited a beat before asking, "What?"

"Until then." Marsh's jaw made a grinding noise. "Until the night he saw me. Then, he...he didn't say anything."

"Nothing?"

"Nothing at all." There was a distance to Marsh's voice, though. As if nothing at all might have been worse than anything.

Greg reached up to put his hand over Marsh's, giving a gentle squeeze to his palm. Marsh settled his fingers at the nape of Greg's neck.

"You okay?" Greg asked.

"Fine."

Greg lay there, touching Marsh while Marsh touched him. He had no idea what Marsh had gone through, or what he was going through now. But for all that he'd been inside Marsh, he'd never felt as close to him as he did right then.

Somehow, the worst night so far of the semester had turned into one of the best.

Greg's breathing had started to slow again when Marsh spoke, quiet and low. "Should I go?"

And Greg was too tired and wrung out from heavy conversation and the lingering echoes of pain. He didn't have it in him to act distant and detached. "Stay? Just for a little while?" It sounded too needy, by far.

But Marsh just slid his thumb against Greg's pulse. "Okay."

Chapter Six

"So what did he do now?" Yulia had managed to snag their usual spot in the student union coffee shop, even though they were meeting up way earlier than they usually did. She was sitting there, staring at her phone, scarcely bothering to glance up as Marsh approached.

"Nice to see you, too," he mumbled as he tossed his bag down on the table and sank into the chair across from her.

She looked at him, entirely unimpressed, then lifted her phone and shook it side to side. "You texted me at eight in the morning. Eight. I didn't know you even knew that hour existed."

"Of course I do. I hear about it all the time." Forget that he had to be up well before it during baseball season, as often as not.

She had a point, regardless. He didn't see it all that often during the fall semester. This morning, though... Something inside him squeezed down hard. He'd spent the whole night watching the clock tick over, had seen every hour pass as he'd sat there in the dark with Greg asleep in his lap. Running his fingers through soft brown hair and trying to remember to breathe past the swell of affection and dread in his chest.

Greg had asked him to stay. Greg had invited him in and let him sit beside him, had told him about his family, and drawn words out of him he hardly shared with anyone, and it had felt so good and so fragile. Even now, he felt like that moment—like he might shatter as easily as so much glass.

And he was even shakier because he'd pressed his advantage and taken what was offered. Greg had only asked him to stay for a little while, but Marsh had remained well past that invitation. He'd finally dragged himself away when the sky started to lighten. He'd gotten an hour or two of sleep in his own cold bed, and then he'd been up, catching the early bus to campus and texting Yulia just for something to do before he went out of his skull.

God, he was tired.

"Is that for me?" he asked, pointing at the second cup of coffee beside her elbow.

She pushed it toward him, and he accepted it gratefully. He'd barely kept his eyes open through his Mideast seminar that morning, and he still had two more classes to make it through before he could head back to the house and crash for a couple of hours before heading to the gym. It didn't strike him often, but damn he missed living in the dorms sometimes. The food sucked and the public showers weren't awesome, but the ten-minute walk to a bed came in handy sometimes.

As did all the alternate exits you could use to avoid running into any brilliant, gorgeous, confusing men you happened to be sleeping with.

Pulling his coffee closer, he popped the lid and blew across the surface of the liquid. With his first slow, leisurely sip, he started counting seconds in his head, suppressing his smirk as he gazed at a point just over Yulia's shoulder.

Apparently she was feeling generous today. She gave him a whole minute to enjoy his caffeine in peace before she was drumming her fingers on the table. Setting her elbows on the edge, she leaned forward, eyebrows raised with impatience. "You never answered my question."

Marsh sighed. "What makes you think he did something?"

Her cutting gaze told him all he needed to know about what she thought of his attempts to put her off.

"Ugh." He put his coffee down with a sharp sound and leaned back in his chair, reaching up to tug his hair before dropping his hand in his lap. "Nothing. Just—I went to go see him last night, because..."

She rolled her eyes. "I don't need to know about your sex drive."

Right. "But he was, um. He...shit, this sounds so cliché. He had a headache." Only not just a headache. Even in the dimness Greg had been so pale, so obviously hurting and vulnerable, and Marsh had been sure Greg'd tell him to fuck off.

"Wait, he didn't want to have sex? That's what's got your panties all in a twist?"

"No. Well, yeah, but. He wanted to hang out anyway."

And Yulia's face got just this little bit of softness to it, and wasn't that the thing about having a friend you'd known that long, one who knew you that well?

"He just wanted to talk," Marsh said. He'd wanted to talk, and for Marsh to sit close and run his fingers through his hair. He'd relaxed into that touch, and all the tender parts in Marsh had just about cracked open.

Yulia waited a beat, and then another. Then she was shifting forward, and her hand was small and soft when it rested over his. "Marsh. People enjoy your company for more than just sex." At his scoff, her expression hardened again. "I enjoy your company for more than just sex."

"You didn't used to."

"I always did, you asshole." She rubbed her thumb across his knuckles, her gaze gentle. "And I'm not the only one."

There was something about the way she said it that made him ache, made all the twisted-up feelings he was still holding on to from last night more impossible to breathe around.

He had to look away, down at the curl of her fingers against his wrist. "He's so smart. And so hot, and he just wanted to talk."

"And I'll never understand why that kind of thing surprises you so much."

He closed his eyes. "I told him about what happened, this summer."

It was subtle, the way her breath stuttered. "And?"

And he'd put his hand over Marsh's and just *held* it. "He was really nice about it." Marsh could have choked on the memory. "And then he fell asleep with his head in my lap."

Yulia squeezed his fingers even harder, and Marsh jerked his gaze from that middle distance he'd been staring into. God, what his face must look like. He felt warm and soft, and Yulia was never going to let him live this down.

"I mean," he started, but she shook her head.

"I know what you mean." She held his gaze for a long, long minute. Because she did know. She knew exactly what that kind of trust would mean to him, how it would rock him.

He cleared his throat, and she pulled her hand away. They each took a sip of coffee.

"So." Her tone was all different, the moment broken. Marsh could have kissed her for letting it drop so easily. "You have my notes for Muller's class?"

Marsh let out a shaky breath, edged with just a shadow of a laugh, and he nodded. He shoved his bag around so she could reach the zipper. "Green binder."

While she scooted over to sit in the chair beside his and started rifling through his things, he dug his phone out of his pocket and skimmed through Facebook. "Hey, did you see Ben posted—"

But Yulia had gone unnaturally still next to him. He glanced up, his smile sliding off his face when he saw what she was holding. Because. Fuck.

"What the hell is this?" she asked.

"Nothing." He reached over to swipe the yellow piece of paper from her hand. She yanked it away before he could reach, but he had the longer arms, damn it, and with another lunge he had it in his fist. He folded the thing up and jammed it in his pocket.

"No. No," she said, "you do not get to 'nothing' me about this." She jabbed her finger into his chest. He swatted her away, but she just grabbed his wrist and twisted, and *ow*. "Marshall Sulkowski."

Prying her fingers off, he tore his arm free, and sat back, annoyed. "It's none of your business, and I'm handling it."

"That's what you said last time."

"I'll call tomorrow. It's just a misunderstanding or something. Crossed wires." Even he didn't believe that lie.

"That bill was due a month ago."

"You think I don't know that?" he snapped, and crap, that was too loud. He cast a look over his shoulder to see eyes darting away from him, then lowered his voice as he faced her again. "Look, I just have to call home sometime when Dad isn't there, and I'm sure..."

"Marsh..." There was a different note to her voice this time. She didn't believe it either.

"I said I'm handling it."

"And what if handling it doesn't work?"

He stopped cold, because he'd been asking himself that every day for a month now. The fight went out of him, and he buried his face in his hands. "I'll figure something out."

Or he wouldn't. How many times had his old man told him he wasn't college material, anyway? He was struggling in all his classes. Maybe this was just the sign he needed to prove he'd been fooling himself all along.

Out of nowhere, Yulia leaned up out of her seat and flicked his temple with her finger. He jerked back, grabbing for her hand. "What was that for?"

"What was that stupid self-defeating look on your face for?" she asked, all fire, and she was darting in to flick him or pinch him again.

And he was laughing. "What?"

"You heard me—" She stopped on an inhalation, and he got around her defenses to tweak her side in retaliation, but she didn't react except to brush him away. She was looking up, past his shoulder at...Greg.

For a second, Marsh just about lit up, because Greg was standing there, and Marsh hadn't expected to get to see him until tonight. It didn't matter how confused he was. He was getting to see Greg early, and this was Greg coming up to Marsh instead of the other way around, and that had to be good, right? Marsh's lips twitched up toward a grin, and he was going to ask if Greg was feeling better, if he had slept all right after the meds had kicked in.

Only, Greg's jaw was stiff, his lips thin. Marsh followed his gaze, flipping things around to see them from Greg's point of view, and the back of his neck went cold. Crap. It struck him all at once, just how compromising this had to look, him and Yulia sitting so close, grabbing at each other and practically wrestling. The happy little ball of excitement at getting to see Greg turned to ice, and he scooted his chair back, but from the way Greg was looking between the two of them, it was too late.

The ice melted and burned its way to rage, because, really? How unfair was that? How completely, totally, fucking ridiculously not okay was it for Greg to be *looking* at Marsh like that, like he'd...violated some trust or something? How could he, when he'd been the one to say they should keep this casual?

Marsh steeled himself and flicked his hair off his brow, tilting his chin up. "Greg. Hi."

"Hello, Marsh." Greg's expression didn't flicker, didn't change in the least, everything about it a mask.

"What are you—"

Greg gestured toward the counter, his hand wrapped around a cup of coffee, and Marsh felt like a dumbass for even starting to ask. Greg pretty much lived on coffee. Of course he'd show up at the only place on campus that knew how to make a halfway decent cup.

Marsh's stomach sank a little further. Greg had already gotten through the line, so who knew how long he'd been standing there. Marsh hadn't noticed him, but he hadn't been noticing much.

What he did notice was the way Greg flicked his gaze toward Yulia again—Yulia, who for once was keeping quiet. Yulia who was sizing Greg up like she was envisioning performing an autopsy on him.

Right. Because she was already convinced that Greg was taking advantage of Marsh, and now this stony performance. Marsh wanted to thump his head against the tabletop. How did he get himself into situations like this?

Saying *fuck it* in his own head, Marsh pointed from one of them to the other. "Greg, Yulia. Yulia, Greg." He didn't bother prefacing either name with an explanation—it was too complicated and he'd only get himself in more trouble if he tried.

Greg nodded perfunctorily, and Yulia's eye twitched. "Nice to meet you," Greg offered, and wow. He wasn't even trying to lie well.

"And you."

Well, at least Greg had tried a little harder than Yulia had.

Marsh somehow managed to resist the urge to kick Yulia or to reach out toward Greg, to touch the bone of his wrist and stroke the tender spot between forefinger and thumb. To knead a little of that tension out so maybe the lines around Greg's eyes would ease.

Greg's gaze was really on Yulia, but he angled himself toward Marsh. "Well. I'm heading back." His eyes shifted to the side, and he met Marsh's gaze. "Will you be at the house tonight? Or do you have...other plans?"

"I'll—" Marsh faltered for a second. Of course he'd be going home. He wanted to go home right now, but he had classes he had to get through. And apparently when he did get home, he was going to have a whole different kind of headache to deal with, versus the one he'd nursed Greg through the previous night. Just the thought of that made his fingers twitch and his heart clench. "Yeah. I'll be home."

"I'll see you then, I suppose."

"I suppose so." And it hardly mattered that Greg looked like he wanted to crush the cup in his hand or that Marsh was as turned around as he could remember being, because beneath the annoyance, there was heat in Greg's gaze.

Marsh sat up straighter as his body registered the promise behind the threat. If the way Greg's eyes darted down, toward Marsh's mouth, was any sign, he heard the promise just as clearly.

Greg's hand lifted just an inch, but then he was curling it up and dropping it back to his side. He shook his head, then turned to Yulia. "Yulia," Greg said, nodding toward her.

"Greg."

One more nod at Marsh and a look that lingered, practically crackling with heat, and then Greg was pivoting neatly and walking away. All the air left Marsh's chest in a rush. As soon as Greg passed through the doors, Marsh gave in to the impulse and let his head fall forward until his brow made a satisfying *thunk* against the tabletop.

Yulia patted his arm gently, and he groaned. "So that's the guy who's ruthlessly fucking you and uninterested in more?"

"The one and only."

"You have *got* to be shitting me," she said under her breath, clucking her tongue.

And he knew there was more to what she was saying, but he didn't want to hear it right now. He *couldn't*, not without snapping at her or breaking something, or...or...he didn't even know, but it would be bad.

"Don't," he said, voice brooking no argument. "Just don't."

She gave a muffled little huff, but she held her peace, shifting to rest her hand over the back of his neck and rubbing gently with her thumb.

He arched into her touch as he fumbled out with a hand to grip her knee. He'd be so lost without her.

And thanks to her, he was even more fucked than he had been before.

Chapter Seven

"Three days! Three days, I'm trying to figure this out, and it turns out the issue wasn't even with my machine. It was Jason's goddamn vacuum pump." Ronnie twisted as he climbed the stairs of the porch, looking at Greg over his shoulder. "Can you believe it?"

"Always the vacuum pumps," Greg empathized, but he wasn't really paying attention. Ahead of them, the door to the house loomed.

Not for the first time, Greg wished he hadn't agreed to carpool in to school today. The whole ride home, Ronnie had been going on and on about the problem he'd been having with his lab equipment. Normally, Greg would have been interested, would have been doing way more than the perfunctory nodding and humming he'd managed this afternoon. He flicked his gaze up at the door again as Ronnie kept on rambling.

The day after a bad migraine, Greg was never at his best, but he wasn't usually this distracted. He didn't usually feel like his skin was too tight or like he wanted to punch something. He didn't simultaneously want to throw a certain sandy-haired shortstop against a wall and either throttle him or...*fuck* him.

He'd known he and Marsh weren't serious or exclusive or anything, but to see it in front of his own eyes, and with a woman no less... To be offered no explanations or apologies, to be denied, and right after letting Marsh see him so broken down and vulnerable, after asking him to stay...

Not that he'd expected Marsh to jump up and kiss him in the middle of the student union, but the casual distance had been something else entirely. It'd made him feel cold in a way he hadn't in a long while. It'd reminded him why he never did this sort of thing.

He tightened his grip on the strap of the backpack slung over his shoulder. Ronnie was still talking as he fit his key to the lock and pushed the door open. Greg held his breath as the hallway came into view.

And there, standing right in the middle of it, was Marsh.

Greg drew himself up a little taller even as his insides ran amok, sweat prickling on his skin, and it was too warm. His gaze locked with Marsh's, and for a second, it was just the static in the air and the rushing of blood in his ears as he stared.

Hell, but he really didn't want to fuck this up.

"Greg? You listening, man?" Ronnie turned to him expectantly, and the world snapped back into focus.

Greg forced himself to look away from Marsh. Ronnie was standing there, one side of his mouth tipped up, and damn. Greg had never expected to keep this a secret forever, but they'd managed a couple of weeks of sneaking in and out of each other's rooms without anyone the wiser. Now, twice in one day, they'd been put in front of witnesses, and suddenly, under that scrutiny, what they were doing felt like something too thin and too flimsy, so much plastic left out in the sun.

Ronnie looked between the two of them, eyes darting from one to the other, and then he chuckled. "Guess I'll talk to you about those sulfur inclusions tomorrow, then."

Greg shook his head, because he had to think. "No. I'll...I'll find you." He gestured toward Marsh and his throat went even drier. "I just have to talk to Marsh for a minute about..."

"Statistics," Marsh volunteered, and Greg's head jerked up. The whole tutoring thing had been Greg's excuse originally, but the lie came so easily to Marsh's tongue now. Greg bit down on the inside of his lip.

"Right."

"Sure." Ronnie gave Greg a quick clap on the shoulder before heading to the stairs, mumbling as he went, "Probability of one ain't that hard to calculate."

Oh, hell. Greg flipped Ronnie off, then looked to Marsh, who was still standing there. He'd changed into a tight T-shirt and track pants, and the lines of his shoulders and his arms made Greg's head swim. The sound of footsteps on the stairs receded, and then there was the closing of a door. Marsh's eyes darkened, and after a long moment, he turned on his heels, disappearing around the corner and into his room.

Greg stood there, frozen and wanting and feeling like a cad for all of this. He wasn't a casual-sex kind of guy, and now his best friend knew what he was doing. Everyone in the house probably knew. This was a distraction from the work he had to do and the lessons he had to plan and the presentation he had to finish. And he didn't care.

His feet took him the dozen or so steps to Marsh's room, and then he was sliding inside and closing the door, flipping the lock and turning, letting his bag slide off his arm.

Marsh was only a scant few feet away, and he was beautiful, but there was tension in every line of him. He rubbed the back of his neck, biceps flexing as he did, and did he have no idea what he looked like when he did that? "So you're, um, feeling better?"

So obsessed with following the lines of those muscles, Greg almost missed the thread. He caught it and burned, remembering. Marsh had seen Greg at his weakest last night. He'd touched him and tended him and kept him from having to lie there, alone and in pain.

He'd gotten Greg to ask him to stay.

And just like that, Greg felt like he was spinning out of control. He was fucking a man who was way out of his league, and he had no claim on him, and last night he'd needed him so much.

Today, he needed something else entirely. Greg lifted his gaze and focused it in on the plush red of Marsh's mouth.

He needed to be tall, he needed to be in control. He needed to make Marsh *his*, if only for a few minutes. An hour. Whatever he could get.

Drawing his shoulders up, he crossed the distance between them until they were mere inches apart, lifting his hand and splaying out his fingers. He hovered there with his palm just over Marsh's heart, only Marsh was radiating this whole aura of uncertainty, this electric field like he wasn't sure if he was ready to be touched. Greg pushed past it, and when he made contact with that warm, solid expanse of Marsh's chest, he felt his own shiver echoed in Marsh's body.

"Better," Greg said, focus intent on Marsh's lips. He was so hot beneath Greg's hand, his pulse strong, and Greg slid his touch higher, curled his fingers into the dip of his clavicle, wanting under his skin, wanting *inside* him. "But I'd be even better if..." He trailed off, mesmerized by the bob of Marsh's throat.

"Yeah?"

"Yeah." Greg darted his tongue out to wet his own lips. His fingers tightened, and he didn't waste any time or leave any room for mistake. He put his other hand right on Marsh's groin, cupping where his cock was not quite hard yet but not quite soft. "You gonna let me?"

"Hell, yes."

Channeling all the anger and possession he'd been feeling since that afternoon, he tugged on Marsh's neck, and Marsh came, leaning into it. The kiss was all teeth and the hard clash of lips abutting, and he pushed his tongue right inside. Marsh tasted like heat and sex, and it was so good Greg could have screamed with it, could have rolled over and taken it, if that had been an option. But it wasn't. He was here to do the taking. He was here to seize control.

He kissed Marsh savagely for another minute, rubbing and feeling the full, stiff length of him unfurl through his clothes, and then he pushed him away. "Strip," he ordered.

Marsh didn't hesitate. He pulled away and was working his shirt up over those abs and those arms, and for a second, all Greg could seem to do was stare. That was for him.

Greg pulled his own shirt over his head and looked around. "You have…?"

Pushing his pants over his hips with one hand, Marsh gestured toward the bed. Only he didn't have a nightstand. Greg refocused, and—oh. The duffle bag there. Greg's stomach did a little flip.

"Front pocket," Marsh said, and fuck, Greg didn't want to think about that. He didn't want to think about how many other people Marsh was doing this with, or where he was going to do it with them. Not now, not in this pocket of time when Marsh was his.

He didn't think he let any of that show on his face as he stalked over to the bag and pulled at the zip. Sure enough, he found a little bottle of slick and a line of condoms. Greg tore one off and didn't think too much about the rest as he threw it on the bed, putting the bottle down beside it. He stripped the rest of his clothes off without looking at it or at Marsh, until a hot hand on his hip startled the breath from his lungs.

Marsh pulled back. "Are you okay?"

How the hell was he supposed to answer that? He was perfect and terrible, and about to have sex with exactly the man he wanted to be having it with, and he felt like he was holding on to his chance with him by his fingernails.

Holding his tongue, he turned, reaching out to pull Marsh in. Kissing him with all the desperation he felt.

Marsh was naked and so fucking gorgeous, and Greg made an undignified noise when all that flesh pressed up against all of his. It was a hot slide and a glide and a searing kiss that rattled him to his bones, blanking his mind against the rising tide of worry. He was here, right now. Right where he wanted to be.

Focusing on that and nipping at Marsh's lip, he ran his hands over the firm expanse of thigh and hip, then curved around Marsh's ass to nudge his fingertips into the crack. Greg wasn't good at talking, he never had been, but as he probed, dry, at Marsh's hole, he groaned. "Wanna fuck you so bad."

"Yeah," Marsh said, and Greg was never going to get over that.

He kept his reverence and his disbelief at bay, though, as he maneuvered Marsh toward the bed. He followed, getting onto his knees at the edge of the mattress, and then nudging at Marsh to get him on his stomach. Marsh lifted up, bracing himself on his forearms, the muscles in his back and biceps thrown into stark relief. Greg wanted to trace every inch with his tongue. He climbed over Marsh and settled, knees to either side of Marsh's hips, and bit down at the place where neck met shoulder. "You look so good," he couldn't help saying. "Feel so good."

"Gonna feel even better around your cock." Marsh dropped his head forward, leaning into every touch.

A wave of arousal crashed over Greg, and he had to lift up, had to get away before he rubbed himself off against Marsh's ass and came all over his skin in a rush, too soon and too much. Exercising all the restraint he didn't feel he had, he levered himself lower on the bed, dragging his tongue along Marsh's spine. He reached over him for the lube and slicked his fingers up. Moaning into Marsh's ear, he got his hand between them and zeroed right in on his hole.

"Yeah." Marsh let out a rasping breath as Greg forced a finger inside. He was so tight, so hot and smooth, and he was shaking his head as Greg fought for the patience to work him open. "Not too much. Wanna feel it."

"Fuck." Greg shook with it. "You trying to kill me?"

Squeezing around Greg's finger, Marsh let out a little laugh and twisted to look at him over his shoulder. "Just might be."

Just for that, Greg pressed another finger in, thrusting in and out and feeling for his prostate. When he hit it, Marsh gasped and swore. "Enough, enough." He fell forward and scrambled for the condom, ripping it open and passing the circle of latex over his shoulder.

And he was looking at Greg, those clear blue eyes staring at him, and Greg felt naked and shaky, and he wanted this too badly.

He accepted the condom and shifted away to roll it on. He poured lube into his palm and gave himself a long stroke, then pressed slick fingers into Marsh again, watching as they disappeared, watching the shine of his skin and the stretched pink rim. Marsh gave another impatient grunt and arched into the pressure, and that was it.

Greg drew his hand back and wiped his fingers on the sheets, repositioning himself between Marsh's spread-wide thighs. He took himself in hand, placed a palm on Marsh's hip. Sucking in a breath, he guided himself into place.

God, but Greg loved this. The way that perfect clench tried to keep him out, and then the soft place inside when Marsh's body started to suck him in, and it was all the velvet grip and yielding heat. Greg caught himself with a hand at Marsh's spine as Marsh choked and took him all the way inside. Plastering himself against Marsh's back, Greg breathed into his shoulder as he rested there. Marsh's arms trembled, but after a few tense moments, he gave a little nod. With a long, low moan, Greg retreated just an inch before driving forward. Marsh was only barely prepped enough. He was so tight, the friction too good to be believed as Greg moved inside his body.

And it still wasn't enough. Marsh braced himself a little better and pushed back into the thrust. "Harder, damn it. Not gonna break."

And Greg practically growled as he scraped teeth along Marsh's neck. He was the one doing the fucking here. He gave a sharp slap at Marsh's side, and Marsh leaned into it.

"I'll fuck you...how I wanna fuck you." Greg reached up and threaded his fingers into Marsh's hair. "You gonna take it?"

"Aren't I?" And it was still too much cheek.

Greg yanked and Marsh gasped. "Yeah," Greg said. "Take it like a pro."

How many other people do you take it from this way?

"Fuck yeah, I do." The way he said it, it wasn't just sex, wasn't just pride at the way his ass clenched and flexed, and the way he moved and let Greg have what he wanted from him. It was something darker. It lit the possessive flame inside Greg's chest and stoked it hotter, made him drive into Marsh harder.

Marsh grunted, but he was still pushing into Greg's strokes, still asking for more.

"You like that?" Greg asked.

"Yeah. God, yeah."

"Because I love it." Greg could hardly believe the words coming out of him. Shit, this was just like last night all over again. Even if he wasn't sick with pain, he was aching, and asking for things. Things he shouldn't want and shouldn't be saying out loud. He snapped his hips against the unbearable pressure in his balls and in his heart and in his lungs. He closed his eyes and buried his face against Marsh's skin. "I love it," he confessed again. "I love fucking you. Love touching you. Love your ass and your arms and your—"

And Greg clamped his jaw shut, because he couldn't love Marsh. He could do this—could take what he could get and do it willingly, could settle for just the scraps he got when he wanted everything, but he couldn't love him, too. It was too much to bear.

And so he *wouldn't* bear it. He groaned and reached under Marsh's body, curled a sweat-slick hand around his cock and jerked it in hard, punishing strokes. He needed to make Marsh feel this. Needed to leave something of himself, even if it was only a memory for when Marsh went out into the world and was amazing and incredible and everything Greg wasn't.

Without acknowledging the sudden desperation in Greg's touch or the brutal pace of his cock, Marsh pushed into the circle of Greg's fist. His head snapped up, and his spine arched in one bright, long, beautiful line.

"Greg!" Marsh cried out, and fuck, fuck, his dick spasmed and pulsed, hot fluid flowing over Greg's fingers and dripping on his wrist.

Greg let go. Braced himself on the bed and on Marsh's shoulder and yanked him hard into his thrust. All he could hear was his own name in that warm, thick voice, all he could feel was Marsh's body surrounding him, Marsh fucking himself back onto his cock. Greg pressed forward another stroke, a dozen, and then he was stifling his scream in Marsh's neck as he came like a storm, like a whiteout.

As he came hard enough to forget he didn't get to keep this.

Almost.

As soon as he could think straight, he pulled out and collapsed to the side. Marsh dropped to his stomach and flailed an arm out toward him. Rested a hand over his still-thundering heart, and Greg settled his own atop it. He held on.

It took a minute for the world to slide out from under him and for his throat to start to close. He squeezed his eyes shut tight. Marsh wasn't his, and he wasn't the pathetic little boy who got used by men who were cooler and bigger than him. He wasn't the kid who needed taking care of, like he had been. He was his own, and he was making it all right on his own. This was a distraction—one he could indulge in, because when it wasn't making him feel so incredibly alone, it made him feel good, and that was all right.

But there were things he couldn't afford to be distracted from. His life, his work, always his work—that was his ticket to making it out and making good. To making his parents proud. And it didn't matter that he wanted to lie there forever, sated and held and pressed up, skin to skin, against a beautiful man.

Greg grasped Marsh's hand in a crushing grip, and then he let go.

He slipped out from beneath the arm slung heavy across his chest. Focusing on the task, he dealt with the condom, stomach turning at the wet slap as it hit the bottom of the waste bin. He picked up his clothes and pulled them on. He'd go clean up and find some food or at least make some coffee, then he'd chase Ronnie down and see what he'd been on about. After that, he'd have time to figure out those graphs and grade those quizzes and finish up his presentation.

The sound of sheets rustling came from the bed. "You're off then?" Marsh asked, voice neutral, and Greg hated that. It burned him, how Marsh always seemed so unaffected, even as Greg was pushing everything down inside himself to make only a piss-poor attempt at the same kind of detachment.

"Yeah."

"I don't have to be at the gym for another hour. You hungry?"

Starved. "Nah. I've got—"

"Work to do, yeah."

"Yeah."

Greg looked over at Marsh, draped out, naked, across that bed, and he wanted nothing more than to crawl in after him and kiss his mouth. He could see it—lazy nights eating takeout in bed and watching action flicks and fucking into the night and curling up together to sleep. Maybe someday, with somebody more like himself, he'd be able to have that.

"You do make time to eat occasionally, right?"

Greg stopped short, diverting his gaze up to Marsh's face. It was just an idle question. Teasing, probably. He'd heard it all before. *Don't you do anything but study, nerd?* "Occasionally," he replied, desert-dry.

Marsh's brow furrowed. "Okay, well. If you say so."

"I just did."

"Whatever." With that, Marsh's expression smoothed back out, and he sat up, gathering the sheet around his waist, and it felt exactly like the dismissal it was.

Whatever, indeed. "See you around," Greg gritted out. He headed for the door and was about to yank it open, but then remembered. He eased the door just a crack and peeked. Coast was clear. "Later."

"Later," Marsh echoed.

Scooping his bag up off the ground, Greg let himself out. Bile burned, and he shut the door behind him with as close to a slam as he could bring himself to. He glanced down the hall, one way and then the other. His stomach churned with hunger and discontent, and he couldn't bring himself to feed either. The thought of standing in the kitchen, making food, knowing Marsh was possibly still naked right through that one thin wall...

Fuck it, warm Mountain Dew and an energy bar it was. Greg hoisted his book bag onto his shoulder. He took the stairs up to his room two at a time.

He had real work to do.

Chapter Eight

"Coward. Come on." Marsh mumbled the words low under his breath as he hovered on the third step from the top. He'd been hovering there for a while now. Because he was a coward. Damn it all.

He cursed himself again beneath his breath, resolving to just do it already. He took one more step before retreating. This was ridiculous. "It's not that fucking hard. Just go over there and..."

And put himself out there. Crap, he hated this.

For what had to be the hundredth time, he glanced at the crack of light spilling out from beneath Greg's door and took a deep breath. This wasn't a big deal. He'd done this how many times now? Gone up to that door and knocked and given a leer, and Greg had always invited him in. Even that once when it had just been to let Marsh run his hands through his hair. He'd never turned Marsh away, but it was different today.

Because the thing was, Marsh had been keeping track. All the signs had been there, the entire time they'd been fucking around like this. Greg worked like he was possessed, only stopping when his body forced him to. Only pausing when Marsh came by, offering a few minutes of stress relief and heat and the chance to thrust, hard and fast into his mouth or ass. The chance to kiss and touch and make it all go away for a little while.

It was such a little while, though, and ever since that night with the migraine, ever since that blindingly hot, possessive fuck the next day, it had been getting worse. A week had passed, and the circles under Greg's eyes had been darkening.

The moments when he'd taken time to come down Marsh's throat had gotten briefer.

And he wasn't eating.

Marsh punched his thigh and tried to get his nerve up again. He was going to go over there, and he was going to make an offer, but it wasn't going to be his body. It was going to be something different, something Greg had only accepted the once. And he didn't know what he was going to do when Greg told him to fuck off.

The sound of a door opening farther down the hall finally kicked Marsh out of his stalemate with himself. Swearing silently, he jogged down a couple of steps only to course right back up them, turning the corner at the top of the landing to see Jason stepping out of his room.

"Hey!" Jason did a little double take, as if surprised to see him there. Marsh didn't know how anyone was still surprised to see him ducking in and out of Greg's room.

He smiled anyway. "Hey, man." He strode right past Greg's door as if he didn't care, as if all his concentration hadn't been on that single spot for the last ten minutes, and held out his hand.

Jason gripped it, and Marsh gave his palm a quick clasp before letting go. "Haven't seen you around much."

Jason had been Marsh's only real link here when he'd first moved in. A former athlete himself, he'd at least spoken the same language Marsh did, even if he also happened to be fluent in geek.

"Been keeping busy. Practices and classes and stuff," Marsh eyed Greg's door, then forced his gaze away. "You heading out?"

"Yeah, gotta check on an experiment. Probably gonna swing by Wendy's on the way back though, if you want something?"

"Nah. I...got plans."

For the first time, Jason had that knowing look everyone seemed to get. "Cool. Catch you later."

Marsh stepped aside to let him go, and the jig was up now. Greg would've had to have been cranking his music pretty loud to have missed any of that, and Marsh didn't have any other excuse to be up here.

Time to man up.

Jason headed to the stairs, and way too cognizant of his audience, Marsh moved to stand in front of Greg's door. He gave himself the time for one big, deep breath before knocking, the same three quick little raps he used every time.

"Yeah?" Greg's voice was pinched, and the nervous energy in Marsh's gut solidified.

He pushed the door open anyway and plastered on an easy smile. "Hey."

Greg was sitting at his desk the way he always seemed to be these days, those sexy, nerdy little glasses sitting low on his nose, and his hair was sticking up like he'd been running his hands through it, and—Marsh's smile faded a little. It'd been a couple of days since he'd been up here, and had there been as many soda cans and papers strewn around the last time?

Mumbling something under his breath, Greg slid the glasses off his face and folded them up, one hand going up to his hair. Marsh wanted to walk right up to him and do it for him, slide his fingers through unruly strands and press them down where they belonged. Or maybe mess them up a little worse. He could never decide.

"Sorry." Greg rolled his chair away from his desk a little. His gaze shifted from his laptop screen to Marsh and back. "It's really not a good time." His eyes drifted lower, and the muscles in his jaw flexed. "Not that I don't want to but—"

"No, no." And hell yes, Marsh *wanted to*, but that wasn't why he was here. Even if that was all Greg really saw him as. He didn't twitch when Greg's shoulders dropped a little, like it was a relief that he wasn't going to have to fuck him, and God. What the hell was Marsh doing here?

"I just—I was." This wasn't that fucking hard. Marsh jabbed the heel of his hand into his thigh. "I was gonna order something. Chinese, maybe?"

Greg was already shaking his head, gesturing to the couple of wrappers next to one of the cans of soda as if protein bars were an acceptable substitute for actual food. Marsh lifted his chin and braced his arm on the door.

He'd come here for a reason, and it didn't have anything to do with himself. No matter what they were to each other, no way in hell Marsh was watching someone he...cared about self-destruct. Not this bad, and not when it was in his power to do something about it.

He lifted one eyebrow. "Are you seriously about to try and tell me that those things are a meal?"

"They got me through undergrad."

Christ. "Um, no. Look, when's the last time you took a break? Like, a real one?"

"I don't have time—"

"Bullshit." Because Marsh had played that game. Back his first year when he'd been trying so hard to make the starting lineup and not fail even the bullshit jock classes he was taking for his gen-ed requirements, he'd pulled this crap. "You're going to make yourself sick like this."

"I'll be fine."

"Just like you were fine last week when you couldn't stand to have the lights on?"

And fuck. Greg's face went hard all at once, and wow, Marsh did not have the right to say any of that. He didn't have the right to say anything. But he was going to say it anyway.

"I'm sorry you had to see that," Greg started, mouth pinched, but his ears were red, and screw it. Maybe this was about Marsh overstepping, and maybe it was some BS instinct on Greg's part to keep up some kind of image, but whatever.

"I'm not." Marsh sucked in a breath through his teeth. "I'm not sorry, okay, because it was fine, and I was...I was glad. Not that you were sick. Just that. You let me..." *You let me take care of you even when we weren't naked.*

This was coming out all wrong.

Marsh jutted out his bottom jaw and crossed his arms over his chest. "Look, I'm ordering Chinese. I'm getting twice as much as I need, and one of the things I order is going to be sweet and sour chicken. If you can find it in your busy schedule to come down and eat some of my food in an hour, great. If not, it's going in the fridge as leftovers that I will not eat, so you can decide to not get an ulcer on your own schedule, and you won't even have to look at my face while you do it. Whatever. Your choice."

With that, he whirled around, intent on stomping down the stairs when the low voice behind him stopped him.

"I thought you told Jason you had plans."

Marsh's ribs seemed two sizes too tight, because there was something wavering there. What had Greg thought? That Marsh was stopping by for a quick fuck before heading out?

He gripped the doorframe and twisted his neck to look over his shoulder. His reply came out a little weak. "I may have been being optimistic. About those plans. Was hoping my date would say yes."

The statement hung in the air, and he hadn't meant to call Greg his date. He wanted to pull the words back into his mouth, laugh it off, say he was only joking. But Greg nodded, and the stiff set to his mouth gave way to the first real smile Marsh had seen in a week. "I'd hate to make a liar of you, I guess." He twirled his glasses in his hand. "Sweet and sour chicken, you said?"

Marsh breathed out a little sigh of relief. He'd been pretty sure that was Greg's favorite, considering how he hoarded it whenever there were leftovers. "Yup."

"I'll try to finish this up."

"Okay."

Okay.

Feeling a hundred times lighter, Marsh pulled the door closed behind him, then all but floated down the stairs. He gave a little salute to Jason, who was shrugging into his jacket. Jason had probably heard everything, but Marsh couldn't bring himself to care. Not right now.

He made his way to the kitchen and grabbed the menu for the Chinese place down the street, retreating to his room to call in the order. He winced at the total when the lady on the line rattled it off, but he could swing it. He'd have to scrimp a little, but it'd be all right.

With food on the way and Greg coming soon, Marsh flopped belly-down on his bed and pulled the book he'd abandoned earlier closer. He glanced at the clock. Forty minutes to read four chapters. Unlikely, but he'd do what he could.

And what he could ended up being...pretty good, actually. By the time the doorbell rang, he had three pages of notes scribbled out about Indo-Pakistani relations in the seventies and an idea for the paper he had to write by next week. Satisfied, he shoved his notes between the pages of the book and set the whole pile aside before bounding up and reaching for his wallet.

By the time he made it to the door, Greg was coming down the stairs, and Marsh had the biggest shit-eating grin on his face as he stepped forward to take the food from the delivery guy. He couldn't even manage to feel like a dork about it. He'd been so sure he'd have to go up there and pry Greg out of his desk chair with a crowbar, but here he was. He paid the dude and turned to go back inside.

Greg was standing there, looking a little better than he had before, hair tamed and glasses nowhere in sight. He had his own wallet out. "What do I owe you?"

"I got it." He sure could have used the couple of bucks, but he wanted to do this. Calling Greg his date had been a slip of the tongue, but the fact of the matter was, this was the closest they had gotten to one.

Greg frowned but tucked his wallet into the pocket of his jeans. "You sure?"

"Yeah, no problem."

"Okay. I'll get the next one then."

And Marsh had been wrong. *This* was the biggest shit-eating grin. He hid it by looking into the bag to make sure everything was there. Check, check and check. He tilted his head down the hall. "You wanna be civilized and do this in the kitchen or in my room?"

"Your room is good. If you don't mind."

"Sure." That was fine. He didn't love having the place smell like takeout, but it was private. Made it even more like a date.

Greg shifted. "Unless. I mean, I'm not expecting...anything. I just don't feel like running into anyone else. I've been dodging Ronnie about helping him out with one of his projects for days." He smiled weakly.

Maybe less of a date then. Marsh's grin receded a bit, but he hid that, too, as he led the way into his room. Greg went off to grab drinks while Marsh set out a picnic on his bare floor. He could have done better if this had been a real date—he would have done better. But this was what he had. Sometimes, you just made do.

When Greg returned, he closed the door behind himself and locked it, then folded himself down on the floor beside Marsh, passing over a beer. Marsh took it and popped the top, watching as Greg shoveled some of everything onto a paper plate. Sure enough, the plate was piled high by the time he was done. Marsh hadn't seen him come down for a real meal in ages; the guy was going to be skin and bones if he didn't let someone take care of him.

As soon as Greg was done, Marsh assembled his own plate. He backed up, resting it in his lap as he leaned against the bed, legs stretched out in front of him, feet just grazing Greg's thigh. Greg didn't move away. He was too busy digging in.

Marsh scooped up a forkful of noodles, watching Greg the entire time. The guy ate like he was starving, and with him sitting so close, the dark patches under his eyes and the lines around his mouth were even starker than they'd seemed before. It wasn't Marsh's job to mother-hen, but damn. He chewed and swallowed and took a pull at his beer.

"So," he said, before he could stop himself. "What are you working on?"

Greg chuckled. "What am I not working on?"

Nudging Greg's leg with his foot, Marsh let the corners of his lips drag down. "Really?"

"You actually want to know?" One of Greg's eyebrows rose, and he paused with his chopsticks halfway between his mouth and his plate.

"I asked, didn't I?" Sure, he probably wouldn't understand it or anything, but it didn't mean he didn't want to know. "I mean, unless you don't want to tell me, or don't want to talk to me." *Or think I'm too stupid to get it.* "Or whatever." He shrugged.

Greg finished getting the piece of chicken to his mouth and chewed it contemplatively for a few seconds. He fished a napkin out of the bag and wiped his mouth with it, then set his plate down and leaned back, bracing himself with one arm, the other held out in front of him as he started ticking things off. "I'm TA-ing a class, and their second exam is coming up, so everyone wants extra help, and that's on top of my normal teaching responsibilities. Quizzes to grade, problem sets to get ready." He extended a second finger. "My advisor is on my ass about getting a new data set analyzed." A third finger. "One of the other guys who works at the computer help desk with me has mono so I'm covering an extra shift a week." Four. "I'm a week behind in the one class I'm taking this semester." His thumb came up, waggling beside its brethren. "And I have to give a big presentation in a couple weeks that I'm still only halfway done with."

Jesus.

Marsh swallowed the lump of vegetable matter he'd stopped being able to properly chew about four bullet points ago. "Is that all?"

Shaking his head, Greg let out a laugh that sounded like the guy could barely catch a breath. Like he was about to go over the edge. "You do what you gotta do, right?"

"Or in your case, you do what about five different people should be trying to do."

"It could be worse."

Marsh boggled. "How?"

"Ugh, you had to ask?" Greg stretched to drum his knuckles against the wood of the open closet door. "Because you said that, some freak storm or something is going to hit and fry my motherboard."

"Um." Gesturing toward the ceiling with his bottle, Marsh asked, "You wanna go do a quick backup or something?"

"Maybe after." Greg folded himself into a normal sitting position again and resumed his meal. He got another mouthful of rice and sauce up to his mouth, gulping it down before admitting, "Too busy eating."

"You needed it."

Greg paused, looking over at Marsh out of the corner of his eye. Marsh swallowed and looked away. After the way Greg had reacted earlier to Marsh implying he'd given himself that migraine last week, maybe Marsh shouldn't be drawing extra attention to the total shit job Greg was doing taking care of himself.

Only Greg didn't overreact this time. "Yeah," he said after a second. "I did. Um. Thank you. For that."

"No problem." Marsh focused in on his plate over the low thunder of his heart. Still half-watching Greg, he pushed his own food around on his plate. "It's incredible, you know."

Greg just furrowed his brow.

And oh hell, now Marsh had to explain. He lifted one shoulder and set it back down, staring at his dinner as if the bit of pepper on the end of his fork was the most interesting thing in the world. "How hard you work."

Greg made a little scoffing noise. "I should be doing more."

"I'm not sure how you could." Really, how were there enough hours in the day? "You do all these things, and you still have friends. Ronnie and them."

"I'd go crazy without someone else in the asylum with me."

"Still..."

"And they're not my only friends," Greg said, and it was low. Serious in a way that caught Marsh's attention and made him look up. Greg rested his chopsticks on the edge of his plate, his hand lowering, and it stuttered in the air for a moment. Then it settled, warm and solid on Marsh's ankle, and Marsh could feel it all the way up his spine.

Marsh couldn't help but squirm at the implication, forget how much he wanted it to be true. "You hardly know me," he protested. "I'm just the guy who—" *you fuck* "—lives downstairs. And occasionally makes you eat."

"And take other breaks."

Marsh's neck felt warm. "And take other breaks." He cleared his throat against the lump forming there. "Anyway, you work really hard. And that's...really something." He sucked his bottom lip into his mouth and ran his tongue over it. "I mean, I take the bare minimum of classes I have to." It was part of why he was as screwed as he was now. "Professors give me a break because I'm a dumb jock, and I'm still just barely getting by."

The room went unnaturally still, and Marsh tightened his grip on his fork. He suddenly felt way too hot. Damn it all, he really didn't need to help Greg figure out that he was an idiot. What the hell was he doing? Why did he ever open his mouth?

He chanced a glance up, and Greg was frowning, his expression strangely intense in a way that made Marsh's insides twist.

Then Greg stabbed a piece of chicken with a chopstick, piercing it through, and his voice was strained. "You're not a dumb jock."

Marsh didn't know where the shock of laughter came from, but his throat was raw so it must have been him. "Sure. If you say so."

"I do."

"Well, you're wrong." He shrugged like it didn't matter, when it mattered more than anything else. More than anything at all. "If it wasn't for baseball, I never would have made it into college at all. Even with that, I'm barely hacking it."

"Marsh." The urgent tone in Greg's voice made Marsh look up. Greg reached over and snagged the book Marsh had been reading off the pile beside his bed. He read the title off. "*A House Divided: Indian-Pakistani Relations in the 1970s Era of Détente.*" He leveled Marsh with a skeptical look. "Idiots don't read books with titles like that."

Marsh grabbed the book and set it aside. "It's not exactly rocket science or whatever you guys do."

"I *like* rocket science. I got a C in history when I was in tenth grade."

Rolling his eyes, Marsh argued, "Like that's really held you back."

"And like you not wanting to do rocket science has really held you back. You like history, right?"

The truth was, Marsh did. He always had, had thought the stories of flags and armies and spies and negotiations were just so *cool.* He'd hidden histories behind his comic books when he'd been a kid. Written papers when the rest of the family had been gathered around the TV. "I guess."

Greg shook his head, and there was a sadness to it. "You sell yourself so short. You know why I work so hard?"

Because he was a genius, and because he was good at this school stuff. Wasn't that always why brains did what they did? "Because you're smart?"

"Being smart is why all the work pays off so well." Greg was sitting up straight now, all his attention on Marsh, and a fire lit his eyes. "I work so hard because I don't want to be the guy in the overalls taking your credit card at the oil change place."

And that hit a little too close to home. "There's nothing wrong with that."

"Of course there's not." He sucked in a breath, gaze wavering. "That's what my dad does."

Marsh's head jerked up. "Your—"

"My dad. Twenty years, and he's still working a dead-end job at a crappy chain, and he coughs all the time at night, and his hands are always dirty. And he works so hard, but he can never get ahead. My mom's a nurse, and she does okay, but the minute they figured out I was good at school, they told me I had to...I had to make it out. They gave up so much for me, so I didn't have to have a job in high school, or in undergrad."

Fuck. Marsh's eyes were stinging, and he couldn't even name why.

"I work because they're counting on me," Greg said. "Because I have to take the chance they gave me. I have to."

Marsh's chest burned. "They have to be so proud of you."

"They are." Greg sounded so confident about it, like that was something he'd never had to doubt the way that Marsh had. "And I earn that. Every day."

What the hell was Marsh supposed to do with that? What, except scoot across the floor and take Greg's face in his hand and kiss his mouth. And he didn't deserve this. Didn't deserve to have someone so smart and downright *good* sitting on his floor eating takeout with him, but by some miracle, he did. He nipped at Greg's bottom lip and pressed their foreheads together and tried to say all the things he couldn't quite, because there weren't words for this. If there were, he'd never found them.

But then again, he'd never gotten so close to someone who made him want to say them before.

When he pulled away, his face felt warm, and something in his chest did, too. Greg squeezed his hand. "What was that for?"

"Just because I wanted to." It came out a little too honest, but with everything else he was holding in, maybe there wasn't any way around that.

Marsh took his hand back and retreated over to his side of their takeout picnic. He downed a couple of bites that didn't taste as good as Greg's lips had and that didn't ease the deeper hunger that never seemed to go away now.

"Well," he said after a minute. "Whatever your reason..." And he wasn't supposed to feel this way. Brains were brains and jocks were jocks, but really, he'd never felt like he was on the good side of that dividing line. "I respect it. I don't know if I could ever work that hard."

"Sure you could. If you found something you cared about enough to want to."

Marsh thought about that. What the hell did he care about that much? There was baseball, sure. He loved the moment of calm when he was up at bat, the thrill of his blood rushing through his veins as he rounded a base. There was the thread of history unwinding before him, intricate and twisting. The looks on the faces of those kids he'd helped learn how to judge a pitch.

"How did you know?" Marsh heard himself ask.

"Know what?"

"What you wanted to do? When you grew up, or whatever."

Greg's face softened, and Marsh felt more out of his league than usual. Younger and more ridiculous.

"Science is always what I was good at. My dad…he's a mechanic, right? He used to take me to the shop with him sometimes, and he'd show me how things worked when he had time. I got really into it, but not just that. I wanted to know *why* things worked the way they did. I found some books on it, and I had a couple teachers along the way who gave me extra stuff." He shrugged. "I don't know. It just made sense to me in a way nothing else did."

"Must be nice." Marsh tried to swallow the rueful edge to the words.

"It is, in its own way. But people who are good at a lot of things…I've always envied them. Sure, I figured my stuff out early, but it was partly because it was the only thing I was ever really good at. Makes it easier. But try telling that to my high school English teacher."

Marsh couldn't even imagine Greg struggling at anything.

Greg paused. "Have you done any internships or anything yet? Those are a way to figure out what you might want to do with yourself. Or at least try things out."

"Nah." Yet another way Marsh had fucked himself over. Any summer internships he might have applied for he'd had to pass over in favor of his damn baseball schedule and trying to fit in some paying work around it. "Though…"

"Yeah."

"It's nothing." Marsh's gaze drifted to the box in the corner of his closet. "I mean, it's not *nothing*, just some stuff I did at summer camps the past few years. Teaching kids." There was a whole crew of them, junior high age mostly, that showed up for a couple of weeks in the middle of Marsh's training camp. He and some of the other guys would volunteer to work with them between practices in the afternoon. "Mostly just helping them with their swing, but there was some other stuff, too. That was pretty okay." More than pretty okay. It was the best he'd felt about anything, other than on the field.

"That's definitely something. Teaching is cool."

Marsh chuffed. He couldn't really picture himself in front of a classroom, or in a tie, or being responsible for anything.

Except that sometimes, he could. "It was," he said, after chewing contemplatively. "Cool, I mean. At least the summer camp stuff." He pointed his fork toward his closet, and his ribs felt tight just bringing it up. Because he didn't tell anybody about this kind of stuff—about what a sap he could be sometimes. "The kids all, like, wrote me thank-you letters at the end of it. I still have them. They cheer me up sometimes." Times when Marsh had needed something to remind himself he wasn't a complete and total waste.

Greg twisted around, looking where Marsh had directed him. His eyes alit on the box of letters before he turned back around, poking his chopsticks at his rice and looking down. "That's awesome. The kids I teach, I consider myself lucky so long as they don't hurl rotten fruit."

"Sure." Marsh bet Greg was a great TA. He was smart without acting stuck-up about it. Approachable.

A beat of silence passed before Greg said, "You'll figure it out."

Marsh grunted noncommittally, his stomach dipping at the quiet tone of encouragement.

Because he *had* to figure it out. Unconsciously, he glanced at his bag. The still-unpaid bill was practically burning through the nylon now, and he wasn't going to get many more chances.

He had decisions to make, but how was he supposed to? How was he supposed to know what to do about any of this when he didn't know what the point of it all was?

Even if he signed the paperwork and hocked himself into debt for the rest of his life, what was it for? A useless degree? A piece of paper to hang on his wall while he ended up as bad as his own dad, thinking about the glory days when people thought he was hot stuff just because he could hit a ball?

Back when he was fucking someone who was going to go on to win a Nobel someday?

God, he was getting whiny—even in his own head he could hardly stand the timbre of it. He pushed his plate away and drained the rest of his beer.

On the other side of the room, Greg was finishing up his own meal. He licked his lips and set his chopsticks down. Fidgeting, he drummed his fingers against his knee. Barely done, and already he was eyeing the door.

Marsh forced himself to smile. He tried to keep the disappointment from his tone as he asked, "You gonna get back to it?"

"Probably should." Greg's posture eased, one side of his mouth quirking up. Probably relieved he hadn't been the one to have to come up with an excuse to go. "You don't mind?"

"Not gonna kick you out, but no. You got enough stuff to do."

"That's an understatement." Closing up the containers that still had food in them, he waved toward the door. "Want me to put this stuff in the fridge?"

"Yeah, sure." Marsh started gathering up the trash.

Greg stood, and Marsh didn't look at him.

But then there were feet in his vision, a hand on the scruff of his neck. Marsh flickered his gaze up, and Greg curled his fingers into the hair at Marsh's nape, tipping his head back.

"Thank you." Greg bent over, pressing his lips to Marsh's. And it felt like the thank-you was for more than just the food.

"Anytime."

Another kiss, and then Greg straightened up.

"Don't work too hard," Marsh admonished once Greg was at the door.

Greg turned to him, and his smile was tired, so tired, but there was light in his eyes. "Don't worry. I've got it all under control."

Chapter Nine

Greg had told Marsh he had everything under control. He'd even managed to say it like he believed it. But one short week later, and everything had started spinning out, accelerating to the point where he was running to stay in place.

Just thinking about it made him want to scream.

It was like when his dad had thrown that seventh ball into the mix when Greg had been learning how to juggle as a teen. That crystal moment just before it all collapsed, the timing one millisecond off, and everything was ready to come crashing to the ground.

He couldn't concentrate, couldn't breathe, couldn't sleep. The only times he felt like he had a grip on anything at all were times like these... Times like this. Right now.

He closed his eyes against it all and nosed harder at the tender flesh beside the crest of Marsh's hip, twisting his fingers deeper into the slick, soft give inside. It was all heat and the rush of having someone—having Marsh beneath him. Even still, he was ready to flame out, ready to burst.

Because he only had control here—here in the space between Marsh's parted legs, smelling musk and scraping teeth along the marks he'd left the day before and the day before that—because he was holding on to it so tightly. Clinging and grasping on, forcing himself into a shape he was never meant to fit. The casual paramour, the pushy top, the *fuckbuddy*, and God, he hated that word.

Almost as much as he loved, loved, *loved* the noises Marsh made. The choked inhale when Greg stroked his prostate and the groan as he danced fingertips up and down the length of his cock. The way Marsh clutched the sheets and the times when he grabbed Greg's hair.

Greg soaked it all up and bundled it, precious and necessary, and hid it deep inside himself, in amongst the reserves that would get him through, somehow.

"Greg—Greg, Christ." Marsh was dripping sweat, his hair falling into his eyes. He looked wrecked and fucked-out and desperate, the sheen to his eyes so perfect that Greg could read things into them that he shouldn't, not if he wanted to stay sane. "Please."

Marsh was begging, and Greg's cock bobbed against his hip. Greg gave another quick twist of his wrist before pulling his hand free.

And Greg didn't have time for this. There were so many things to do, but taking Marsh apart this way was like a drug, and he didn't know when he'd get his next fix. He didn't know when Marsh would realize what was going on here and walk away. When Greg's oasis in the desert dried up completely, leaving him scrabbling at sand.

A skitter of pain seared its way through his chest at the thought of it, there and gone in a flash. Refusing to dwell, Greg shook his head and swiped his fingers across the sweat-slick plane of Marsh's abdomen. Wrapped a hand around his cock and gave it one wet stroke that had Marsh keening.

"Come on," Greg grunted, shoving at Marsh's hip, and Marsh went over willingly enough. Greg rolled a condom on and got himself wet, and then wrested Marsh's legs apart. He bit his lip at the first rough push inside. Marsh was so hot and tight, flat on his stomach as he let Greg take him and fuck him and fuck his own problems out of his mind. Greg lay himself out across the sheets of rippling muscle, every inch of them pressed together as he fit his mouth to the hollow of Marsh's ear.

Every time was the best time, but this was more. This was Marsh panting and perfect underneath him, and Greg *needed* this. With everything else in his life seeming to slip through his fingers, he held fast to it with everything he had left.

"Do it," Marsh groaned as Greg paused. "C'mon, fuck me, fuck me."

It broke the spell.

Sex. Greg was here for sex and not salvation, and he was too close, Marsh's skin too hot, and there was too much of it pressing up against him. He reared back, fitting hands to thighs to push Marsh wider, getting his knees beneath him.

Just once, he wished he could be the one lying on his back, letting himself be exposed. Taking it. Slow and sweet, and with his hands on Marsh's face, kissing his mouth and giving him all the things he was so tired of trying to hold on to.

But not tonight.

He closed his eyes. With one hand braced on the bed and one on Marsh's shoulder, Greg fucked into him, fast and brutal and efficient and just like everything else.

When Marsh came, it was with a cut-off cry that sounded like Greg's name but that could have been *God*, or anything. Greg focused in on the sound of it and on the feel of hot flesh through latex and away from the jagged edges in his chest. His balls ached as the swell of climax arched its way through him. He buried himself deep and gave in and let it go, and for a shining moment, he felt *amazing*.

Like somehow, someway, everything would be okay.

Sagging, he let his head rest on Marsh's shoulder, and Marsh made a wrung-out humming sound low in his lungs. Greg gave himself a second.

Then he pulled out, and it was over, and he was weak-kneed and exhausted and more brittle than he had been before. He disposed of the condom and started looking for his clothes.

Marsh flopped over onto his back, one arm draped over his face. "Damn, I needed that."

"Yeah," Greg gritted out. Because he had. So badly. He *needed* this.

He didn't know what he was going to do.

Greg squinted and shoved his glasses higher on his nose, but he couldn't make heads or tails of this proof. Or the chicken-scratch handwriting it was written in. He rubbed his eyes and focused again. Just another dozen papers to get through and he could try to get some more work done on his simulations, and then—

A voice rang out from the vicinity of the hallway. "There you are!"

In his mind, Greg went back in time, turned off all the lights in his room and closed the door. Lacking a time-turner, he opened his eyes and looked up at Ronnie standing in his doorway.

"Here to steal my clothes again?" he asked hopefully, cursing all the while. No way it was going to be that simple.

"Actually, that's not a bad idea." Ronnie strode in and ambled to the closet where he started poking around. "But, no."

"What can I do for you, then?" *Nothing. I can't do anything for you. Not tonight.*

"Please," Ronnie said, dripping derision. He flipped a few hangers to the side, but really all of his attention was on Greg. "You know damn well I've been trying to pin you down for a week now to help me figure out why that damn high-vac experiment is giving wonky data."

Greg wanted to cry. He hit *save* on each of the seven different windows he had open and shoved the stack of quizzes he'd been grading to the side. Desk now clear, he dropped his head onto it and ground his brow into the wood. "And I suppose there's no putting you off?"

"Nope. Armed guards at every exit."

Armed? Probably not. But Greg could totally see a couple of the other guys from the department assembled to keep Greg from making a run for it. Ronnie could put Jason up to it, for sure. Greg eyed his window. If he survived the fall, he could be in his car and all the way to the Canadian border by dawn. Hell, Marsh had been acting run-down, too, of late. Maybe he'd be interested in a life on the lam from professors and doctoral candidates alike.

Ronnie stopped fiddling with Greg's wardrobe and wandered back over, settling in to lean his hip on the corner of Greg's desk. Greg's resolve cracked. He really liked Ronnie, was the problem. All his dreams of taking his gay lover and absconding for the border evaporated in a regretful haze.

"Fine," Greg mumbled, turning his head to the side. "Your place or mine?"

"All my stuff's downstairs. I may have commandeered the dining room."

"We have a dining room?"

"Sure." Ronnie grinned. "That space next to the kitchen with the giant table that's always covered in papers and bits of dead computers?"

"Oh right. That dining room." With a groan, Greg rolled his chair away from his desk and stood. "Let's do it, then." As he followed Ronnie out, he cast one doleful look at his own paper-and-electronics-strewn workspace. His gut churned. He'd give Ronnie an hour, and then he'd have to beg off. Even at that, he'd be up until one in the morning if he was going to get everything prepped for his class tomorrow. Maybe he could work on his presentation while he was doing his shift at the helpdesk in the morning.

Juggling his to-do list in his head, he ambled down the steps, pausing for a second in the hallway. He cast his gaze longingly toward Marsh's door. What he wouldn't give to blow Ronnie off and, well, blow Marsh instead. He quashed that train of thought with a vengeance. Not tonight—hell, probably not this week. Just the thought of going so long without touching all that skin made a little note of distress work its way across his ribs, though. He sucked the inside of his cheek between his teeth.

Hoping Ronnie hadn't noticed the way his gait had faltered, he turned away from the siren song of Marsh's door. Ronnie was already in the dining room, paging through one of a half-dozen marble notebooks. "So," he said, not missing a beat even though Greg had missed quite a few, "here's where we are so far."

Greg forced himself to focus as he slipped into one of the hard-backed chairs. Fortunately, once Ronnie got into the specifics of the issues he was having, it wasn't that hard to get immersed. Greg pored over the sheets of data, comparing one set of graphs with another.

"Have you thought about..."

They talked through a bunch of ideas, and as usual, Greg's mind latched on to a train of thought and refused to let it go until he had the problem figured out. Finally, after Greg didn't even know how long, Ronnie slapped a hand down on the table. "I think that might be it."

"Yeah?" Greg sagged with relief. He leaned back in his chair to peer around the corner into the kitchen, and— "Shit. Is it really midnight already?"

"Maybe?"

Shit, it was. Forget giving Ronnie an hour; he'd given him three. Greg was so screwed.

"Hey. You okay, man?"

"Yeah," Greg lied. So he'd just get the problem sets ready for class tomorrow. Grade the quizzes while he was at work and sneak in the presentation-tweaking during his nonexistent lunch break.

Or there was the whole running-away-to-Canada plan. That was a sound plan.

Ronnie frowned. "You don't look all right."

"Sorry." Making his eyes focus, he looked at Ronnie. "Just got a lot left to do tonight."

Ronnie shook his head and clapped a hand on his shoulder. "You work too hard."

"Tell me about it."

"Anything I can do to help? You saved my ass tonight. I totally owe you one."

Greg wished. He scooted his chair away from the table. Nothing he was doing was the kind of stuff he could delegate. "Nah, I got it."

"Is it stuff for the symposium, or...?"

Ronnie'd had a paper accepted for the conference coming up in a couple of weeks, too, so at least he could relate. "It certainly isn't helping. I mean, it's great and all. It'll look nice on the CV. But..."

"But none of us needed one more thing to worry about this close to the end of the semester?"

"Pretty much," Greg agreed, chuckling darkly. "Plus, I made the mistake of telling my mom about it."

"Dude, you found time to talk to your parents?"

Shrugging, Greg answered drily, "If I don't call back after four tries, she calls the police." At Ronnie's snort, he soldiered on. "Anyway, she wants to come in for it."

"Yeah?"

"Yeah. I told her she and Dad would be bored out of their minds, but she's insisting." Greg pulled his mouth to the side. She'd been really excited, actually. It had been nice. Inconvenient, but nice. "My little sister is really into sports, so they go to a bunch of her games and stuff and get to meet her friends that way. Apparently they feel bad that they never come to anything of mine."

Ronnie rolled his eyes. "You poor baby with your supportive parents."

"I know, right? Totally oppressive."

As their small talk wound down, he stretched his arms overhead. He was about to stand and head back to...a bedroom—he hadn't completely decided which one yet, when Ronnie tossed his pen down and clasped his hands behind his neck. "You hungry? Wanna order some food or something?"

Greg didn't even really think before saying, "Nah. Marsh brought me something earlier."

It took a beat too long for Greg to recognize Ronnie's silence, to take in his raised eyebrow. "Did he now?"

"Yeah." No big deal. Just something housemates did for each other sometimes.

Ronnie's look was appraising. "So that's getting pretty serious, huh?"

Honestly, it wasn't as if Greg had ever really seen it as a secret. He'd gone knocking on Marsh's door enough times. Hell, he'd ditched Ronnie explicitly to go knock on Marsh's door. But he didn't want anybody getting the wrong idea—least of all himself.

"It's just a thing." Greg didn't mean to act defensive about it, but his guards went up.

"Just a thing."

Greg lifted one shoulder and lowered his gaze. "What else would it be?"

For a long moment, Ronnie sat there in silence, and Greg's face felt hot. Finally, Ronnie shook his head. "Whatever you say."

Greg swallowed and stood. It was just a thing, that's what they'd agreed to that second night, when he'd gone to Marsh and licked him out and come inside his mouth. He glanced toward Marsh's room, though, and it wasn't just his sex drive that engaged. It was more. It was always more.

His chest hurt, and he was too young for a heart attack, no matter how hard he pushed himself. Who was he kidding? He knew what he felt, and he knew what he needed, and it was...pointless. Marsh was his refuge and his relief and he was the man Greg turned to when he was tired and alone and wanting someone to touch him. Someone to make him smile and forget whatever was troubling him.

Because Marsh could do that. Marsh with his body and his hands and his quiet. His self-deprecation and his eyes, the ones that lit up whenever Greg came knocking, even when everything else about Marsh seemed to be trying so hard to play it cool.

Marsh, who was probably lying in his bed right now, dressed in only his boxers, the sheets pulled up to his stomach.

"All right," Greg said, throat dry. He took one step toward the hallway. "I've got to get back to work."

"Sure." Ronnie didn't sound convinced. He smirked down at the paper in front of him. "Tell Marsh hi for me."

And Greg stopped cold. He had been edging that way. He had so much to do, but all he wanted was to lose himself for an hour. To kiss Marsh and get him naked and spread out on his sheets. To let go.

Something sank inside him. That's what he'd done the past three nights. Four. Had it been every night this week? So often, when he should be working, he found himself in Marsh's bed, and it made him feel better, and then every time after they were done, Marsh would roll over or Greg would make himself get up.

And he might have needed the comfort and the sex and the companionship, but he didn't need *that.* Not tonight. Just like he didn't need Ronnie suggesting he and Marsh were getting serious, when he could only wish.

He closed his eyes and curled his fingers tight against his palm. He had things to do.

Looking up again, he turned himself away from where he'd already subconsciously moved to face Marsh's door. He started up the stairs and at the top, forced himself to keep trudging on. He shut himself in his own room, where he dropped into the chair before his desk.

He had things to do.

And no time to worry about anything else.

Chapter Ten

You call your mom yet?

Ugh. Marsh blinked a couple of times at the message that had popped up in the corner of his screen. He'd just been getting into a groove on this paper, too. Running a hand over his face, he hit save and clicked over to the chat window he and Yulia kept going in the background pretty much all the time. She must have just gotten home. Otherwise, she would have been bugging him hours ago.

Hi, honey, he typed, *nice to see you, too.*

She didn't skip a beat. *So have you?*

Fuck off.

Eloquent. He closed the window and closed the top of his laptop, because, seriously? Why the hell had he opened his mail in front of her that morning?

He shoved off the bed and started pacing around his room, stretching one arm over his head and then the other. The walls were feeling a little too close. He chewed on one of his nails. Maybe he should go for a run. He cast a glance at his door, open just a crack in case anyone came looking for him. Not that that had happened in the past couple of days. Maybe he should go to Greg's room. See if he was home and if he wanted to...

No. No.

Greg was busy, and Marsh wasn't that pathetic. He could handle this shit on his own, and he could wait until Greg came to him. Or at least until tonight.

He hit the corner of his room again and stopped, doing an about-face. Pushing down the bile that wanted to rise up, he strode straight over to his bag and yanked it open, then dumped it out onto his bed. Books and notebooks, and there, wadded up near the bottom. He pulled open the folded yellow paper.

Third notice. How many more notices was he going to get? The page crinkled in his hand as he tightened his grip.

Yulia's prompting floated back to him. He'd been putting her—and the bursar's office, and his coach, and everyone—off for a while now. With his free hand, he touched the rectangle of his phone tucked away in the pocket of his jeans. He'd been telling her he'd call his mom, that this was all a big misunderstanding, but he kept not doing it.

What would Mom say, anyway? Would she tell him the truth? That Dad wasn't going to flip the bill anymore for his meathead of a son who also happened to be a queer?

Shit. He dropped his head into his hand. He'd been putting the call off for a reason. She wouldn't put it in quite those terms, but it was going to be something like that. Hearing it from her lips, though... It'd be too real.

He balled the bill up in his fist and crammed it into the bottom of his bag, tossing all the books in on top of it again. Damn, it was hot in here. The walls felt even closer now, and he tugged on the collar of his shirt, just trying to get some air on his skin, but it didn't help.

He had to get out of there.

Pushing his bag aside, he made for the door and threw it open. The house was as quiet as it usually was in the late afternoon, and somehow that only made it more oppressive. He headed to the kitchen and made a beeline for the fridge. The cool air flowing out as he yanked it open was a shock against his skin, and thank fuck for that. He paused, sucking in air. His ribs didn't feel quite so tight.

Everything was fine. The overdue tuition bill, it was all just a mistake, and if it wasn't he'd deal with it. Get some loans. Or take it as the sign it was.

God, it was going to suck, missing the last season he was eligible to play.

Whatever. He reached into the fridge and sorted through the bottles and cans taking up the whole top shelf. Beer wasn't a good idea right now, tempting as it was. Soda would be good. Something cold, just anything to help calm him down.

He'd just gotten his hand around the neck of a bottle of Sprite when noises at the front of the house made him startle. He grabbed his drink and shut the door, then retreated a few steps to the side until he could see around the corner and down the hall. The front door swung open, and strands of conversation wafted in.

"No, seriously, you saved my ass."

"You would have figured it out eventually," another voice said, and that was Greg. Of course it was Greg.

Marsh tugged at his shirt and ran a hand through his hair as Greg walked in, followed closely on his heels by Ronnie, the both of them embroiled in something way too technical for Marsh to comprehend. Greg lifted his gaze and swept it around the place as he took his jacket off, there in the entryway. He skipped right past Marsh, then stopped, swinging back. He trailed off. Ronnie looked up, too, and closed his mouth.

Marsh puffed his chest out and raised the hand still wrapped around his soda in greeting. "Hey."

"Hey," Greg echoed, and there was a gruffness to it. A quality of tone that reminded Marsh it had been *days*.

"Hey," Ronnie said, but neither of them were looking at him. With a dismissive sigh, he pushed past Greg toward Marsh.

Marsh stepped aside as Ronnie headed to the fridge, all of his focus squarely on Greg. On the lines of his body. His shirt was tucked into his stupid khakis, and even that didn't make him any less attractive.

The bags under his eyes, though... Well, even those didn't make him less attractive, but they did give Marsh pause. He hesitated.

Greg looked away. He gestured at his bag, then pointed upstairs. "I'm heading up. Work to do." He took a step toward the landing.

And Marsh wasn't going to show his disappointment, he wasn't. "Sure."

Greg stopped short, twisting. A softness clung about the edges of his mouth. "Though, later. If you want. I'll be around."

"Oh." It was embarrassing, how even that thin of an invitation set Marsh's blood aflame. His throat went dry. "Sure."

"Okay."

"Okay."

The silence carried on a second too long, and then Greg was making jerky movements to the stairs, turning. His ass flexed with every step as he climbed.

From behind Marsh, there was a pop and a hiss and then a curse. Marsh whipped around to see Ronnie darting toward the sink, overflowing soda in his hand. He pointed to Marsh. "Can you—?"

It took Marsh about a second too long to register that he was standing right next to the paper towels. He tore off a couple of sheets and stepped forward, holding them out. Ronnie grabbed them, then flipped the sink on, rinsing his hand and then swabbing the toweling over everything. He sucked at his thumb and twisted around to look at Marsh. "Thanks," he said.

"No problem."

Tossing the towels in the trash, Ronnie moved to stand with his back to the cabinets, ass resting against the countertop. He lifted his drink up to his mouth and tilted his head toward the other room. "He head up already?"

"Greg? Yeah. Guess he had stuff to do." It came out sounding a lot less bitter than it felt.

Ronnie shook his head, chuckling as he took a sip. "So what else is new?"

"Tell me about it."

"That guy's going to work himself into an early grave if he doesn't slow down."

"Yeah." Marsh frowned. "But what do you expect?"

Because in his world, that was how it was. Brains worked hard. That was what they did.

Ronnie scoffed. "For him not to have an aneurism before he's thirty?"

Aneurism. Wasn't that the thing with the blood vessel bursting in your head? Something about it struck a little too close to home, and Marsh furrowed his brow. "He have another migraine or something?"

"Not that he's admitted to me." Shrugging, Ronnie set his soda down. "No, it's just this...thing. Symposium." At Marsh's blank stare, he waved his hand. "Whole bunch of academic types all working on the same kind of stuff we are, it's like a conference, I guess. The university is hosting it this year, and they opened it up to some students from the department. Greg and me both, we're presenting at it."

Greg had said something about that, hadn't he? Something about a big presentation. Only he hadn't said how big it was. "That's...cool."

"It's awesome, and it sucks, because it's a whole bunch of extra work. Your boy there has it even worse. His parents are coming in and everything, and he's pretending it's not a big deal, but he always stresses out when they come into town. Thinks he has to prove something, I guess."

Marsh didn't even flinch when Ronnie called Greg Marsh's boy, even if it set off a flare of warmth inside his chest. But he couldn't stop his eyebrow from lifting at the idea of Greg thinking he had to...what, impress his parents or something?

"Because he's clearly such a disappointment?"

"Right?" Ronnie said in response.

Marsh took a long gulp of his drink and turned his head to gaze back over at the stairs. He drummed his fingers against his leg. "When is this—what was it called again?"

"Symposium. And it's in like two weeks."

"Wow. That's soon."

Really soon. Really, really soon, considering Greg had yet to make more than a passing reference to it to Marsh.

Then again, why would he? Marsh gulped hard and ground his teeth together.

"Yeah." Ronnie set his can down in the sink. "Speaking of which, I should probably go see if I can get some work done for it."

Marsh blinked for a second, then recovered his composure. "Sure."

"Catch you later."

Nodding, Marsh let him walk by, but he didn't watch his retreating form as he headed up the stairs.

It wasn't a new impulse, not by any stretch, but all he wanted to do was storm on up there and crash down Greg's door and...and... Shit, he didn't even know. He just knew he wanted more. He wanted to *be* more.

He wanted to be worth Greg mentioning what was going on in his life to, and he wanted to graduate college, goddamn it. He wanted his folks to show up at his games, and he didn't want to have to call them to beg them to pay what was left of his bill.

He wanted them to be proud.

With one too-quick motion, he drained the rest of his drink, slamming it back, then crushed it against the countertop. He tossed it into the recycling bin and turned on his heel.

He wanted Greg.

And he was hardly really seeing as he climbed the stairs. The coast was clear, the door to Ronnie's room closed, and that was probably good, but he didn't care. Everyone knew something was going on, even if Marsh himself didn't know quite what.

God, what was he doing? Greg wasn't his boyfriend. Greg didn't owe him anything. Marsh hadn't *asked* him for anything. And maybe that was the problem right there.

It was breaking all kinds of rules, but he didn't even knock. He just shoved at Greg's door, and it gave easily enough. Greg was sitting there at his desk, just like he always was, and Marsh's heart ached as he gazed across the room at him. Greg had said he'd be around later, and sure, it had only been five minutes ago, but still.

Marsh's throat felt choked as he closed the door behind him. "Is it later yet?"

Over the tops of his glasses, Greg glanced between the computer screen and Marsh and back and forth. There was uncertainty there, a hesitation that squeezed even tighter on all the tender, on-edge pieces of Marsh. But then he was looking right at Marsh and rolling his chair away from the desk, hand coming up to the button at the top of his shirt. "Hell, yes, it is."

"Thank God." Marsh wasn't shaking at all as he flipped the lock and pulled his own shirt off.

It was a race, clothing flying. When Marsh was down to his boxers, he crossed the distance, tugging Greg up from where he was knelt over, working at his shoes. He caught his mouth, and it was teeth and harshness and miles of skin as their bare chests met.

Marsh let out a sound he could be embarrassed about later, because Greg tasted so good, the heat of his hands on Marsh's spine a relief. One hot moment of kissing until Marsh could hardly breathe, and then he shoved Greg back. Greg bounced on the mattress, and Marsh dropped to the floor before him. He yanked at the one shoe Greg hadn't managed to kick off in the rush of it all, tore at socks. Greg tugged at his fly, and the second it was open, Marsh was pulling those stupid khakis down, and yeah. That was so much better.

He took a long moment, palm flat on the tense plane of Greg's thigh, to stare. Greg always looked good, but he looked best when he was half naked and sweating, all the repression and the tension torn from his skin, and he was just a man. Marsh kissed his way up, over the knob of Greg's knee and along the muscle of his quadriceps. He nosed at the bulge in his underwear, wrapping his lips around the outline of his head through the fabric, then licked a stripe along his tight abs. Climbing onto the bed, he hovered over Greg.

He looked different, he looked perfect, glasses askew, hair all out of place. Unsteady, Marsh reached up and touched the black plastic frames, swallowing when Greg flinched. "Sorry," Greg said, lifting a hand.

But Marsh didn't let him. "Don't." He pinched the corners of the frames, fingers gentle as he eased them down Greg's nose. He smiled as he held them up. "Can't decide how I like you better. With them or without them."

Greg scoffed, his shoulders heaving. He brushed his hair out of his eyes. "Right. Nerdy or nerdier."

Marsh furrowed his brow. "Try sexy or sexier."

Greg laughed outright at that. He closed a hand around Marsh's as he folded the glasses up. Taking them from him, Greg leaned over to set them on his nightstand, and then he was gripping at Marsh's neck, pulling him onto the bed and into a kiss that curled Marsh's toes. Marsh wasn't quite done, though. Cupping Greg's face, he edged forward to press pursed lips to the bridge of Greg's nose. "I like the glasses," he insisted.

"If you say so."

"Just did."

Before he could get anything else out, Greg hitched a leg over Marsh's hip, yanking him down so their fronts met, hard cock dragging against hard cock. "Bet there are other things you like."

And...okay. Letting himself be distracted, Marsh closed his eyes and ground down into Greg, recapturing his mouth and pressing forward with his tongue. With a scrape of teeth against his bottom lip, he agreed, "Damn right there are."

There were so many things about Greg he liked. He liked his voice and his eyes and how *into it* he always got when they were like this. He liked his smarts and his hands. He liked his glasses and how he never seemed to want to wear them when Marsh was around. He just *liked* him. Entirely too much.

And he wanted...

He bit that train of thought off before it could go too far, refocusing on the friction, almost too good to be believed. But it could be better. Bracing himself with one arm, he got the other into the waistband of his boxers, shoving them down. He nudged Greg's thigh, and Greg lifted up so they could push his underwear down, too. Their cocks lined up, sticky-slick with pre-come, and Marsh groaned as he let himself drop a little, pressing his mouth to the column of Greg's throat. Greg tilted his head to the side, and Marsh couldn't resist. He bit down, sucking hard, because he wanted to still be here after Greg kicked him out. He wanted to always be here.

He wanted to leave his mark. "Jesus," he moaned into the warm flesh as Greg writhed and clutched him closer. Greg spread his legs, and Marsh didn't waste any time. He settled himself between those open thighs and skidded along warm flesh. Christ, Greg was always so warm, the hollow of his hip smooth, his cock a blazing line of heat. Marsh rutted against him, skating his hand over ribs and flank, down to the inside of his knee and back up.

His touch stuttered when he hit the crease of Greg's ass, because Greg arched and groaned, and it hurt, how much

Marsh wanted him. He sucked in a deep breath and slipped his nose along damp skin, over stubble, to the tender place beside Greg's ear. He pressed his fingers closer to the center, brushed them over Greg's hole, and Marsh was so hard.

Everything inside of him constricted, and then he breathed, "Wanna fuck you so bad."

Greg went still.

Greg's eyes popped open, a broad palm on Marsh's sternum, a light shove, and shit. Marsh pulled back, looking down into eyes that were wide, pupils dark, and there was want there. Hell, yes, there was. But there was more.

For a second, Greg worked his mouth, jaw flexing. "I don't—"

He cut himself off, and Marsh's stomach sank. "Fine," he mumbled. He pressed his forehead to Greg's collarbone and breathed and breathed. Some guys didn't like that. Marsh didn't always like that. It was vulnerability, it was exposure, even with a condom. It hurt sometimes, and with the right man working you open, it could be the best damn feeling in the world.

The thing was, Greg always made the best noises when Marsh got near his ass. He loved to get a throat full of cock, and Marsh had thought he'd be willing to, eventually. That he'd let Marsh inside him. But not today.

"Never mind," Marsh grit out, because that was fine. "Never mind." He rasped out a harsh breath and dragged his hand away from Greg's ass. He lined their cocks up and got a fist around them both, swallowing down the sound that wanted to escape at just that pressure alone.

"I mean—"

"It's fine. This is good." He parted his lips and mashed his face into Greg's chest to keep from showing everything he felt. To help him focus on the pleasure instead of the brush-off. Because this felt amazing, even if it wasn't exactly what he wanted. Greg was a hot line, all velvet and smoothness, and Marsh stroked, steady and fast at them both, smoothing the fluid from the tips down around their shafts. "Isn't it good?"

"Yeah." Greg slipped his hand between their bodies, down into that humid space there, and covered Marsh's hand with his own. It just made it all better, made Marsh's sac draw up tight.

And then it was just the pull and push, the shuddering breaths and the subtle motions of hips. The slapping noises as they jerked their arms together. Greg tensed and hooked his calf around Marsh's thigh, urging him closer.

Marsh dropped his head until his brow pressed to the mattress beside Greg's ear, and he twisted his neck. Against the sweaty hair at Greg's temple, he whispered, "You gonna come? Gonna come all over me?"

Greg just keened, scrabbling at Marsh's back, spine arching, his voice thick as he swore and pulsed. The slide went slick with come as Greg's cock jerked in his palm. Marsh sped his hand, Greg's fingers tightening over his, and he bit his tongue as the feeling crested. He spilled across Greg's skin, all over his abdomen and into the trail of hair there, over their intertwined fists, and it was good. Good enough.

Once his vision cleared, he sagged, shifting his weight so as not to crush the man beneath him, tugging his hand free and flopping it to the side. Every time they did this, the pleasure of it turned him to jelly, turned him inside out, so it wasn't anything to float away on that knowledge. To lie there and soak up this warmth and this comfort, all of it so close to what he wanted. He was always so close.

Finally, he couldn't really linger any longer, and it was time. Were this Marsh's room, Greg would already be getting up and looking for his clothes. Marsh should pull away. Should go.

Greg's hand came up and settled, warm and tentative at the base of Marsh's spine, and any will he'd had to leave evaporated.

"You okay?" Greg asked, fingertips tracing an uncertain line up the center of Marsh's back.

"Fine." Fine, and yet not. The same discontent from before was a rumbling deep inside him.

Marsh peeled his sweaty skin from Greg's, wincing at the spatters of cooling come. But Greg didn't let go. His arm stayed hooked around Marsh's waist even as he slid off to lie on his side. He placed his own hand on the center of Greg's chest.

He didn't want to go. He didn't want to always have to go, to feel so uncertain every time he wanted a fuck or a smile or just to see Greg's face or kiss his mouth.

And it was so stupid. They were naked, they'd just shot off all over each other, but the question in the back of his throat hurt in a way that made him feel like he was stripped bare in another way entirely.

"Do you wanna—" he started, and the words lodged, hard and impossible to breathe around.

"Hmm?"

"Do you want— I don't know." Shit. "To...hang out?"

Greg snickered, and it hurt. "Isn't that what we just did?"

"Yeah. Right. Sure." And Marsh felt hollow down to the centers of his bones. "I'll just go then."

"I've got a lot to do," Greg said, staring up at the ceiling. Because he couldn't even look at Marsh.

Marsh pulled away. "Of course."

Then Greg was turning his head to the side, focusing dark, gorgeous eyes on Marsh. His hand tightened on Marsh's side. "You don't have to leave."

"But you just said—" Marsh felt dizzy.

"I've got a lot to do," Greg repeated, "but you can...stay. If you want to."

Christ, that was all Marsh wanted to do. But he couldn't seem to make his throat work. The offer didn't feel real.

Greg shifted his whole body over, tugging Marsh down and nosing in. Their lips brushed. "You can stay."

The hollowness seeped away, replaced by something full. Something he hadn't felt in so long. Maybe ever. He found Greg's hand in the space between them and intertwined their fingers, the block in his voice box melting away. "That'd be nice." Because this really wasn't that much of a stretch, was it? They'd watched a movie together, that once. They'd eaten dinner, and they'd fucked, never the both one after another, but they could do this, too, couldn't they? The fucking and the dinner? He reached up, nice and slow. Rested his fingers against Greg's jaw. "Dinner?"

"Takeout?"

"Is there any other kind?"

And Greg laughed, and it was free in a way it hadn't been. Rich. Greg put his hand over Marsh's wrist, holding it gently, and it felt like a lifeline. "That sounds nice."

"Yeah." Marsh exhaled nice and slow. His own smile felt free, too. "It does."

The nicest thing he'd heard in a long, long while.

Chapter Eleven

"Hey."

Greg looked up from his screen, over the rims of his glasses. He had to fight the urge to pull them off his face, and just that had his cheeks warming. *I like the glasses,* Marsh had said, close and soft and warm. He tapped his finger against his mouse to keep his hand from reaching up and fidgeting with the frames.

Marsh stood there in the doorway, nudging it open another couple of inches. Not like when he'd stormed in a week or so ago. Oh, no.

Thing was, though, Greg liked the storming and the stripping and the kisses so deep he hardly knew where his body ended and Marsh's began, but he kind of liked this better. The quiet knocks and the hovering.

The way Marsh tugged at the strap of his bag as he asked, "Do you mind if I—" He gestured toward the inside of the room.

"No. Not at all." Because he didn't just not mind. He loved it.

He loved that possessive, intense sex last week had turned into possessive, intense sex and takeout. And then sex and takeout and studying in the same room together. And now, apparently, to just studying, and how fucked up was it that Greg felt as warmed by that as he had by the rest of it?

Marsh smiled and stepped inside, pushing the door behind him to leave it ajar. Dropping his book bag off his shoulder, he took a couple of steps into the room, eyes wary as he crossed over to Greg. Every motion was forecast, like he thought Greg was going to push him away. Marsh leaned in and pressed a light kiss to the corner of Greg's mouth. Greg was the one to reel him in, clasping a hand to the side of his neck to give him another, firmer kiss. "Hey."

"Hi," Marsh echoed, the one side of his lips twitching up. "Busy?"

"Always."

"I won't bother you too much then."

Greg kind of wanted to protest, to say it was never a bother, but he really did have a lot to do tonight, so he smiled and nodded, letting his hand slip down Marsh's chest before returning it to his keyboard tray.

Not that he was going to get a lot of work down for the next few minutes, anyway. Unreasonably aware of every movement, Greg watched Marsh in the reflection on his computer monitor as he settled in, sitting cross-legged on the floor, back propped up against Greg's bed. He pulled out a book and flicked it open, then lifted his head.

"You good?" Greg asked, twisting so he could look at him straight-on.

"Yeah."

Greg turned to face his desk and all the work spread out across it, but his chest felt full in a way he could scarcely explain—in a way he didn't dare to even try to explain, worried it would upset this fragile balance.

Because he could drown in this. In quiet companionship, in the knowledge that Marsh was there in the background, turning pages and scribbling notes. It eased the tension in Greg's shoulders, leaving him less overwhelmed, less distraught. Less alone.

Even as Greg fought down his smile over that, he couldn't help feeling a little twitchy. Maybe it was *too* quiet? He tapped his finger against his mouse. "You want any music or anything?"

"Doesn't matter to me."

Music would be good. Only... "Anything in particular you like?"

"Whatever."

Not helpful. Greg brought up his MP3 collection and skimmed through it, and his heart sank. He never should have asked. He'd heard pop and R&B coming from Marsh's room often enough, and he didn't have anything like that. "Um. How do you feel about...jazz?" It was good studying music, no distracting lyrics or anything. And it was hopelessly, painfully dweeby. Greg cringed in anticipation of Marsh's answer.

"Seriously, anything is fine."

"Okay." Still feeling a little squirmy about the whole thing, he brought up a quartet he liked for when he was really trying to concentrate and set the volume on his speakers to something sort of medium-low. And it sounded like a pretentious coffee shop, the kind intellectual douchebags went to. *You* are *an intellectual douchebag.*

Marsh didn't respond except to turn his page, and Greg forced himself to breathe past the knot in his throat. There wasn't any reason to be self-conscious. Marsh had said anything was fine, and the things Greg liked were *fine.* It didn't ease the stricture in his chest, but he could work with that. He *had* to work with that.

Refocusing, he brought up his calendar and wished he could go back to worrying about Marsh and what kind of music he preferred. The countdown was on now—just two days until the symposium started and only three until he was scheduled to present. His commitments were blocked out in blue and yellow and green. Double shifts at the helpdesk and classes to teach, the sessions his friends and colleagues were speaking at that he needed to attend. On top of that, he hadn't been able to wriggle his way out of hosting duties for the symposium in spite of how hard he'd tried, and he was stuck manning the registration desk for a few hours the first day and escorting bigwigs to sessions the day after that. Oh, and picking his parents up at the airport and taking them to dinner.

No problem. No reason to panic at all.

He snuck a glance over his shoulder at Marsh. He seemed absorbed in the notes he was taking, the cap of his pen between his teeth, hard blue plastic against the soft plump of his lips. And it was so tempting to put all this off and stalk over there instead and remind himself how soft those lips could be. God, he wished he had time for that tonight. Greg looked away again and minimized the calendar, then scanned the rest of the programs running in his taskbar. It was probably time to give up on lost causes and ignore his research for the next few days. He had everything prepped for the class he had to teach first thing in the morning, so that left just the presentation he *had* to get squared away tonight.

He pulled up PowerPoint and started scrolling through the slides. Just looking at them made his stomach roil. Being asked to present was an honor, he reminded himself. It would look good on his CV, and it would put him in front of the people he'd be applying to for post-docs in another year or two. It was important.

And just the idea of getting up in front of all those important people made him want to break out in hives.

At least the slides themselves were more or less set to go at this point. He clicked back up to the beginning and made himself page through more slowly, practicing in his head what he would say. The bullet points would keep him from getting too lost, even if he had a fit of nerves, but he really wanted to be able to do the majority of the talk without looking.

He didn't want to fuck this up.

"You want to give it to me?"

Greg whipped around at the sound of Marsh's voice. He'd been so obsessed with Marsh's presence, yet somehow, as soon as he'd started thinking about talking in front of a few hundred people, he'd forgotten all about it. "Excuse me?"

Marsh pointed at the computer screen. "Is that your presentation? For the…thing? Symposium? Thing?"

"What do you know about that?"

Marsh's expression flickered, something hurt and foreign passing across his face before smoothing out. "Ronnie mentioned it, I think. Said it was what you were so busy with." His gaze darted off to the side and back again. "I mean—"

"Yeah, that's what it is."

"How long is it supposed to be? Your talk?"

"Twenty minutes, plus questions. No big." Greg's pulse sped just thinking about it.

Marsh nodded. "Yeah, that's not so bad. So do you…?" He tipped his head toward the screen. "Want to give it? Like, for practice? I could listen. I mean, I probably wouldn't understand it or anything."

Greg's gut twisted. Marsh would probably be bored out of his mind. "Nah, I mean, I'm still working on it."

"Really? Isn't it soon?"

"Friday." Greg was seriously starting to feel queasy about it.

"You've got to have at least part of it done, then." Marsh smirked, but there was a shadow to his smile. "Come on. I'm a good listener. I won't fall asleep on you or anything."

Greg wasn't so sure about that. His work was so *boring*. And he just…he *couldn't*. He shook his head. The idea of doing this in front of Marsh made his stomach flip dangerously and the back of his neck sweat. "Nah, I mean, I have to give it in front of my advisor on Wednesday. I'll probably make Ronnie listen to it tomorrow or something."

Something in Marsh's face shifted, and he blinked. "Oh. Sure. Cool." His jaw looked tight, and he glanced away again.

It sent Greg scrambling for excuses. "I mean, you'd just be bored. And you couldn't comment on the science or—"

"Yeah, of course," Marsh cut him off. His knuckles were white around his pen, and it made Greg feel all twisted up inside. "Whatever."

He tried to imagine again what it would be like to practice this in front of Marsh, but he just wasn't ready for that. He still had too much prep to do. Too little confidence about how Marsh would react to hearing it. Trying to be as conciliatory as he could, he gave a wincing little smile. "Thanks for offering."

Marsh had already buried his gaze in his text again, his foot tapping out a rhythm against the carpet that ratcheted up Greg's anxiety even further. "Like I said. Whatever."

"Okay..." Nothing about that felt final, but there was a dismissal there. Greg lingered for a few seconds, then turned toward his screen, only his attention was shot. Five times, he started to twist to look over his shoulder, but that was stupid. There wasn't any reason to feel nervous like this.

Then Marsh asked, "So, can anybody go to these talks?"

"Sort of." He'd asked about this when his mom had insisted she and Dad were coming. "People visiting from other campuses are supposed to have badges, but no one's really going to be checking. And anybody who goes to school here can sit in."

"But it'll be just you science types?"

Greg chewed down on the inside of his lip. Science types. Right. "Not necessarily. Some of the other guys will probably invite some of their friends."

"Oh."

The word hung in the air, and Greg didn't know whether that was the end of it or not.

"You're talking on Friday, you said?" Marsh asked.

"Yup." Friday. Three days. He checked the clock. It was almost midnight. So, swiftly approaching two days. Christ.

"I only have the one class on Friday."

"O…kay?"

"So if you need any help or anything. You know." Marsh shrugged, like it wasn't a big deal, but his voice was heavy.

"The guys from the department are all assigned to take care of all the hosting stuff. I think we'll be fine."

"Right." And that word was even tighter. "When are your folks getting in?"

"Thursday night." Greg sighed and rolled his eyes. "Wanted to make sure they could take me out to dinner before. You know, because I'll have so much free time then."

"Sure."

"I mean, I shouldn't be complaining. I appreciate the support and everything, you know, but…"

"Yeah," Marsh said, cutting in. "Supportive parents are…are great." The corner of his mouth twitched up, but it was as much a grimace as a smile, the cant of it hard to look at somehow, and Greg shifted his gaze away. "That'll be nice then, dinner with them. On Thursday. Are you going to get Ronnie or any of them to go?"

Greg hadn't really thought of that. "I don't know. Maybe I should ask them."

There was a snap, and Greg furrowed his brow as Mash cursed. His pen had split open, but it wasn't leaking ink, at least.

"Hey, are you okay?" Greg asked.

"Shitty pen," Marsh said, but he wasn't meeting Greg's gaze.

"Better ease up there." Greg laughed, trying to make the sound light, but everything was strained. He didn't know why it was strained.

"Yeah." Marsh stood in one fluid motion and tossed the shattered plastic in the trash next to Greg's desk, and Greg couldn't help it. He reached out, putting a hand to Marsh's waist, but Marsh twisted away, arching back from the touch.

Greg swallowed hard, and it tasted like bile. "Marsh—"

"I'm gonna go." Marsh retreated farther. He bent to pick up his book and his notes and jammed them into his bag.

And he'd come in there, less than an hour ago, all tentative knocks and uncertain kisses, and now this. What had Greg done wrong?

"Hey, we can—" But the thought died on his tongue. What? He didn't have time tonight to go out or watch a movie or do anything interesting. Anything someone like Marsh would think was interesting.

"Nah, I just… I need to work on this paper, and I left my laptop downstairs."

Only, as Marsh crammed things in his bag, Greg could see the corner of the laptop right there. He could see the cord.

"Oh," Greg said, and now he was really going to be sick. "Okay."

Marsh edged toward the door, and he didn't make a motion to lean in for a kiss or even a touch. "I'll, um, see you around."

"Right."

"Good night." Marsh had the door open already, one foot through it. Had he always had one foot on the threshold? He looked out into the hall. "And um, good luck. On your presentation and stuff."

"Thanks." A clanging bell rang out in the back of Greg's mind, because, really, when had this all started? The distant look in Marsh's eyes and the grip that could snap a pen in half? "If you do want to listen to it, I can—"

"Nah," Marsh said, laughter ugly in his throat. "Like you said, I'd just be bored by it anyway."

Of course. Something deep inside of Greg went cold. "All right. Good night, then."

One jerky nod, and then Marsh was gone, the door closing behind him, and Greg was left to sit there with his work and his commitments, staring at the place where Marsh had stood.

He threw his notebook across the room and swore.

The sounds of fucking *jazz* music followed Marsh into the hallway and down the stairs, and how fitting was that? Greg listened to jazz. The only thing worse would have been Mozart or something. Hell, Greg probably had that, too.

Who did Marsh think he was kidding?

Something thudded upstairs, but he ignored it. He swung by his room to grab a jacket. Out of spite, he nabbed his earbuds, too. He stormed out of the house, not really seeing anything, and stood in the cold, waiting for the bus. It took forever; late-night buses always did. When it finally stopped, he climbed aboard and slipped into a seat far enough back to not have to make eye contact with anyone, but not so far back that he'd be stuck with all the drunks.

Scrunched up in his seat, fingers half-numb, he fiddled with his phone and brought up the stupidest album he owned. Something he'd wasted his money on before he'd known how limited it was, springing for the whole record just because he liked the single. Awful, cheesy synth-pop flooded his ears through the headphones, and yeah. That kind of music at least he understood.

He leaned his head against the window and stared out into the darkness, slouching down in his seat and tapping his foot along with the beat.

He got off at Yulia's stop and trudged his way to her apartment. It was late enough he didn't bother knocking, just let himself in. He dropped his bag by the door and stripped out of his jacket and toed off his shoes.

Yulia's room was dark, but whatever. He took off his jeans and snuck in under the covers beside her, wrapping his arms around her middle and burying his face against the curve of her spine.

"Marsh?" She slept so lightly. She reached an arm behind herself and petted his hair.

He just squeezed her tighter.

Getting a firmer grasp on the back of his neck, she asked, "What's wrong?"

"Nothing."

"Crawling into my bed at one in the morning on a school night isn't nothing," she said, but her voice was colored by her yawn, the words trailing off. He half-thought she'd fallen back to sleep before she mumbled, "You're gonna have to tell me eventually."

He stayed silent for the longest time, like holding it in would keep it from being real, but words were clawing at his throat. Finally, so quietly he could barely hear it himself, he said, "He doesn't want me to meet his parents. Or go to his conference." He shuddered, and this was pathetic. Just bottom-of-the-barrel stuff, but he couldn't seem to stop it from looping over and over in his head.

"Shh." She turned inside his embrace, moving to lie on her back and wrangling him until his head rested on her abdomen. It didn't ease the shaking any, but those awful, self-indulgent words about how shitty Greg had made him feel retreated into his throat, and he could keep them there. "Shh," she murmured again, and her fingers were magic in his hair.

She didn't have to tell him she wasn't going to have sex with him. He couldn't have, even if he'd wanted to. Couldn't even imagine it. Sex was ruined. Everything was ruined. All he wanted was to lie there and be miserable and wish that things were different, somehow.

After long, long minutes of silence, her fingers faltered against his scalp. He closed his eyes.

"You have to talk to him, you know," she whispered in the darkness.

Squeezing his eyes tighter, he said, "I know."

Chapter Twelve

Five minutes. If Greg left right now, he'd be exactly five minutes late for work. He rubbed his temples in tight circles, then dug his knuckles into his eyes. When he looked up again at the kitchen clock, it was blurry around the edges, and he blinked hard to clear the haze from his vision. The slightest hint of an ache was building behind his left eye, but it wasn't bad. He dug into his bag for the little bottle there. He got the cap off and shook an ibuprofen into his hand. This didn't feel like a killer one. If he nipped it in the bud, it should be fine.

Seven minutes. He swallowed the pill down with the rest of his coffee and glanced at the front door. It sounded like—

The door opened, and Greg was on his feet, gaze riveted, and the nascent headache had nothing on the way everything else hurt. Marsh stumbled in, hair sticking up on one side and flat on the other, eyes red, and Greg's heart broke right in two.

"Oh." Marsh stopped short, hovering in the hallway before the turnoff for his room. He ran a hand over the crown of his head and tucked the thumb of his other hand into the strap of his backpack. He was still wearing the clothes from the night before, when he'd stormed out of Greg's room. "Hey."

"Hey." Licking his lips, Greg darted his gaze toward the door. "Just getting home?" And how stupid was that? Marsh had just come through the front door, and he sure as hell hadn't been home when Greg had checked on his way downstairs to start up the coffeepot and to apologize. He still wasn't quite sure why Marsh had reacted so strongly, but a few things were clear. He shouldn't have dismissed Marsh's offer so quickly.

He should have asked him to stay until he figured out what was wrong.

Marsh nodded. "Yeah. Um. Had to go to Yulia's, and then it was late and..."

Greg's whole lower face felt frozen and cracking with the fakeness of his smile. Everything inside him felt brittle, and he was running ten full minutes late now, and for what? He should've just left. Seeing Marsh come in like this wasn't helping anything, and Greg had nothing to say.

He wondered if Marsh smelled like her sheets.

This was killing him. It was time to go. Cut his losses and get out of here before he could show exactly how much this all hurt. He gripped his keys so they dug into his hand.

Except then Marsh shuffled his feet, readjusting his bag on his shoulder. "We're just friends, you know. Me and Yulia. Best friends. But that's it."

Greg's heart hammered hard, and he nearly lost his hold on his keys. "Oh?"

"Yeah." He shrugged and looked toward the ground. "Tried it the other way a few times, years ago." He chuckled darkly. "Didn't work out for a reason."

"Oh."

The twisted-up little knot of despair in his chest didn't exactly let go, but it shifted its shape. That was good news. Amazing news, and it cast that whole afternoon in the café when he'd stumbled on the two of them in a whole new light. Changed this morning and last night up, too.

Marsh wasn't screwing around with someone else. Greg's lack of interest in sex last night hadn't driven him into someone else's bed. At least not for that.

But he was jealous all the same. What did Marsh tell her? Why did he feel like he had to go to her when he was mad at Greg?

Why couldn't he just *talk* to Greg?

Why the hell didn't Greg just talk to him?

All the words he'd been rehearsing, earlier that morning resurfaced. He shoved his hands into his pockets. "I'm sorry, by the way. About last night. You seemed upset, and I..." *Don't know how to make you stay. Don't know what you want from me.* In the end, he chickened out. Fell back on his usual excuse. "I had so much work to do."

It was Marsh's turn to look brittle. "It's cool. I get it."

Greg wasn't sure Marsh did. Not at all.

His phone beeped at just that moment, though. He glanced at the clock. Fifteen minutes late. It was probably work, asking him where the hell he was.

Tonight, he and Marsh would talk more. Maybe. If Greg had time. He ground his thumb into his temple against the sharp flare of pain there.

"Sorry," he mumbled, gesturing toward the door. "I'm running crazy late."

"Yeah. Sure."

Greg grabbed his bag and strode forward. As he walked past the living room, a beam of sunlight cut through the open window, making him wince.

A warm hand settled on his upper arm.

"Are you okay?" Marsh asked, and he was so close, his face all concern.

All Greg wanted to do was lean into him. Bury his nose against his neck and breathe him in. Take him up to his room and draw the curtains closed. Fall asleep in his lap while he ran his fingers through his hair.

Maybe, if he wasn't still mad, Marsh would even let him.

But this close, he smelled ever so faintly of lavender.

"I'm fine," Greg lied. He shot him the best grin he could muster. He was pretty sure he wasn't convincing anyone. "I'm fine."

The whole way to the door, he kept telling himself that.

"Your father and I are so excited, sweetie."

"I know, me too," Greg said, cupping the phone close to his ear.

A series of sharp raps on the glass behind him made him jump. He whirled around, twisting his phone to angle the microphone away from his mouth. Ronnie was standing at the window between the conference room and the hallway. Once he had Greg's attention, he tapped on his wrist and jerked his thumb back into the room behind him. Had it really been fifteen minutes already? Greg nodded and sighed.

He cut off whatever story his mother had been launching into. "Sorry, Mom. I have to run. Group meeting's starting."

"At eight o'clock at night?"

Greg didn't like it any more than she did, and he shrugged even though she couldn't see it. "You do what you have to do."

"I know. I just hate to see you working so hard."

All Greg could do was laugh and rub the heel of his hand into his forehead. It was his fault they were meeting so late this week. He'd had to pick up another extra shift at the helpdesk, and Dr. Chu had been nice enough to switch things around to accommodate him. Every now and then, being in a smaller research group had its perks.

"You and me both," he replied. "Anyway, I'll see you tomorrow. Your flight gets in at six?"

It was going to be tight, getting to the airport in time. He'd have to run out the instant his shift covering the registration area at the symposium was done, but he should be able to manage it. Probably.

"Yup. We'll see you soon."

"Sounds good." Greg rolled his eyes when Ronnie knocked on the glass again. "Later."

He hated shooing his mom off the phone like that, but he'd said it himself. You had to do what you had to do. Once she'd gotten off a quick goodbye, he hit the button to end the call and pocketed his phone before heading into the conference room.

Dr. Chu was sitting at one end of the big table, Ronnie and the rest of the members of the research team scattered around the edges. Greg did a quick headcount, and yup. He was the last one. "Sorry," he mumbled as he set his bag down and folded himself into a seat.

Chu nodded curtly and began. "Now that we're all here..."

God, Greg was tired. He paid attention the best he could, especially when it came to the stuff about last-minute preparations for the symposium. He scribbled a couple of quick notes and tried to remember not to nod along too much. The haze over his vision from this morning had more or less stayed at bay up until now, but the halos were beginning to shimmer, and the pressure inside his skull had grown to the point where it was getting hard to ignore. He'd been counting on getting his lesson ready for tomorrow's classes before bed, but that wasn't going to happen, not at this rate. His hand twitched toward his bag. He folded his fingers into his palm and squeezed his fist tight. His prescription meds always made him loopy and sleepy, and he hated driving after he'd taken them. But there was no way he could afford to still be useless tomorrow if he didn't get a handle on this now.

Glancing up at the front of the room, he checked no one was paying attention to him, then pulled his phone out under the table.

He typed, *You heading home right after?* and sent the message to Ronnie.

Ronnie glanced under the desk, and a few seconds later, a reply of *Y* came back.

Can I hitch a ride? He hated having to leave his car on campus, but it would be okay. He'd just ride in with Ronnie tomorrow, or maybe Marsh could help him with the bus schedules or something, if he was home.

Across the table, Ronnie caught Greg's eye, brow rising in concern. Greg shook his head to try and communicate that he was fine, even though his stomach was starting to go sour. Ronnie frowned but nodded, mouthing *okay*.

Relieved, Greg dug into his bag with as much stealth as he could muster. He palmed one of the little pills and uncapped his water bottle, bringing it to his mouth and slipping the tablet onto his tongue. Now all he had to do was not vomit it up and hope no one tried to talk to him anytime soon.

Of course, that was when Chu turned to him. "Greg?"

"Yes?" He sat up at attention and cringed at the sudden explosion in his head.

"How's the data coming on those new low-pressure trials?"

Of course. The trials he'd blown off until next week. "Um, okay." How to stall, how to stall? "It's slow-going," he admitted, "with everything going on this week."

Chu's mouth tilted down. "Our collaborators at Dow have been contacting me. How soon can we get them something?"

"How soon do they need it?" The roughness of his voice belied his worry. It was the juggling analogy all over again—he could almost see the spinning balls over his head, the graceful arc they made and the way they were all just hanging in space, all waiting to come crashing down.

Chu frowned. "Stay after for a minute when we're done here."

"Right." He needed out of there, not an extra few minutes of trying to come up with excuses. The room was too warm and the bright light of the projector was steadily boring a hole into his skull.

Ronnie was looking at him with real concern now, and Greg had to drop his gaze.

The meeting dragged on for Greg didn't even know how long. Finally, Chu closed his notebook, and Greg heaved a sigh of relief before remembering he was supposed to stay. The sharpest edges of the migraine had dulled, but noises were still too loud, lights too bright, and he wanted nothing more than to crawl into bed and close his eyes.

As everyone else filtered out, Greg forced himself to his feet, but only to drag himself up to the head of the table where Chu was waiting for him. Ronnie tilted his head to the door, and Greg gave him a weak thumbs-up.

"Dr. Chu?" he asked as he approached.

"Greg. Talk to me some more about that data."

Greg rubbed his fingertips along his hairline. "I'm working on it, but this week is just a mess." No point lying. "I haven't had time."

Looking up from his papers, Chu leveled him with an even stare. "How many hours have you been working outside your assignments here in the department?"

Sighing, Greg admitted, "Too many. It's just temporary, though—"

"It might be time to think about curtailing those." The set of his mouth was full of implications, and Greg withered. Technically, he wasn't supposed to be working at all outside of the research and teaching he did for his fellowship, but his car had needed a massive set of repairs over the summer, and Chu had allowed it.

"Yes, sir," Greg ground out.

"I don't like rescheduling meetings around outside involvements, but having results delayed due to them is another issue entirely."

"I know."

There was a long moment's pause. "I'll put off the Dow people, but I need data soon."

Greg's stomach sank. He couldn't stay any longer tonight, and the next few days were scheduled so tightly he'd barely have time to breathe. The image of his calendar swam up in front of his vision, the blocks of color jammed together without gaps. There wasn't any wiggle room, but he'd have to find a way to carve out some time. "I'll get right on it."

Waving his hand, Chu looked down at the calculations strewn out in front of him. "It can wait until tomorrow. Go home. Get some sleep. You look like you need it."

"Yes, sir," Greg said, sagging.

He didn't wait around to see if there was anything else. Just managing to keep it together, squinting all the way, he stumbled his way out to the hall. The harsher fluorescent lights made him want to whimper. Then there was Ronnie, getting a hand on his elbow and steering him toward the exit.

"Migraine?"

"Yeah."

Ronnie shook his head as he ushered them outside. "You should've told me. I would've covered for you."

"Chu rescheduled the meeting for me. And I couldn't afford to miss any more. Plus, it wasn't bad until I got in there."

All the warning signs had been there, though. He'd been pushing it, and he'd known it.

Ronnie made a little humming noise, and then went mercifully quiet. Somehow or other, they made it to Ronnie's car, where Ronnie held the door open and put a hand up so Greg wouldn't bump his head. When he moved to help with the seatbelt, Greg batted him away. "Not an invalid."

"Sure could use someone to take care of you," Ronnie groused, but he let Greg get himself situated. He touched Greg's shoulder before he eased the door closed.

And there was nothing to that touch, nothing at all, but it was kind and warm, and it reminded Greg of the last time he'd had an episode this bad. Marsh had been so nice to him then. What he wouldn't give to be able to crawl into his bed tonight. To have the guts to ask him to sit with him and talk to him and touch his face again.

Forget his outside commitments. Marsh was what had him so turned around, making him feel all these things. Reawakening all these desires, not just for sex but for basic human intimacy.

Greg had been hoping they'd have time to talk tonight. A chance to get back on even ground. He would have scoffed aloud if it wouldn't have hurt his head. He didn't trust himself to have a conversation with his houseplants tonight. He definitely didn't trust himself to have one with Marsh.

That was okay. He'd get through this one on his own.

The ride home passed in a long, aching blur as he pressed his brow to the cool glass of the window. He could feel Ronnie's gaze on him every time they stopped, but he couldn't bring himself to open his eyes, dizzy from the motion of the car.

Finally, they came to a stop, and with a jangle of the keys, Ronnie flipped the ignition off, surrounding them with blessed silence. Greg could have stayed there all night, curled up in the seat, head sheltered under his arm, but Ronnie came around and opened the door. Greg couldn't suppress the sound of distress he made as he forced himself to his feet.

He'd go to the bathroom and clean up, and then he'd go to bed, and maybe his pillow would still smell a little bit like Marsh, and he could lie there in the darkness and wish he could die while he imagined phantom fingers in his hair, and he'd be fine.

With Ronnie carrying Greg's bag, one hand on Greg's shoulder to steady him, they made their way inside. He didn't glance down the hall toward Marsh's room or go beg him to come upstairs and hold him until he felt warm and safe and able to breathe. He stumbled up the stairs exactly the way he'd planned to. Past his own door and on toward the bathroom.

He rinsed his mouth out, then turned the tap onto pure hot and wet a washcloth with it, wringing it out before carrying it with him back toward his room. Hot compress. Darkness. Sleep. He'd be fine, and somehow or other, tomorrow, he'd get caught up. He just had to make it through this week.

Only he didn't even make it to his room. Because there, sitting on the floor beside his door, was Marsh.

Chapter Thirteen

There was something wrong.

Marsh had been sitting in his room, trying to study and mostly just bouncing a tennis ball off the wall, listening for Greg to get home. The minute the key had turned in the lock out there, he'd been on his feet, every muscle alert, words clawing at his throat. A full day of stewing had been more than enough for him to get a grip.

Greg had made him feel like shit last night, but this morning he'd looked so vulnerable and exhausted. He'd apologized. And most confusing of all, he'd looked so goddamn relieved when Marsh had clarified that he and Yulia weren't sleeping together. It made Marsh hope—hope for things he'd never imagined he could have.

And he couldn't bear to let those hopes grow for another minute. Not when he still felt so unsure of him.

They had to talk, and Marsh was going to ask all the questions he should have asked ages ago. Whatever happened, at least he'd know. He'd ask Greg what the hell they were doing together. If it really was just sex, then, shit, that would hurt. But it would be an answer, and one he could live with. It was all he had ever expected anyway. And if it was more, well... Marsh almost didn't want to think about it, but if it *was* more, he'd ask why he couldn't meet Greg's parents. Why he couldn't kiss him in the living room or listen to him practice his stupid talk for his stupid symposium—so what if he couldn't understand a word of it? He just wanted to listen. To get to be part of Greg's world.

Only, now Marsh was sitting on the floor by Greg's door, and Greg was walking toward him, and his eyes were ringed with more than just fatigue. There was tension in his shoulders and in his bones, and he was pale as death. Marsh scrabbled at the floor to stand up. Something was *wrong*. Every instinct told Marsh to go to him, to shake him and ask him what the hell was going on.

The instant Greg caught sight of him, though, everything in his face shifted and changed. For a fraction of a second, the lines around his eyes and mouth went soft. But then it was like he had some kind of mental argument with himself, and all that openness was hidden away.

He balled his hand up into a fist around something and hid it behind his back. Marsh didn't really even have time to think about it. He was frozen in place, and Greg was striding past him, looking for all the world like he was on a pair of legs he'd borrowed after his last ones had given out on him, but his shoulders were square, his spine straight.

"Not a good time," Greg said, jaw clenched tight.

"Are you okay?" Marsh let Greg slip by him and into his room, one hand out, fully expecting at this point to get the door slammed in his face. Greg hadn't been this stiff and this defensive since before that first night. There was a space bubble around him a yard wide, his whole body radiating static and pushing off touch. Yet, for just a second, as he turned back around to face Marsh, his eyes were open and soft and imploring, practically begging for a kind of comfort Marsh didn't even know if he could offer.

And just like that, it was gone. Greg's gaze went hard again, his brows dropping. He met Marsh's eyes for a second, then looked away. "I'm fine. It's just not a good night."

Marsh held his hands up in front of himself. "I only want to talk."

But Greg was already shaking head and retreating farther into his room. "I'm so busy tonight. Can't it wait?"

The thing was, sure. It could wait. Marsh had *been* waiting. He was tired of it, though. Tired of not being important enough for Greg to make a little time for him except when he was horny.

Hadn't Yulia been telling him this entire time that he'd been selling himself short? Always assuming the worst about Greg's intentions and never asking for an explanation.

Enough was enough.

The whole time he'd been going back and forth in his head about whether or not to press, Marsh had been hovering on the threshold to Greg's room. Greg gave a withering sigh, and his shoulders drooped. "Close the door if you're going to stay, or go if you're going to go. The whole house doesn't have to hear this."

He'd been about to barge his way in anyway, but that made him pause. "Do you want me to stay?"

"Doesn't matter to me."

And that didn't sound like Greg. Buying himself a second, Marsh did as Greg had asked and stepped into the room, turning his back to close the door and flip on the light. Facing Greg again, Marsh looked him over, searching for whatever he had missed. There had to be some kind of sign of what was going on in his head. "Did something happen? At school, or work, or…?"

"Nothing I can't handle."

Marsh was trying so hard to stay calm, but oh that got his hackles up. His voice rose in spite of himself. "Yeah, I'm not real sure about that."

"Look, whatever. I'm not up for sex, and I'm not good company right now, and I don't want to say anything I'm going to regret. If you want someone to hang out with, you've got your team, or Jason." His chest rose and fell with his breath, like he was giving in to something he'd been fighting for so long now.

"Or why don't you just go over to Yulia's place, like you usually do?"

Were they back to this?

"I told you, her and me, we're friends. There's nothing going on there."

"It doesn't matter."

Marsh wanted it to matter. "Hey." He reached out, wanting to get a hand on Greg's arm. To *touch* him and ground himself somehow. "I'm worried about you, okay? Is it the symposium? Or your parents? Or...?"

"What do you know about any of that?" Greg asked. He sidestepped Marsh's effort to touch him, and that was a slap. Was a sharp sting that tasted like rejection and like bile and like so many other moments in Marsh's life.

Something inside of Marsh snapped. He yanked his hand back, clenching it, digging his nails into the meat of his palm. His throat ached. "How would I know about anything? Since you never tell me about any of it." He gestured widely toward the door, toward the hall, toward all of the world outside this one damn room. "I hear about the whole symposium thing from Ronnie, about your parents from fucking *Ronnie*. And I mean, sure—" his voice cracked, "—I get it, it's boring, or too hard for me, or maybe you don't want me involved with any of it—" *Maybe you don't want your parents to have to know you're sleeping with a broke fuck-up who's probably not even going to graduate college.* He drew in a breath, all fire and ash, but the words couldn't seem to make it past his tongue.

Not that they needed to. Greg's expression was wretched, even worse than it had been that morning. "Don't want you involved with it? Is that what you think?"

"What the hell else am I supposed to think?" Marsh was ready to tear his hair out. He didn't understand this at all, and being in the dark was leaving him miserable. He threw his hands up.

But Greg was shaking his head for real this time, and it looked like an agony, and a bell started ringing in the distance. An awareness. Marsh raised his eyebrows and opened his mouth.

Before he could make a sound, though, Greg spat, "Christ, how stupid are you?"

Marsh reeled. Because that was a blow. That was a hand reaching into his ribs, and he'd figured Greg saw through his attempts to fit in with the brains he lived with, but he'd never been sure before. He caught his footing, but it was a narrow thing, and Greg was still talking.

"You never stay," he said, "and you're so cozy with— You think I don't know? I try not to care, but that's not— That's not who I am."

Marsh blinked as Greg cut himself off. The laugh rose up in his lungs. "Are you still talking about Yulia?" Then he really listened, and he boggled. "Are you *jealous*?" Because that was insane.

Didn't Greg know Marsh was a sure thing?

Flinching, Greg jerked his gaze to the side. And his knees just about buckled underneath him.

"Shit," Marsh hissed, stepping forward again. Greg caught himself, but his face wasn't just pale anymore. It was positively grey, and his eyes were all wrong. "Greg?" He got a hand under Greg's arm this time. Greg still batted at it, moving as if to push him away, but Marsh wasn't about to be put off. He steered Greg to the side and got him sitting on the edge of the bed, and that seemed to help. The clench to Greg's jaw went a little less rigid.

Marsh glanced down at what Greg's hand was still folded around, and he furrowed his brow. A washcloth? He darted his gaze up, searching Greg's face, suddenly seeing the sharpness of the lines there, and even Marsh could put some signs together. He swore again and swept a hand over Greg's brow. "Migraine?"

"Yeah," Greg finally sighed. "Bad one." His skin was clammy beneath Marsh's hand, and Christ, Marsh was such a tool, goading him into an argument when he was like this.

"How long has it been coming on?" Marsh asked, fussing, trying to get him down on his back.

"Since this morning. But it wasn't bad until an hour or so ago."

"An hour?" Marsh winced along with Greg at his own raised voice. "But you just got home."

"Group meeting. Had to."

"'Had to', my ass," Marsh grumbled under his breath as he started working at Greg's clothes. Get him comfortable. Get him into bed.

Greg's hand settled over his, and Marsh looked up. "Told you sex wasn't on the table tonight." And there was humor there in Greg's eyes, slitted as they were. There was a wryness there in his tone.

Marsh shuddered out a little sigh. If Greg could joke, that was good. That was something. "You asshole," he groused as he helped Greg get his shoes and jeans off. The undershirt and briefs could stay. He'd be comfortable enough that way.

Then Greg was mumbling, "You don't have to take care of me."

Pausing, Marsh reached up and touched Greg's face, because there was a question there. A self-sacrificing, self-denying kind of vulnerability that Marsh understood entirely too well. He ran his thumb across Greg's cheekbone. "I want to. If you'll let me."

Greg pushed into the touch, and the lines around his eyes and mouth finally eased. It was all the answer Marsh needed.

Maybe not the answers he'd come here for in the first place, but the things Greg had said, in his irritation and his anger and his pain... This thing between them, what was happening right now, it was more than just a fuck. "Just a fuck" didn't ever have the ability to hurt this much.

Marsh lingered for a minute, fingertips gentle against Greg's skin as he stared at his face, for once letting the hope bloom in his chest. Finally, he drew back, moving to take the cloth from Greg's hand. "Be right back."

"'Kay." Greg lay down, closing his eyes and curling in on himself in a way that made Marsh ache.

The closed eyes... Marsh could have smacked himself. Last time this had happened, Greg had lain in the darkness, swaddled in it. And Marsh, like an idiot, had turned on the light without even recognizing the damage it had done. Rag firmly in hand, he rose from the bed and walked over to Greg's desk where he flipped on his desk lamp and angled it down so it would cast as little light as possible. Just enough for Marsh not to break his neck. On his way to the door, he killed the overhead, and could actually hear Greg's little noise of relief.

Jesus.

Marsh let himself out, closing the door behind himself to block the brightness from the hallway. On his way to the bathroom, he passed Ronnie's room. Ronnie was sitting at his desk, and he twisted around, one brow raised as he gazed at Marsh.

"He okay?" Ronnie asked.

Marsh lifted his shoulders marginally. "He will be. I think."

"You done screaming at him?"

Marsh just chuckled. "You've met the guy. Think there was any other way to get him to calm down and let someone give him a hand for a second?"

Ronnie gave him an appraising stare, then shook his head. "You might just be all right, Sulkowski."

That tiny bit of approval shouldn't have made him feel so good. With a nod, Marsh gestured down the hall and Ronnie waved him away.

In the bathroom, Marsh got the hot tap going and re-soaked the washcloth, then wrung it out. Turning off the faucet, he caught his own reflection in the mirror. He ran a damp hand through his hair before he could stop himself. He shook his head. Didn't matter what he looked like. Not now.

He crept into Greg's room as quietly as he could. While he'd been gone, Greg had pulled the covers up to his waist and stretched out on his back, one arm draped over his eyes. Taking care not to jostle the bed too much, Marsh sat down beside him and swept light fingertips over his wrist before tugging it away. Greg caught his hand and gave it a little squeeze, then let him go.

"It's hot," Marsh warned. He folded the cloth into a thin strip and laid it out across Greg's brow. Groaning, Greg patted the sheets until he found Marsh's leg.

"Thank you."

"No problem. Anything else you want? Did you take something?"

"Yeah." Greg paused, seeming to think for a minute. "I can take another one, though." He pointed toward his desk. "Do you mind?"

Marsh rolled his eyes and stood. At Greg's desk, he wasn't quite sure what to do, though. "Are they in a drawer, or...?"

"Yeah. Top one on the left. Little orange bottle."

Marsh pulled the drawer open, flicking at the contents until he found the bottle. Squinting, he read the label. "Maxalt?"

"Yup."

He trusted Greg well enough, but read the label to double-check the dosage. Sure enough, it allowed a second pill if the first proved ineffective. He pressed down before twisting to pop the lid and shook out a single capsule. "You took one already?"

"Yeah. Helped a little, but..."

"I can see how much it's helping."

"Believe it or not, it was worse."

Not for the first time, Marsh thanked God he didn't have to deal with this kind of thing. Only, if he could, he would. Right now, at least, if he could take this away from Greg, he would. The guy had enough on his plate, and seeing him laid out like this did things to Marsh.

Before he could examine it too closely, he closed the bottle and put it back. "Why didn't you take a second one earlier?"

"They're really strong. Hangover's a bitch."

Well, that Marsh could relate to. Last time he'd twisted a knee sliding into home, they'd given him codeine, and he'd been high as a kite, then sick as a dog as soon as it wore off. He shoved the drawer closed, maybe a little too hard. As it slammed, the computer monitor on the desk went bright.

Without really meaning to, Marsh swept his gaze over the screen. It was a calendar of some sort, and Marsh blinked.

Every single hour for the next three days was blocked off. Every one.

Marsh whistled, then felt like a dick, because wow, this was an invasion of privacy. He reached over to turn off the screen, but even after it went dark, he couldn't get what little he had seen out of his mind.

He turned back to Greg. Strong, smart Greg who worked and worked and worked, and who was going to have an ulcer before he was thirty— Greg, who literally made himself sick with stress.

Greg, whom Marsh...cared about. So much. Vulnerable and hurting in his bed. Not even naked or anything, he looked fragile.

And Marsh didn't want to simply take the pain from him. He wanted to *take care* of him. Keep him safe and protected, even from himself. He might not be able to understand the work he did, or even the fundamentals of it— He sure as hell couldn't do it for him. But there had to be something. Deep behind his vision, that schedule still glowed.

He kept it there as he retreated to the bed and got in. Greg held out his hand, and Marsh pressed the medication into his palm, then reached over to grab the glass of water sitting on the nightstand. Greg took that, too, sitting up with a little moan. Marsh leaned in and held the compress in place as Greg swallowed and passed the glass over, lying down again with a grunt.

Marsh hovered there for a moment. Greg had said he didn't have to do this, and ever since then, he'd only given silent, tacit approvals. Smoothing the damp fabric down over Greg's brow, Marsh asked quietly, "Can I?" He brushed his fingertips over Greg's scalp, and the answer seemed unequivocal. But he wanted Greg to say the words. To ask. "Last time it seemed to help."

"Yeah," Greg said, voice rough. "Yeah. That'd be...nice." His throat bobbed, like there was an emotion there underneath his acceptance of this barest comfort. This touch that was only human decency. Only affection.

Maybe there wasn't any *only* about it.

Holding tightly to that thought, Marsh settled in, his back against the headboard just the way it had been the last time. He worked his way around the obstacle of the compress and traced out familiar paths, along the edges of Greg's face and through his hair and down, sweeping over his neck to the place where his shoulders met the collar of his shirt before sweeping up and completing the circuit all over again.

Greg turned into the touch, breath deepening, and Marsh's thoughts drifted. They were little thoughts, pointless thoughts, ideas about the shape of Greg's cheekbone and the point of his jaw. About how good it felt to have Greg here and resting and trusting. Protectiveness welled up in him all over again.

He wasn't good at putting words to feelings. He'd never known how to ask for what he wanted—what he needed, even. But this, this he could do. In little ways like this, and maybe in bigger ones, he could show Greg how he felt. He could give Greg what he needed.

To all appearances, Greg looked asleep, but Marsh knew better. His breathing was a little too fast, the corners of his mouth just a shade too sharp. He seemed peaceful, though. It seemed wrong to break the quiet or to pull Greg out of whatever haze he'd fallen into, but Marsh let the bubble in his throat press its way up and out. He stilled the motion of his hand. "When's your alarm set for?"

"Six," Greg mumbled, then sighed. "Should probably make it earlier. Didn't get anything done tonight."

"Yeah, no." Marsh resumed his stroking, daring to brush a thumb against Greg's bottom lip. "You need the sleep."

"No time to sleep."

Marsh pushed a note of laughter through his nose. "You know, I was wondering how you kept ending up laid up like this, but I think you just answered my question for me."

"I can handle it." A note of defiance colored his tone for the first time since Marsh had wrangled him into bed.

Marsh dug his fingers in a little deeper at the spot behind Greg's ear that always made him seem to melt. "Never said you couldn't." *Just that maybe you shouldn't. That maybe you don't have to.*

Greg made an unhappy, snuffling noise, but he didn't try to move or pull away. *Shh*-ing him, Marsh kept touching and petting. Once Greg had settled down again, Marsh whispered, "Sleep. It's okay." *Let me worry about the rest.*

Slowly, Greg's breath evened out, and the trust was staggering. Of course, Marsh was just about to violate it grossly, but even that couldn't stem the tide of wanting. Of...loving. Marsh's eyes felt warm, the corners prickling. He blinked it back, though, focusing on the contours of Greg's face beneath his fingertips, committing it to memory. Just in case.

He kept going long past when he felt confident Greg was asleep, psyching himself up. Finally, he whispered, "Greg?" At the lack of response, he nodded to himself. Moving gingerly so as not to wake Greg, Marsh pulled his hand away, then edged toward the side of the bed. Greg didn't so much as stir, and Marsh breathed a little easier.

Okay. First things first.

He found Greg's phone in the pocket of his pants on the floor. He pressed the button to wake it. No passcode. Phew. A couple of flicks through the screens to find Greg's alarm, and yup, it was set for six o'clock, all right. Marsh glanced at the time. It was almost midnight. He turned the alarm off and set the phone down on the nightstand beside Greg's head, then double-checked there wasn't another alarm set on the clock next to the lamp. Satisfied, he turned around. Greg was still lying there, chest rising and falling, the cloth draped over his eyes.

Marsh picked his way over to Greg's desk and turned the monitor on, squinting against the sudden glow. Another peek over his shoulder to check that Greg hadn't moved. Marsh exhaled long and slow, then sank into Greg's chair.

The calendar program was still front and center on the screen, and the array of appointments was just as dizzying as it had been the first time. Pushing past the guilt at looking at Greg's things like this, Marsh read through it all. Shifts at the help desk, classes to teach, meetings with advisors. Even nominally free blocks of time were dog-eared to get things done. Christ. Marsh rubbed a hand across his brow. Greg hadn't been kidding about not having time to sleep.

But there had to be some give. Greg wasn't going to make it if he didn't get a break.

Marsh scanned all the way through the end of the week, ticking off one obligation after another: man registration desk, pick parents up, eat with parents, escort visiting professor, give talk. It kept going on and on, until finally, come Saturday morning, Greg's parents would be back on an airplane, and a few slivers of white, un-booked time shone through between the crush of appointments and responsibilities. Greg just needed to make it until then without another migraine. Or a panic attack. Or a stroke, the way he was going.

Marsh's finger hovered over the mouse. Boundary-pushing or no, he reached over to the keyboard and took a screenshot, then emailed it to himself. It was something to work with. Marsh was going to have his hands full between now and when Greg woke up, and Greg was going to be mad. Probably *really* mad.

Turning off the monitor, Marsh swiveled around in the chair. He caught sight of Greg's face, untroubled in sleep, and his heart welled up. Even if Greg was mad...it'd be worth it.

He stood and walked over to the bed. The compress had long since cooled and was leaving Greg's skin clammy. Marsh pulled it away and tucked it into his hand. He leaned over and pressed a kiss to the center of Greg's forehead, lingering for a long moment with his eyes clenched shut, soaking this in. He couldn't resist a quick brush of his lips over Greg's mouth, and then he pulled away.

Greg shifted, turning over onto his side and reaching out. "Leaving?" he mumbled.

"Have to," Marsh whispered, smoothing his hair from his face. "But I'll check in."

"'Kay." A pause, and Marsh thought he'd fallen asleep again, but then Greg's eyes fluttered. "Thank you."

Marsh could hardly breathe through the way those words pressed in on his chest. "Anytime."

Forcing himself away, he crossed toward Greg's desk. He turned off the lamp there, casting the room in darkness, then retreated to the door. And it would have been so much simpler to stay. He'd all but been invited, but "all but" wasn't enough. He wanted Greg to ask him one night, when they were sweaty and tangled together.

He wanted Greg to forgive him for this.

Without another look back, he opened the door and let himself out.

Chapter Fourteen

Bright.

The first shred of awareness coming over Greg as he surfaced through too-thick layers of sleep was the sheer amount of light in his room, and that...wasn't right. Too groggy yet to figure out why, he curled in on himself, fumbling for the covers to drag them up and over his head, and that was better. Warmer. Darker, at least, and that was good.

He swallowed, only to choke on the desert that was his mouth. His eyes felt full of sand, and maybe he really had come to in the Sahara. It would be the best explanation. Unless...

Right. Migraine. God, how had he even gotten home last night? All he could remember was a blinding pain and auras surrounding everything, and Chu reaming him out, then—it had been Ronnie, hadn't it? Ronnie who'd taken care of him and gotten him into a car. Just the memory of the way the streetlights had pulsed brought up echoes of bile. He held it back, though, going perfectly rigid against the surge of nausea.

Another agonizing minute or two, and then it passed. He brought his hand up and poked gingerly at his temples. It didn't hurt, but numbness lingered, and there was a shakiness in his bones. He'd taken a second pill, then, only he couldn't remember digging around for the bottle, he just remembered hands. Warm. Gentle.

The wave of wooziness hit him harder this time, but it wasn't only physiological.

Marsh. Marsh had found him, and they had fought. God, they'd been yelling at each other, and he could hear the words.

Marsh had said his symposium was boring and he didn't want anything to do with it or— No. That wasn't it. Not quite.

He'd thought *Greg* didn't want *him* to have anything to do with it, and that was absurd. Ridiculous. He'd told Marsh as much, hadn't he?

What had he told Marsh? That he wanted nothing more than for Marsh to be interested? To be able to look up while he was speaking and find Marsh in the audience and not be afraid that Marsh would be judging him, bored and unaffected and trying to figure out how to let Greg down easy?

That he wanted Marsh to stay?

He must have said something, because Marsh *had* stayed. There was a dim recollection, there in the back of his mind, of the room lit by the glow of his monitor. Of coming awake in the dimness with Marsh's lips against his brow. Of Marsh saying he had to go, and Greg being sad, disappointed beneath the exhaustion and the pain, but grateful, too. Grateful Marsh had stayed as long as he had. That he'd taken care of Greg.

Greg had to find him. He had to ask Marsh what he'd said in his delirium. He had to see Marsh's face.

Throwing off the covers, he jerked upward, but the vertigo nearly floored him. He caught his head in his hands and closed his eyes, swaying, and he was shivering so hard he could barely manage to even sit right. Christ, it was bright.

It was bright.

Shit. Shit shit shit. He braced himself and peered between his fingers at the clock. It was past ten. Four hours later than he'd planned to be up. This was bad, this was unrecoverable. He was screwed, and his stomach spasmed. Once, and then again, and he had to close his throat, but not against nausea. Against breath and sound, and he was *laughing*. High and uncontrolled, and his stomach hurt, everything hurt. He could barely sit up straight, and it was ten AM, and he was screwed. He was completely and utterly screwed. His abdomen cramped, and he eased a hand down to cradle it, sobbing and in hysterics all at once. He'd worked so hard.

The laughter was just starting to give way to cold, hard fear about having to call work and try to explain why he was two hours late, when a series of quiet knocks rang out against his door. It struck him—if it was Marsh, he didn't know what he would do. He must have turned off Greg's alarm. He'd taken care of Greg, but this was too much. Blame settled, cold and angry and coloring everything red. He loved Marsh, more than he should, but he'd have to...

What? Break up with him? Marsh wasn't going to want to sit there and let Greg rant at him. Even if Greg tried to be calm and rational, he wasn't going to be able to keep it together. It would devolve into yelling, and Marsh would walk away. Greg's hand trembled harder where he had it pressed against his cheek.

He had to do something, say something. Whoever it was knocked again, and Greg worked to find his voice. Before he could, though, the knob twisted, the door canting inward, and—

And Ronnie of all people poked his head through the crack. His left eyebrow was sky-high. "Sounds like you're awake?"

"Yeah." Greg exhaled slowly. He dragged his hands over his face and looked at the clock again. "Finally."

"You needed it."

"You're not the only one who thinks so." Unable to keep the bitterness from his voice, he shifted forward, testing himself and his balance before setting his feet down on the carpet. His head swam, but he had to get up. He *should* have gotten up four hours ago. A pathetic little whinge broke free of his lungs.

"Whoa," Ronnie said. "Easy." He'd gotten across the room awfully fast, had set something down on the floor, and then his hand was on Greg's shoulder, steadying him.

Greg shook his head. "Gotta—"

"Gotta plant your ass there and take it easy for a minute? Why, yes. Yes, you do."

"No, you don't understand."

"*You* don't understand, but if you'd listen for three seconds, maybe you would. Here." Ronnie reached over, going for whatever he'd set down on his way in, and— Greg furrowed up his brow. Since when did they even own a tray?

Wherever the tray had come from, Ronnie grabbed a cup of coffee off of it and passed it to Greg, and Greg's eyes widened. God, *coffee*. Greg couldn't even suppress the little moan as he wrapped his hands around the mug and brought it to his lips, taking a careful sip of it. He took another, bigger one when the liquid didn't burn his tongue.

Pulling it away from his mouth, he sighed and braced his elbows on his knees against the lingering shakiness in his limbs. The coffee was a tawny caramel color, just the right amount of cream, no sugar, thank you very much. Anything still left of his migraine started to dissolve on his tongue.

"There's food, too."

Just like that, Greg's stomach made itself known. He'd been too sick to eat last night, and now that he'd been reminded food existed, he was ravenous. Stretching to set his mug down on his bedside table, Greg held out his hand for the plate of eggs and toast and fruit Ronnie was holding out to him. It smelled like the best thing ever. Still wary, though, he tested himself on the toast first. Only once he'd gotten it down without any threat of consequences did he tuck in to the rest of it, trying to eat slowly but fairly shoveling it in.

Making a little chuckling sound, Ronnie stepped away to fall into Greg's desk chair. "Marsh said you'd probably be starving."

"Don't even get me started on Marsh," Greg managed between bites. "He turned off my alarm. Speaking of which—"

Balancing his plate on his knees, he made a move for his phone, but Ronnie swooped in and stole it first.

"After," Ronnie admonished, pointing at Greg's plate.

Greg gave him a look, though it probably lacked gravitas what with his fork hanging out of his mouth. He chewed and swallowed, then insisted, "I'm late for work."

"Taken care of."

That made Greg stop cold. "Excuse me?"

"Taken care of. You've officially called in sick. Your boss said to tell you to feel better."

Greg's brows felt like they met his hairline. "You talked to my boss?"

"Not personally, but I was asked to relay the message. Not only that, but you've been told to take as much time as you need, since you've been so accommodating these past couple months." Ronnie's level gaze dripped accusations. And sure, Greg had been filling in for other people a little more than he needed to, strictly speaking, but someone had to do it.

"They needed me," he offered weakly.

Ronnie was having none of it. "Anyway, you don't need to worry about work today."

It took a minute for that to sink in. And then about thirty seconds to move on to what else was fucked so far this morning. "I was going to get my lessons put together before work."

"Which, considering Jason is covering your class, is just as well."

"Jason? Why would he—"

"Because he heard you needed the help."

"I don't need..." Greg trailed off, unable to finish that sentence. He did need the help. He'd been desperate for a way to keep everything he was juggling aloft, but he hadn't asked for it.

He worked hard. He pushed himself. It was what he did. People stepping in to offer…no one did that. If you didn't take care of it yourself, nothing ever got done—how many times had he learned that?

Suspicion was a point of ignition in his brain. Slowly, setting aside his demolished plate, he turned to Ronnie. "And what else do I not have to do today?"

Ronnie's grin went shark-like. He sensed Greg had cottoned on, now. "Well, I'm taking your shift at the registration desk—and don't even try to argue. I owe you one for that help you gave me with my low-pressure experiment last week. I owe you a lot more than one."

"We all do favors for each other," Greg argued, though he wasn't sure why. The dizziness now wasn't about a migraine hangover or low blood sugar. It was the sheer novelty of being able to breathe without feeling like he was about to be crushed.

"And you do more favors for all of us than anyone else. Don't you get that? Every time, man, you always come through. You never say no. It's why I come to you so often—and don't think I didn't get a reaming out about that—"

Wait, what? "Who reamed you out?"

Softening his smile, Ronnie shook his head. "Who do you think?"

Greg threw up his hands. "Everything that's happened since I woke up this morning has been a mystery to me."

Ronnie's pause was longer this time, more considering. "You're a smart guy. What do you *think* is happening here?"

"I don't know," Greg insisted, getting frustrated now. "You're staging an intervention—"

"I'm not doing anything. Not me. Greg, seriously?"

"Look—"

"I'm just the one conveying the message, because your boyfriend had to go to practice and didn't want to wake you up."

Everything suddenly went very quiet in Greg's head, all his thought processes stuttering on a word that should have stopped meaning anything back in high school, if he'd, you know, been dating in high school. If he'd ever managed to keep anyone's interest for any substantial period of time. Then all the objections and the equivocations crowded back in. "Marsh? He's not— We've never said."

Ronnie leveled him with a look that could peel paint. "From what I heard last night, you two haven't said *anything* you need to. But let me tell you this. That boy took care of you last night, and when he was done, he came out fighting and he took every single person who's been taking advantage of you or asking too much of you to task. I'm not too proud to admit that included me."

And that didn't make any sense. Greg had been trying not to bore Marsh with too much of the minutiae of his schedule. He hadn't been able to hide that he was a giant ball of stress, no, but he'd never asked for any of this.

Maybe he could have. All along, maybe Marsh had been waiting for him to.

"How—" he started.

But Ronnie was still enumerating all the things Marsh had done. "He came storming to my room with a printout of your calendar for the next week—and we are going to have words about how the hell you let things get that bad, by the way—and told me in no uncertain terms that I needed to find people to help cover for you. He got the number for your help desk people from me, and—"

Once again, though, Greg was stuck. His stomach was doing somersaults. "My calendar?"

"Focus." Ronnie snapped his fingers in front of Greg's face. "He did this. All of this."

Greg batted Ronnie's hand out of his space. He rubbed at the bridge of his nose, because this was a lot to process and a lot to think about, and none of it made sense.

Continuing, Ronnie said, "He made sure that for the next few days all you have to do is give your presentation, entertain your parents and get Chu off your back. Oh, and not make yourself sick again."

"But..." There was one thing Greg couldn't seem to work through, and it was a stupid question to ask. He swiped his hand over his face and turned his neck to look at Ronnie. The question came out anyway. "Why?"

Ronnie shook his head, shooting him a wry smile before shoving up to stand. "If you don't know, you're gonna have to ask him." He pointed at Greg's plate. "You done with that?"

"What? Oh. No. I'll deal with it."

"Okay." He grabbed the empty tray and headed to the door. "When do you have to pick up your folks?"

"Um..." Shit, right, that was today. "Not until five."

"Cool. I'm heading to campus in another hour so I can cover *someone's* shift. You want a lift?"

Right, he'd need a ride. His car was still parked in front of the science building, and he had to... He stopped the thought, blinking at the direction it had been drifting. He didn't have to do anything except feel better and dig himself out of this hole. He felt *light*. When was the last time that had happened?

"Yeah," Greg said. "That'd be great."

"Cool. Find me when you're ready."

"Will do."

Ronnie left, and Greg stared into empty space. Absentmindedly, he scooped some eggs up with his fork and reached for his coffee cup. Sitting and eating breakfast. It was a novel concept, considering how things had been going of late. It was a luxury.

His heart squeezed hard. He wasn't entirely sure what he'd done to deserve it.

Chapter Fifteen

Greg crawled along, weaving his way through the cars lined up in front of arrivals, eyes peeled the whole way for— Oh. He grinned and waved, throwing his blinker on as he nudged his way into the rightmost lane.

Clearly too impatient to wait for any of that nonsense, his mom stepped off the curb, tugging his dad along. Greg checked over his shoulder, and the car behind him was loading someone, too, so whatever. He wasn't in immediate danger of losing a mirror or a bumper. Switching off the turn signal, he tapped the button for his hazards and popped the trunk.

He was barely out before his mom was wrapping him up in a crushing hug. God, that felt good. He breathed her in, lemon and powder and home and squeezed her even tighter. "Hey, Ma," he managed to get out.

"It's so good to see you."

And that shouldn't have gotten to him so much, shouldn't have made his throat feel rough. "Yeah, it is." He closed his eyes and filled his lungs, only letting her go when a horn sounded in the distance. They were triple-parked. There wasn't time to revert into a five-year-old who just needed his mom.

She caught him before he could pull away entirely, though, making a little *tsk*ing noise as she looked him over. "You've been working too hard again, haven't you?"

"Am I ever not?" He laughed it off. If he looked bad now, it was a damn good thing she hadn't seen him yesterday.

"Leave the boy alone, Elaine," Greg's dad insisted. His mom made a little noise of protest but stepped aside, letting him pull Greg in for a quick one-armed hug. "Hey, there."

"Hey, Dad." It wasn't the same bone-crushing embrace his mother had given him, but it was secure and accepting and familiar, and that was just fine.

Another car honked behind them, and Greg dropped his arms, shooing his parents into the car. His mom shoved his dad toward the front over his protests, and Greg chuckled to himself as the two of them bickered about it. Dad always hated letting her take the back seat, but in a tiny car like this it didn't really work any other way. "Might as well give up," he said, buckling himself in. "Lord knows she's not going to."

"Chivalry is well and truly dead," his dad lamented as he finally acquiesced. "And your mother killed it."

"Oh, hush."

Greg flicked off the blinkers and put the car into drive, nosing his way forward and around someone else who'd given up and started loading passengers in the left lane. He stole a glance at his dad, who was eyeing the dash appraisingly.

"Think we'll have time for me to take a peek under the hood before we go?"

Greg shrugged. "Would love it if you could, but I'm doubting it."

"What's the mileage up to now?"

Too high. Greg rattled off the numbers and answered a few other random questions about what the heck that rattle was and when it had started. His dad hummed, and Greg caught his mom's eye in the rearview mirror. "Burgers okay tonight?" He had a place in mind—simple and affordable and just down the street from their motel.

"Sounds great," his mother answered. "But we're going somewhere nice tomorrow."

Greg shook his head. "You don't have to."

"Nonsense. It isn't every day we get to see you."

True, but they'd only managed this visit because Southwest had been having a sale, and his mom watched for those like a hawk. Money was as tight as ever, and the two of them were getting up there. He didn't even like to think about what their retirement account must look like. His mom was still insisting, though, and he opened his mouth to argue again.

"You said it yourself, son," his dad cut in, smirking. "She's not going to give up."

The man wasn't wrong. Conceding for now, Greg sighed and asked, "So how was the flight?"

His mom started in on a story about one of the flight attendants, or someone they'd had to sit next to, and Greg nodded and smiled in all the right parts, grateful for the chance to concentrate on driving. And on other things. His phone was sitting in the cup holder, and it was dumb, but every now and then he chanced a peek at it, checking if the light was blinking. It never was. And that was fine, it wasn't like he was expecting to hear from anyone. As promised, Ronnie had taken his shift manning the registration table at the symposium, and the help desk had been able to find people to cover for him. Jason was handling his teaching responsibilities through the middle of next week. Really, no one should be bothering him, and he knew damn well that Marsh was in classes or doing off-season training with his team at the gym all day. But it seemed too weird not to have anyone breathing down his neck, asking him for something.

It still seemed impossible that Marsh had done so much for him and then not said a thing.

Stupid. He was being stupid. He'd see Marsh tonight. He'd take his parents to dinner and drop them off at the motel, and then he'd go home and... Well, he didn't know what then. But something.

"Greg? Are you even listening?"

Starting, Greg flashed back over the conversation he'd only half been paying attention to for the past few minutes. "Yeah. Of course. The guy next to you needed a...seat belt extender?"

"Right. Anyway, so." His mom launched into her story again, and his dad cleared his throat. He rolled his eyes the way he often did when Mom was feeling particularly loquacious, and Greg let one corner of his mouth tilt up.

Yeah, this was all familiar, all right. It was kind of perfect.

She was still rambling by the time Greg pulled into the parking lot of the diner he'd picked out, and she only paused for breath as they headed in and followed the hostess to a booth. Side-eyeing his dad, Greg picked up his menu, wondering not for the first time what marvel of combinatory genetics had managed to suppress all of his mother's social chromosomes in the process of creating him.

She made it all the way through placing their orders before his dad cleared his throat. She squinted at him for a second, then shook her head and tapped her fingers to her forehead, turning to Greg. "Look at me, babbling like that. We're here to see you, honey!"

"You're not babbling," Greg lied.

"Yes, she is."

His mother threw a napkin at his father without taking her eyes off Greg.

"How are you? How's everything going?"

Where to even start? "I'm...okay." He was, actually. Sort of. Confused and tired but okay.

"You're as bad as your father," she admonished. She waved her hands. "Fine, fine. Tell us some more about tomorrow."

"Well." He frowned. He was a little fuzzier on the details than he probably should be. "There are talks all day. There were a few today, too."

"Anything interesting?" his father asked.

Greg tilted his head side to side. "I only sat in on one session, but what I heard was pretty good. Not sure if it was *interesting*, but if you're curious about high-temperature nickel alloys or implications of tungsten inclusions in manufacturing..." At the blank look on both their faces, he trailed off and twisted his napkin between his fingers. "It was okay."

"Sounds...fascinating," his mother said, her left eye only twitching a little as she smiled at him. She'd always been really nice about that kind of thing, humoring him when he started going on about science stuff. "Why just the one session, though? That slave driver of an advisor locking you away in your lab again?"

"He's not a slave driver." Greg paused. "Well, not much of one. But, um, kind of? I'd gotten behind on some experiments, and he reminded me last night that I needed to keep up with them." He gave a little one-shouldered shrug. "It's okay, though. I think I made some progress today."

Amazing what a day without distractions could do for his ability to focus. Well, without too many distractions, in any case. He'd been watching his phone more carefully than usual, keeping half an eye out for a message from Marsh, or from anyone else who needed Greg to do something for them. The silence of the thing had been unsettling after so many people knocking down his door of late.

Since he was thinking of it, he snuck his phone out of his pocket and glanced at it under the table. Nothing. Which was fine. He slid it back away and smiled at his parents.

"I may even have his results for him by the end of next week if I can keep focused," he continued smoothly. And that would be another relief. Another burden off his shoulders.

"Well, don't be too focused," his mother said. "We're only here a couple of days."

"Don't worry. I know."

"Good. And everything else? Your teaching? Your job?" Her eye twitched again when she mentioned the job, and his dad ran his thumb over the corner of his knuckles.

"Both fine." He gave them quick rundowns on how things were going with both. "And they're fine. Really. I've got things under control."

Thanks to Marsh. He still didn't know how to feel about that.

"Well, if you're sure. If the job ever gets to be too much..."

"It..." And should he tell the truth here? They hated that he'd had to pick up something outside of his school and his research and his obligations at the university. He'd hated it, too, but he'd been done with acting as a drain on them and the resources they didn't have. "It's tricky," he confessed. "Chu actually talked to me about it yesterday. I may have to give it up."

"If you need some help while you're still in school—" his father started.

"It's grad school."

"But it's still school." His mother reached out to put her hand over his. "And we are so proud of you. You've gone so far."

Dad chimed in, "And I'm still dying to tell your grandma we have a doctor in the family."

"Not that kind of doctor," Greg said.

His mom squeezed his hand. "Still a doctor."

Turning his palm over, he wrapped his fingers around hers. "I'm trying to make it work."

"But if it doesn't, you'll tell us." His mother fixed him with a gaze that brooked no argument. "There's no shame in asking for help."

That made something stick in his windpipe, and he took a sip of his water in a fruitless attempt to clear it. He should have asked for help a long time ago, back before things had gotten so bad. He'd been too damn proud to, though. Somehow, help had come to him anyway. Swallowing around the constriction, he nodded. "I know."

"Promise? You'll call us if you need anything?"

"I promise."

He was saved from actually having to make a blood oath by the arrival of their food. He'd made time for lunch for once, but the burger and the pile of greasy fries in front of him still had him salivating, suddenly reminding him that he was starving. After a liberal dousing with ketchup, he picked up the burger and took a big bite out of it.

His mom chuckled as she speared a piece of lettuce from her salad, one eyebrow raised. Greg glanced to the side, and, right, his dad was eating like a civilized person, too. "Sorry," he mumbled, grabbing a napkin and wiping at his mouth.

"No, please," Mom said. "Good to see you have an appetite. You're skin and bones."

"Hardly." He popped a fry into his mouth and chewed and swallowed. Besides, he'd been eating way better than he usually did when he was stressed out. "Marsh has been making me eat."

A single beat of silence passed before he realized what he'd said.

"Marsh?" his mom asked, head tipped to the side. "Your housemate, Marsh?"

"Um...yeah?" Crap, he looked guilty. He could feel it.

"Just your housemate?"

Taking a bite to buy himself a second, he thought back on all their phone calls of late, and damn. He'd been casually mentioning Marsh a lot more than he would normally talk about someone who was just a friend. He hadn't said anything really compromising, but his mom had an instinct for this kind of thing. "It's complicated?" he tried, wincing around a smile.

"Uh-huh," his dad said.

His mom had that look on her face like she could smell the blood in the water, but she was too nice to go in for the kill. Instead, she just smirked and elbowed his father. Greg really hoped they didn't have too big of a wager riding on this thing.

That happened sometimes, when his mom had a hunch about his personal life. His dad had had to do the dishes for a month after Greg had come out.

"Well." She directed a sly smile at her salad. "I hope we get to meet him?"

Greg hid his choking cough behind a gulp of water. That shouldn't have surprised him—his parents always wanted to meet everyone. His housemates, his friends, his professors. Marsh was a housemate and a friend, and so much more, and yet Greg hadn't so much as thought about introducing him to his folks. He should have, though.

As he shook his head and cleared his throat, his heart twisted. They needed to talk, him and Marsh. Soon. Talk about what they were and what they wanted, and God, he barely even dared to hope they were on the same page with that.

Marsh had been there for him through a lot—through a lot more than Greg'd had the guts to ask him to help with. Every migraine and every near-panic attack about how much work he had to do, every time he got so busy he nearly forgot to eat. Every time he was lonely and itching for human contact, longing to be touched. Longing for *Marsh*...

Marsh had been there.

Greg set his napkin aside and looked down at his plate. Maybe Marsh would want to be there a little longer. Maybe, somehow, Greg could begin to pay him back.

"I hope so," Greg said. He hoped he could introduce Marsh to his parents as his housemate and his friend.

He hoped he could introduce him to them as his so much more.

A few hours later, Greg stood by the door to his parents' motel room, casting one more regretful glance around at the décor. "Sorry again about you guys having to stay here."

His mom waved a hand dismissively. "Please. As tempting as the idea of staying in a house full of bachelors is..." She cocked one eyebrow as she gave him a lopsided smile. "I think we'll be just fine here."

"Okay," he conceded. She was right, too. He cringed thinking about the state of the place right now. "My session tomorrow starts at one."

"And we'll be there in plenty of time."

"You sure you don't want me to come pick you up? I could probably—"

"No way, mister. You're going to have enough going on as it is getting ready."

His father nodded in agreement, putting a hand on his mom's shoulder. "Cab's all set to come and pick us up at noon."

Yet another thing he felt bad about not being able to do for them. He was really, really lucky they were so understanding. "Okay. I'll see you tomorrow, then."

"Can't wait." His mom stepped away from his dad, moving to stand right in front of Greg and reaching up to put her hands to his cheeks. "You're going to be amazing. We're so proud of you."

His face went warm, and his insides did, too, embarrassment and happiness intertwining the way they always did when she said that kind of thing. "*Mom*," he said in a sing-song-y whine. Only that kind of deflection hadn't worked when he was five, and it sure wasn't going to now he was twenty-five.

"Oh, hush." She pulled him in for a hug and kissed his cheek, and he let it linger the way he had at the airport, soaking it in.

His father cleared his throat, and Greg let go, reaching around his mother to accept a quick, two-pump handshake from his father before edging toward the door.

"Knock 'em dead tomorrow," his dad said.

"Will do." Greg took one last glance at them over his shoulder, then nodded to himself and stepped outside.

The door closed behind him, and he stood there in the darkness, staring up at the vast night sky. Even with the neon lights of the motel and the streetlamps blazing, the stars and the moon shone down at him. He breathed out long and slow. It was time to go home, and his nerves were coiled into knots inside of him. One last check of his phone to find it silent and dark.

He was tired—exhausted, really, still a little wrung out from the migraine and the medication from the night before, but he was thinking clearly. He'd had a day to think, and to work, and a night with the two people in the world who had always believed in him, no matter what. The two people who had always given him whatever he needed.

Marsh had given Greg what he needed, too.

Dropping his gaze, Greg made his way toward his car.

The drive home passed in a blur, and before he knew it, he was pushing through the door of the house he shared with a friend, a co-worker and a lover, and his blood was thrumming in his veins, a faint buzz drowning out his thoughts. His pulse sped as he passed through the entryway and strode down the hall.

The door to Marsh's room was closed, but light was spilling out from underneath. Greg closed his eyes for just a second. When he opened them again, all he could see was how he wanted this to go.

He raised his hand and knocked.

Chapter Sixteen

Sometimes, the softest sounds rang out the loudest.

The thudding of Marsh's heart. The rapping of a knock at his door.

Marsh forced himself to relax, clenching and unclenching his hands to keep himself calm.

He'd been sitting on his bed, back braced against the wall now for a couple of hours, trying to focus and get through this one damn article for class and failing miserably. Greg had been planning to take his parents out to dinner. They saw him so infrequently, of course they'd want him to spend some time with them. Of course Greg would want to see his folks. Not exactly something Marsh could really relate to, but sure, he got it. Didn't make it any easier, though, sitting there and waiting.

He'd kept his music off the entire time, kept his ears trained for the sound of the front door. Listened for footsteps in the hall, and he could recognize the sound Greg made when he walked now. How many nights had he spent, wondering if he'd hear it coming down the stairs? And the minute he had—the instant he'd recognized that particular jangling of keys and that quick, efficient gait, his body had gone rigid. His breaths had quickened, his lungs going tight. He'd thought maybe Greg would just keep walking. Head upstairs and not even bother coming to say hello. Maybe he'd want to get some rest.

Or maybe he wouldn't even want to look at Marsh's face.

But no. Greg was right outside his door, and that brought a whole other set of possibilities. Maybe he'd be cool, maybe everything would be fine, or maybe Greg was stopping by to tell Marsh off. Because Marsh had overstepped, Marsh had crossed a line, Marsh wasn't even really his boyfriend anyway, and Greg was so bad at asking for help. How he'd react to having it thrust upon him, well. That was anybody's guess.

Not for the first time, Marsh wished Ronnie hadn't been tied up in classes and stuff for that symposium today, because damn if Marsh wouldn't have loved to pick his brain about this, or at least get some idea how Greg had reacted when Ronnie had told him everything this morning.

Another quick sequence of knocks sounded out, and shit, Marsh had to say something. Now.

He cleared his throat and managed to croak out, "Come in."

The door creaked open, until Marsh could see Greg standing there through the gap. The top button on his shirt was undone, and his expression was pointedly neutral. Marsh looked him up and down, searching for any kind of a sign. Greg's skin was still too pale, the shadows under his eyes lingering, but the furrows on his brow weren't quite so deeply set. Still tired, then, but not actively in pain. Not so raw and ragged as he had been the night before.

Greg gestured toward the room within. "Can I?"

"Yeah." Marsh capped his pen and set his article aside, sitting up straighter. "Of course." He wiped his palms off on his thighs, but then he didn't know what to do with his hands. Clasping them together in his lap, he cracked one knuckle after another before he could stop himself.

And Greg was moving so slowly, a deliberateness to his every action that had been absent of late. He was less harried, and that was good, but it was killing Marsh. Suddenly, all Marsh wanted was for Greg to tear the damned Band-Aid off, because all this waiting and wondering was going to drive him insane.

If Greg was mad, he should just *be mad*, and if he wasn't, he should be over here, preferably in Marsh's lap. He should let

Marsh touch. Kiss. Ease this nervous energy with the heat of his breath.

But Greg just stepped a few feet inside. He closed the door behind him, and Marsh swallowed against the dryness in his throat. Greg settled his gaze on Marsh, and there was something penetrating to it, something searching. If only Marsh knew what he was looking for.

Marsh was being stupid. This kind of uncertainty wasn't attractive. Relaxing his spine, he let go of his knuckles and draped his palms across his knees. He strived for that casualness, the mask he put on at parties and games and whenever Greg was scrutinizing him like this. But his voice still rasped as he asked, "How are you?"

Greg chuffed. "Better. Couldn't be much worse, though, could I?"

"You could, but then I'd have to take you to the hospital, and neither of us has time for that."

For a second, Greg's neutrality slipped, and his gaze darted to the papers Marsh had set aside. "Are you busy?"

"Nah." It wasn't like he'd been able to focus today anyway. If Greg left now, without saying anything, Marsh would be fucked for the rest of the night. "It can wait." Marsh hesitated. "Are you? Busy?"

A minefield opened up in front of him, and he wasn't treading carefully enough. Then again, he'd been the one wishing Greg would rip the bandage off. No reason Marsh couldn't do the ripping his own damn self.

The laugh that escaped Greg this time was less wry, but an achy tremor clung to it all the same. "No, I'm not busy. Strangely enough, my whole schedule seems to have cleared up today for some reason."

"Oh?" Marsh's heart was fucking hammering.

"Yeah. But you knew that."

All right. Good. No more pussyfooting around. "I did."

And there was that level stare again. Marsh felt paper thin, but he wasn't going to bow to the weight of Greg's gaze. The moment seemed to drag on and on, the two of them staring at each other.

Greg was the one to look away first. He jerked his head to the side and crossed his arms over his chest. He brought one hand up to his mouth and tugged at the nail with his teeth. "I don't know how you did it, or why."

Marsh's ribs squeezed hard at the thought. Really? After all this time? Greg still didn't understand. Marsh forced out a breath and scrubbed at his face. "Because you needed it. God, if you could have seen yourself last night."

"I never asked—"

"You didn't have to. Okay?" There wasn't much to lose, now, so no reason to keep this in. Marsh had already laid his cards out on the table, doing this for Greg. "You never have to ask. When you don't take care of yourself...I hate it. I hate seeing you like that."

Greg visibly bristled, and if his walls had come down at all, they were building themselves back up. They looked so damn fragile, though. Like it took everything Greg had left to hold them around himself. And he didn't have much left.

Marsh stopped Greg before he could say whatever awful, self-effacing thing was clearly forming itself on his lips. "And that's not to say I don't want to see you, so don't even start with that. I'm glad you let me see you like that. When you're not at your best." Because even at his worst, Greg was better than pretty much anyone else. "I want to take care of you. I just won't let you work yourself into an early grave. Not if I can help it."

"I'm not working myself—"

"You are. And I saw a way to help. So I did, and I'm not sorry."

Greg still wasn't looking at Marsh, and there was a little pit of dread opening itself up in the bottom of Marsh's stomach.

"I am," Greg said, and the pit cracked even wider. But then Greg was turning, was facing Marsh and looking him right in the eye. And the walls were all down. Everything about Greg softened, his shoulders dropping and a ghost of a smile coming out to curl around the corners of his lips. "I'm sorry I didn't thank you."

All at once, the bed underneath Marsh felt solid for the first time since Greg had walked through his door. A bubble of laughter forced its way out of his chest. "Jesus Christ." He let his head fall into his hands, leaving it there for a long second while he tried to catch his breath. "I thought you were going to chew me out."

"The thought occurred to me." Greg's voice was lit with the force of his smile, and he took a few tentative steps toward the bed. Marsh beckoned him closer, and he dropped down to sit on the edge. When Greg reached a hand out into the space between them, Marsh didn't hesitate to take it, squeezing hard at his palm, relishing the feel of Greg, real and there and not walking away. Greg gripped him back just as tightly. "How did you know?"

"I didn't mean to pry," Marsh confessed. "Last night, when I was getting your medicine, I knocked your mouse by accident and that calendar came up."

"Ah."

"I know I said I wasn't sorry, but I am. I guess. For that part. I know your stuff is private, but..."

Greg shrugged. "If it was that sensitive, I would put a password on my computer before I invited strange men to sleep in my bed." He scooted closer and nudged his shoulder against Marsh's, a teasing little bump.

It wasn't entirely a joke, though. Maybe Greg had asked Marsh to spend the night, but only when he was laid up and sick and not quite thinking straight. "Yeah," Marsh agreed, but it came out a little more serious than he wanted it to.

Picking up on Marsh's shift in mood, Greg went quiet for a second. Then, lower, he said, "It's late."

"Yeah."

"And I have a big day tomorrow."

Yeah, Greg did. Marsh didn't let his feelings about not being invited creep in again. He'd groused enough about that to Yulia already today, and Yulia had given him more than enough shit about it. It smarted, but it probably wasn't personal. Not if the way Greg was looking at him now had anything to do with it.

Maybe, if things went the way he hoped they would, he'd be invited to the next one.

Keeping that hope in mind, he nodded, shifting closer to Greg on the bed. The relief at not being told off for rearranging Greg's schedule was still a heady thrumming in Marsh's veins, and he just wanted to sit here a little longer, soaking in Greg's acceptance and his warmth. He wanted to touch him and kiss him, and maybe more. Mostly, he just didn't want to let him go.

Then Greg had to go and say, "We have to talk, you know."

The warmth receded faster than Marsh could grapple to hold on to it, taking the relief right along with it, but Marsh was only so deluded. Greg was right. They'd needed to talk for a while now.

And there was a low, simmering quality to Greg's voice. One that didn't speak to a break-up being imminent.

Turning his head, Marsh pressed a hesitant kiss to Greg's shoulder before leaning his brow against his neck. Greg smelled warm and clean and so good it scrambled Marsh's thoughts. "Yeah," he said finally, quiet and slow. "I guess we do."

All the words Marsh had been imagining saying hovered in the air, right beside the ones he'd been waiting for Greg to speak. The space around them felt pregnant, ripe with potential.

But Greg exhaled and wrapped an arm around Marsh's side. "Tomorrow? When I get home?"

The air around them crystallized, the unspoken words suspended within it, like flies in amber. They'd hold. At least for tonight, they could wait. Greg was exhausted, and he had a lot on his mind. A lot to get ready for, and he didn't seem up to it right now.

Marsh didn't feel up to it right now, just in case he was reading this whole thing wrong.

"Yeah." Marsh's lips brushed the hollow of Greg's collarbone. "Of course."

"Okay." Incrementally, Greg pulled away. "I should probably go"

Marsh darted out a hand to grasp Greg's wrist. To keep him there. "You don't have to," he said, and this was stupid, but Greg had asked. A couple of times now, he'd let Marsh into his bed, and Marsh could have stayed, if only he'd had the guts to say yes. He swallowed hard. "It's okay if you don't want to, but if you do. If it'd help you sleep or whatever. You could stay. If you wanted to."

Time stretched out like so much taffy, Greg unmoving at Marsh's side, and Marsh's insides churned. Then Greg wrapped his arm around Marsh and pressed his face to Marsh's hair. His grip was almost too tight, but that was okay. That was fine.

"Yeah." Greg's voice was rough, as earnest and raw as Marsh felt, and Marsh shivered from his shoulders to his toes. "Yeah. That'd be...nice."

Marsh clenched his eyes shut and squeezed down tight on Greg's wrist. "Okay."

"Lemme go upstairs and check some things first? Back in...an hour?"

"Sure." And damn, but Marsh didn't want to let Greg go, but he could be reasonable. He'd have plenty of time to hold on to Greg later, when he came back. When he slept in Marsh's bed.

He let Greg pry himself from his grip. Greg put gentle fingers to the underside of Marsh's jaw, tilting his head up. The kiss, when it came, was firm and dry and perfect against Marsh's lips, and Greg's eyes were so fucking soft.

Then Greg walked away, and Marsh let him go. The instant the door was closed, Marsh fell to his side, sprawling out on the mattress like a starfish, limbs outspread. He stared up at the ceiling and imagined he could see all the way out to the sky, and for miles and miles beyond.

This time, when the knock came, Marsh was ready for it. He was lying in bed with the covers tugged up to his waist, dressed in a T-shirt and boxers. The only light in the room was the little lamp on the floor beside his bed.

He quit the stupid game he'd been playing on his phone and set it aside as he called for Greg to go ahead and come in. Greg pushed the door open and stepped inside. In an undershirt and flannel pants, he didn't look like he was trying to be sexy, but he might have been the best thing Marsh had ever seen.

Greg hovered for a second just inside the door, and Marsh rolled his eyes, ignoring the way his chest was fluttering. He scooted to the side and turned the covers down. "Coming?"

Nodding, Greg crossed the room and sat on the edge of the bed. It was like there was some debate he was having with himself in his own head, but when Marsh reached out to touch his leg, he seemed to arrive at some sort of resolution. He fit himself into the space left by Marsh's body, and it wasn't the first time Marsh had had someone in his bed. It wasn't the first time he'd had *Greg* in his bed, but it was different now. Better, for all that they weren't here to have sex.

Clamping down on the things it wasn't the right time to say or do or feel, Marsh reached over Greg to turn off the light. In the darkness, he retreated to his own side of the bed.

And it was easy, wasn't it?

He settled down on his back, then turned onto his side, facing away from Greg. Greg put an uncertain hand to his waist, and Marsh closed his eyes. "Yeah."

Then Greg was melting down, pressing his chest to Marsh's spine, sliding his arm over and around until it splayed across the center of Marsh's chest. Marsh grasped that palm and pulled Greg's arm in tighter, and what did he care that he wasn't usually the smaller spoon?

Lying there, with Greg holding him in the dark, his heart grew and grew until it filled his ribs. Until it was bright enough to light the room and light his life, and anything felt possible.

Even the idea that Greg might want Marsh exactly the way Marsh wanted him.

Chapter Seventeen

Marsh awoke to an empty bed. It took him a second to remember why that was wrong. He frowned as he blinked his eyes open, pushing the covers off and looking around, and yeah. Definitely alone. Groaning, he rolled onto his back and rubbed the sleep from his eyes before flipping onto his other side, and, oh.

The other pillow smelled like Greg, like warmth and whatever he put in his hair. Marsh buried his face in it and breathed in deep. It hadn't been a dream. Greg had been here. He'd slept beside Marsh, curled around him, and it had been...perfect, really.

After a few long minutes of dawdling like that, Marsh pushed himself up. It was already midmorning, and the sun was pouring in through the slats in the blinds, so it wasn't any wonder Greg was gone, but still. Disappointing. He reached for his phone, only to come up with a piece of paper. Confused, he picked it up and unfolded it.

Had to head in to campus early to do some last-minute prep. See you later tonight.

-Greg.

PS—You're gorgeous when you're sleeping.

Marsh read through the handwritten words a couple of times, his lips curling up more and more with every pass. Greg had stayed and he'd left a note, and suddenly Marsh didn't feel quite so bereft after all. Still nervous, of course, and there was that lingering rankle of irritation. He would have liked to have met Greg's parents, and he would have liked to have seen Greg speak, but that was okay. Maybe the next time something like this happened, they'd be on more solid ground.

Or maybe they'd have nothing to do with each other, but it was too early in the morning, and Marsh was feeling too hopeful and good to really think about that right now.

He refolded the note with care and tucked it under the corner of the base of his lamp for safekeeping, then went through the messages on his phone. There was another email reminder from the bursar's office, and a missed called from his coach, and two missed calls from Yulia. He winced as he cleared the alerts. It was all stuff he could put off until later. He rested his phone on his chest. It was a light day for him—just a couple of classes in the late afternoon. He had a few more articles to get through before those classes, but he had time.

With a groan, he levered himself up and grabbed a change of clothes. Somehow, he made it through his morning routine without too much distraction. Shower, breakfast, coffee. The house was empty, so he sat at the newly cleared space at one end of the dining room table with some of his reading and a notebook as he devoured a bowl full of Cheerios.

The articles he had to read were dry as hell, but he made better progress than he had the night before, his thoughts only going to Greg and how he was doing every now and then as opposed to every other freaking second. He was just starting to get on a roll when the doorbell rang. He pressed the button on his phone to check the time, his brow furrowing. It was too early for the mail, and the UPS guy usually came later, too, with those endless boxes of books and electronics and stuff for the resident geeks in the house. Huh.

The doorbell chimed again, and Marsh set down his highlighter, then rose, grabbing what was left of his coffee before padding to the door.

He opened the door to a head of blue hair and two raised eyebrows. "Yulia? What are you—"

Instead of answering, she thrust a bright-green flyer at him. He took it without really thinking, already starting to scan over the text, and as he did, his stomach did a somersault.

"So?" he asked, pushing the paper back at her. His voice cracked, and damn. He'd thought he was cool with this, but apparently not.

"'So?'" she parroted. "You recognize this, right?"

Like he could possibly not. "Yeah, it's the...thing the engineering department is doing." Symposium, he wanted to say. Conference. *Thing* worked, though.

Yulia tilted her head to the side and put her hands on her hips. "The one your boyfriend is talking at this afternoon."

"He's not my—"

"And that his parents are here to see."

"Yulia..." He trailed off, because what was he supposed to say?

Rolling her eyes, she took the flyer back from him, scanned it for a second and then pointed at a line of text at the very bottom. "The 'thing' that is open to all university students?"

Oh. Right. Greg had said something like that, hadn't he? That only people from other universities had to register. But still, what did that have to do with anything? "So?"

"Seriously?" She looked at him like he was missing a couple hundred brain cells. "So you don't need an engraved invitation to go to something that everyone in the whole damn school is welcome at."

"I don't think..." What? That Greg would be okay with him showing up? That Marsh would understand a single word coming out of his mouth?

Nothing good could come of this. It was presumptuous and weird, and Greg hadn't once made any kind of indication that he wanted Marsh to be there. Even if he didn't mind, afterword he might try to ask Marsh what he thought, and then he'd really find out how much of an idiot Marsh was.

"No," he said, shaking his head.

"Why the hell not?"

"Because..." *Because I'm scared.*

He didn't even have to say the words. Understanding was written all over her face. Her expression softened, if only by a little. "Marsh. How would you feel if he showed up to one of your games?"

And it was a crackling lick of warmth that unfurled itself in his chest. Some of the guys had their girlfriends in the stands cheering for them, and Marsh had always thought that would be nice.

Not content to wait for his answer, Yulia poked him in the arm. "Would you *tell* him you wanted him to go?"

Oh. Yeah, with things the way they were right now, Marsh wasn't sure he would. But was that really the point? Marsh knew how *he* felt about Greg. It was Greg's feelings about Marsh that were so hard to figure out.

But last night, Marsh had thought...he'd hoped.

Marsh gulped and worried the inside of his cheek with his teeth. He darted his gaze from the flyer to Yulia's face. "You really think he wouldn't mind?"

"You really wanna date a guy who doesn't want his boyfriend to be there to support him?"

Marsh's stomach stopped somersaulting just long enough to turn to ice. Because he'd known full well he'd been selling himself short this whole time, but, seriously, Greg wasn't the kind of guy to fall in love with the dumb jock. Greg was better than that.

But maybe Marsh was better than the kind of guy who would accept that from someone he...loved. Maybe Marsh was making a terrible mistake assuming Greg would be so shallow.

Marsh stepped away from the door but left it open for Yulia to come inside. "You know, you're annoying when you're right."

"You're just mad because I'm smarter than you are."

"And you're just mad because I'm prettier."

Yulia closed the door behind her. She reached up and tugged on his neck to pull him down so she could plant a big, loud kiss on his cheek. "Go make yourself a little prettier." She let him go, gesturing at the track pants and T-shirt he was wearing. "Your boyfriend's session starts at one."

With that, she took a seat on the couch and started up the PlayStation. When he hesitated, she gave him an expectant look.

Right.

He had someplace to be, and soon. He had a...well, a maybe-boyfriend to support.

And some parents he might have a chance to make a good first impression on.

"You ready for this?"

The whole row of seats shook as Ronnie plopped himself down next to Greg. Greg held up a single finger, keeping his gaze trained on the printout of his slides as he finished silently mouthing what he was going to say. When he got to the bottom of the page, he nodded to himself. There was just the conclusion left to go, and he had that more or less down. Folding the papers in half, he lowered his hand and looked up.

Ronnie was smirking at him, and Greg just had to roll his eyes. He glanced over his shoulder and breathed out a long sigh.

The lecture hall had started to fill up while Greg had been practicing, and Chu and a couple of other bigwig professors were milling around the front of the room near the lectern. Only a few minutes left to go. Greg had been sitting there for about half an hour, practicing his speech and trying to settle his nerves. Great lot of good that had done.

"What time is it?" he asked.

"Five 'til." Sounded about right. Ronnie tilted his head toward the back of the room. "Your parents say hi."

Reflexively, Greg twisted around in his seat, searching until he found them sitting a dozen rows from the top. As soon as his mom caught his eye, she grinned and waved maniacally. Good grief. It was like Greg was still twelve the way he wanted to sink down in his seat and pretend he didn't know her. He was better than that, now, though, more mature. He gave an embarrassed little wave back before turning to face front and dropping his head into his hands.

"Remind me why I told them it would be cool for them to come for this again?"

"Because you're their precious little baby and you secretly love it?"

Fair enough. Greg grunted in answer and shook his head, striving once more for calm. Why did these things psych him out so bad? He was fine, talking in front of people. He'd done it a hundred times before, but those few minutes beforehand, the adrenaline always made him jittery and weird. He vibrated his leg up and down to try to burn a little of it off and tugged at his tie. Was it hot in here? Why was it always so damn hot?

"Hey," Ronnie said, and there was a question in his voice. "Where's Marsh?"

"Marsh?" Greg jerked his head up, and suddenly the room wasn't too hot at all. The blood draining from his face probably had something to do with that. But seriously, why would Ronnie be asking that?

Ronnie scrunched up his face. "Isn't he coming?"

And Greg probably looked like an idiot as his jaw worked without any words coming out. He blinked a couple of times, trying to get it together. Finally, he managed, "Why would he?"

Ronnie's brows darted up toward his hairline. "Um. Because? You're giving a super important talk at a prestigious conference?"

"But." The whole idea was completely failing to compute. "It's on engineering."

And now Ronnie was the one looking at Greg like he was out of his mind. "So?"

"So, Marsh doesn't care about that stuff. It's boring, and he's..." Greg trailed off. Marsh was cool, and nothing about this was even close. It was hopelessly boring and lame, and Marsh had a million better things to be doing, like...

Like...

Oh, hell. A dozen conversations they'd had over the past few weeks swam through Greg's mind. Marsh asking about this conference. Asking about his speech, and about his parents, and did Greg want to practice in front of Marsh, and Marsh's eyes had shuttered so damn fast when Greg had said *no thanks*. Because it was boring. Because Marsh didn't care, and Greg kept slipping into technobabble. Right? Not because...

Greg turned to Ronnie, and the panic seeping in was of a totally different sort. "Was I supposed to ask Marsh to come?"

"You *didn't* ask Marsh to come?"

Oh, hell. Oh hell, oh hell, oh hell. Suddenly, all those little questions took on a different meaning. What if that closed-off look wasn't boredom? What if Marsh had been just waiting for an invitation, and Greg had been too dense to even realize? Had he hurt Marsh's feelings, or— It seemed impossible.

"Shit." Greg fumbled for his phone. Maybe if he texted Marsh now—

"Oh, there he is."

Greg whipped around, and he could hardly breathe, because, yes, that was Marsh. Marsh, in black slacks and a button-down and looking profoundly uncomfortable as he scanned the room. Greg's lungs constricted another inch, because Marsh's friend, Yulia was leading Marsh to a seat in the back, and she had her hand on his wrist, her poise all confidence and purpose, like she was the one leading him along.

Taking him to Greg's talk when Greg had been too oblivious to invite him himself.

Christ, he'd been so jealous of that girl, even after Marsh had told him in no uncertain terms that they were only friends. He'd still envied the way Marsh talked about her, how easy they seemed with each other.

And in the meantime, it looked like she'd been working behind the scenes, getting Marsh here.

"Who's that with him?" Ronnie started.

Greg swallowed hard against the lump in his throat. "His friend."

Of course, Professor Chu had to pick that precise instant to tap on the microphone at the front of the room, sending the *tap-tap* noise over the speakers. The buzzing in the room settled down, and Greg should face forward now. He should be paying attention, but he couldn't stop staring at Marsh, who was here.

Greg hadn't invited him, and he'd come anyway, and Greg felt so overwhelmingly, powerfully grateful it floored him. Marsh cared, and he was here.

Marsh was still scanning the room, and Greg held his breath until those cool eyes finally swept over to point toward him. Marsh sat up a little straighter as their gazes locked, and Greg wanted to run up there and kiss him or hug him or hit him for not saying whatever he'd been thinking all those times he'd mentioned this stupid presentation. For not shaking Greg out of his own self-deluded navel-gazing that had kept him from even imagining Marsh might want to be here. For now, though, all he could do was soften his features and give him a pained half smile that didn't say even a fraction of what he wanted to.

He had no idea what Marsh heard.

But he couldn't dwell on any of it right now. Dr. Chu was at the lectern, and he was holding a hand out toward Greg. Greg's first slide was up on the projector.

Showtime.

As Greg's name was called, he rose to his feet, hardly feeling the clap on the shoulder from Ronnie. What was his talk supposed to be about again? Oh God, he was going to blank. He was going to embarrass his family and humiliate himself in front of Marsh. Maybe he could make a break for it...

Only, his feet were taking him across the room toward the lectern, and he was shaking Dr. Chu's hand. Chu, who was nodding at Greg expectantly as he pressed the clicker for the PowerPoint into Greg's palm. Greg faced the room, and it was only two-thirds full, but that was a lot of people. All the big names in the field he'd met yesterday, people whose papers he had read and cited. Hell, one of the men who had written Greg's first-year materials science textbook was in the fifth row. The projector was bright, and his tie was too tight, and the room was *boiling*.

He swept the room with his gaze, and there were his folks, his mom beaming while his dad sat back with a smug, pleased expression on his face.

And there was Marsh, sitting with his elbows on his knees, his chin braced on his steepled hands, and his attention was rapt. Was absolutely focused on Greg. His brow was furrowed, but as their gazes met, Marsh smiled.

Greg took a deep breath and looked over his shoulder at the words on the screen.

Just like that, it all came back to him. He was in his room practicing. He knew this. He *had* this.

Facing the crowd again, he nodded. And then he began to talk.

Chapter Eighteen

There were a lot of different words Marsh had associated with "science" over the years. Crazy. Ridiculous. Impossible. Never, in a million years, had he ever thought he'd find it sexy.

Sure, there had been glimpses of that just recently. Those few rare times Greg had broken down and told Marsh a little bit about what he did day to day, but even then, it had been more adorable than hot. Especially considering how hesitant and tightlipped Greg tended to be.

But now Greg was standing up in front of a room full of people who probably had more smarts in their pinky fingers than Marsh did in his entire brain, and he was *owning* that shit. He looked good, all put-together and grown-up, and goddamn but Marsh could think of things he wanted to do to him in that tie.

Because this was the man Marsh had been coming home to for weeks, almost months now. The man who sat on his floor eating crappy takeout, the man Marsh had had inside him, the man who'd slept in his bed last night, and Marsh was never going to be worthy of any of that, but in that instant he wanted to be. So fucking bad.

For a good twenty minutes, Greg talked about phase transitions and alloys and a whole bunch of other stuff Marsh couldn't even begin to understand. Marsh did his best to keep up and failed miserably, but the rising tide of insecurity didn't tow him under, because he was just so proud of Greg. So happy for him.

"So, in conclusion..." Greg went through a few last bullet points, his posture somehow self-assured and confident in a way Marsh hadn't really seen before. Marsh's heart swelled, because, yeah, even Greg knew he'd done well. Wrapping things up, he clicked forward to a blank screen. "I think we have a few minutes for questions?"

Apparently, that was science-speak for "I'm done", because people started to applaud. At that, Greg stood back, his hands clasped in front of him, and for the first time since the beginning of the presentation, he looked right at Marsh. Marsh clapped even harder, his chest fit to bursting, and he beamed, trying to tell Greg how amazing he was without any words at all.

Yulia leaned in and whispered, "Your boy is *smart.*"

"I know," Marsh said out of the side of his mouth, and his cheeks hurt with the force of his smile.

As the applause died off, the professor-type who'd introduced Greg stood, and a bunch of hands went up. He called on some old guy in a tweed jacket with actual, honest-to-goodness elbow patches, who rose and started rambling about something apparently related to what Greg had talked about.

As the guy asked his question, Marsh watched Greg. He stood there, unflappable as anything, nodding from time to time, so Marsh drifted to take a look around at the other people in the audience. A small minority were doodling or staring off into space, and one guy near the front was clearly fighting to stay awake, but most everyone was listening in with apparent interest on their faces.

Then Marsh spotted them. Over by the aisle and a few rows down, there was a couple of middle-aged people who were dressed nicely but not quite right for the crowd. Other than the shockingly pink sweater she wore, the woman was unremarkable, but the man next to her… Marsh swallowed hard. Well, at least it was nice to know Greg was going to age okay. The guy's hair was thinning a little, but his eyes were bright, and the lines on his forehead just made him seem distinguished. He looked kind and sharp, and the shape of his nose and chin were so familiar it almost hurt.

The man asking his question finally sat down, and Greg started to answer. It was way, way over Marsh's head at this point, so he nudged Yulia, shifting so he could say in her ear, "See the lady in the pink? Over to the left?"

Yulia craned her neck. He could tell the second she spotted them, because she turned back to him with a smirk. "You mean the one sitting next to Greg Senior?"

"That's gotta be them, right?"

"Definitely."

As people took their turns asking questions, Marsh divided his time between watching Greg and watching the reactions of the people who had to be his parents. It stopped Marsh in his tracks, the way they looked at him. Like he hung the moon, like he was just as incredible as he was. Like he was their son, and they loved him so much it hurt. Even if he wasn't so amazing, they'd love him exactly that much.

And Marsh had to look away.

It wasn't much longer after that before the professor leading the session called time. "Anyone who would like to speak further to Mr. London will be able to find him after the session." He introduced the next speaker, and Greg took one last sweeping glance around the room, pausing to face the spot where his parents were sitting, then turning toward Marsh. Marsh gave him the best smile he could before Greg dropped his gaze and retreated to take his seat up near the front.

Someone else had claimed the podium by then, and it suddenly dawned on Marsh. He really should have known there would be more talks to sit through, but it wasn't until the new title page flashed across the screen that the gravity of the situation sank in. He groaned and peeked over his shoulder in a panic. No one was making for the exits. No one. He leaned in closer to Yulia. "How many speakers are there?"

"Runs 'til three o'clock."

Fuck. Another hour and a half? He could make a break for it. God knew he had plenty of excuses with how much reading he was supposed to do before his three-thirty class, but no. The whole point of showing up at this sort of thing was getting to congratulate the person you'd come there for when it was over. If Greg was a girl—or if Marsh had planned ahead at all—Marsh should have brought him flowers or something, though that would have really given everything away.

Marsh crossed his arms over his chest and tapped his foot as the new guy started droning on. In for a penny, in for a pound. Marsh would stay. He'd go up to Greg after and tell him he'd been amazing. Maybe, if Greg allowed it, he'd even shake his hand. Or give him a hug. A nice, manly hug. Greg probably wouldn't want that, though, not in front of everyone, but that was fine. Greg'd still know Marsh cared. He'd know Marsh came for him.

Like there was any other reason he'd sit through two hours of lectures on engineering.

"Every man for himself," Marsh muttered to Yulia. "If you, y'know, wanna make a break for it."

She smirked and nudged him with her shoulder. "And miss the show at the end? Not on your life."

Great.

Somehow or other, Marsh made it through the three speakers that came after Greg, though it was touch and go at points. Finally, the session came to a close. The instant the guy at the front said, "Thank you for coming," Marsh was out of his seat.

"Don't act too sorry to see it end," Yulia grumbled as she stretched her arms overhead and cracked her back.

"And I thought two hours of sitting still during a history lecture was bad."

"It is. This is just worse."

Huffing in agreement, Marsh surveyed the room, spotting Greg up front, not far from where he'd been sitting. The guy with the elbow patches had already cornered him, and Marsh shifted his weight from one leg to the other. People were either making their way to the exits or lingering around in loose clusters, having what looked like awfully serious conversations. A couple of science-y-looking types had gathered a few feet away from Greg. They probably wanted to talk to him too, and about things that mattered.

Maybe Marsh should just go. Greg had seen him after all. He eyed the door.

"Uh-uh." Yulia tugged his elbow and started making for the aisle. "We did not sit through that for you to chicken out."

"But he has people to talk to," Marsh said, cringing at the whininess in his own voice.

"Yup, and you're one of them."

"I'll see him at home?"

Yulia rolled her eyes and kept edging toward the front. "Yes, you will, *after* you've said hi and told him he looks really hot in a tie."

"He does, doesn't he?"

Mumbling something that sounded a lot like *hopeless* under her breath, Yulia skirted around some of the scientists loitering near the podium. Elbow-patch guy passed Greg a card and walked away, and Marsh took a deep breath. Okay, he could do this, just a quick hello and a congratulations and then he could go. He threw his shoulders back and stepped forward—

Only to have Greg's parents cut in front of him, inserting themselves into Greg's space.

And fuck. Marsh should go. He should *really* go.

Greg's mom caught Greg up in a hug, and Greg's cheeks bore the faintest hint of a flush as he let himself be drawn in.

He clasped her close and said something in her ear. But then he looked up, over her shoulder, and his eyes alit on Marsh.

Marsh should *go*.

Only a hand shoved Marsh forward, and he stumbled, hopping twice to regain his balance, until before he knew it, he was standing right in front of Greg. Greg pulled away from his mom, and Marsh froze in place. He was ready to point to the exit and mouth something about seeing Greg back at the house. But the corners of Greg's lips twitched up, a smile so tentative and unsure, and Marsh would do anything to make it solid and sound.

Greg patted his mom's shoulder and said something Marsh couldn't quite make out. He stepped toward Marsh.

And this was it. Game day, with a star pitcher on the mound. Marsh fixed his courage up and stood his ground, and everyone else in the room seemed to fade away.

"You came," Greg said. He was so close, just inches away. It would be so easy to cross that space, put a hand forward and...

"Yeah." Marsh's lower lip wobbled, and his expression felt fragile and soft, the way his heart felt whenever he looked at Greg and saw him for exactly who he was. "You were amazing."

Marsh twitched, wanting to step forward and pull Greg in. Greg's arms rose, and Marsh looked him right in the eye as he made to do the same, because he needed permission for this. In the end, Greg closed the space between them, catching Marsh up in a hug that was tight and perfect and warm. Marsh wrapped his arms around him and squeezed him for all he was worth. A happy shiver made its way up his spine.

Greg cupped a hand around the back of Marsh's neck. "I can't believe you came."

"Wouldn't have missed it," Marsh swore, and it wasn't quite a lie. If he'd gotten it through his skull earlier that it was even an option, he wouldn't have hesitated. He would've been here, come hell or high water.

Greg drew back just a little, and there was something frowning to his mouth. "I'm sorry I didn't invite you. I didn't think—"

"It's fine."

"But I'm glad." And Greg's hands were still on Marsh's neck and waist. This didn't look friendly. This looked so obvious, only Greg didn't seem to care. "Thank you."

"Anytime," Marsh said, his throat thick.

Greg's eyes were searching, his one eyebrow lifting. Marsh held his breath as Greg moved to take Marsh's hand in his, and it felt like electricity. Like something he thought he'd never have.

"Is this all right?" Greg asked. He tightened his grip on Marsh's palm to clarify, and wow, that was *so* all right.

"Yeah," Marsh managed.

Greg twisted away, letting air between their bodies, but as he did, he put his lips beside Marsh's ear. "I know this is way too early, but do me a favor?"

What? "Um..."

The rest of the room crept back in, and suddenly, there Marsh was, holding Greg's hand in the middle of a lecture hall, with Greg's coworkers and all these professors and, right, Greg's parents. All at once, Marsh's throat got unbearably tight.

Greg smiled, huge and wide as he turned to the woman in pink and the man who had his nose and his chin. Voice tremulous, he said, "Mom, Dad. I want you to meet someone." He squeezed Marsh's hand. "Marsh. This is my mom and dad."

Chapter Nineteen

It didn't make any kind of sense. Greg had left the podium over an hour ago, had managed to sit still through three more presentations, but his heart was thrumming, and he felt like he could take on the world. He *was* taking on the world, holding on to Marsh for all he was worth, and these were liberties he wasn't sure he was allowed, but fuck it. Fuck it all.

For a long moment, even with the buzz of conversation in the room, everything seemed to stop, the space around them going quiet as Marsh's jaw dropped and Greg's mother blinked. And maybe Greg had really stepped in it now, but he squared his shoulders and kept that smile firmly planted. Everybody stared at everybody else, and Greg darted his eyes from one of them to the other to the next. Greg's dad coughed.

And then everything was moving again. Greg's mom snapped out of it first, shaking off the stillness as the widest grin stole across her face. "Marsh," she said, and her gaze went to Greg. "*The* Marsh."

"Yes, Mom." Greg kept his eye roll to himself.

"Um." Marsh fidgeted, acting nervous in a way Greg had rarely seen on him. But he kept his hold on Greg as he shifted forward, extending his free hand. "Hi. Yeah. Marsh. Marshall. Sulkowski. Nice to meet you."

"And nice to meet you, too." Mom took his hand in both of hers and pumped it up and down. Her gaze kept darting between Marsh's face and Greg's. "We've heard so much about you."

"You have?" Marsh asked, brow furrowed, like that was really so surprising to hear.

Greg cleared his throat. "Just a little. Here and there."

"More than we hear about anyone else, these days," his dad interrupted, slinging an arm around his mom and holding out his own hand.

Greg's mom finally released her grip, and Marsh reached forward to shake with Greg's dad. "Nice to meet you, sir."

"And the young lady?" Greg's mom asked.

Oh. Right. Greg twisted to see Yulia standing right behind them. With a grin, Marsh gestured for Yulia to come on over. "This is my best friend, Yulia. She's here keeping me company."

Greg lost track of the conversation for a second as he stood there, holding Marsh's hand and feeling like an ass all over again for having been so jealous of her. She glanced down at where Greg's and Marsh's fingers were entwined and shot Marsh a smug smile before stepping forward. Greg's mom reeled her in, and then there was a whole other round of introductions that Greg kind of glazed over for.

"Honey?"

Greg snapped to attention at his mother's voice. "Huh?"

"Marsh has to come to dinner with us, right? Tell him."

"Um." Swallowing hard, Greg turned to Marsh. The expression on his face was vaguely shell-shocked. That tended to happen to people when Greg's mom bulldozed them like this, but it made all of Greg's misgivings reassert themselves with a vengeance. It was too soon for Marsh and his parents to even be meeting, much less for Marsh to have to sit through the inquisition Mom would put him through if he agreed to this. "You don't have to—"

And Marsh's face fell.

Greg started backtracking immediately. "I mean, I'd love it if you did. But if you have plans, or if you don't want to or—"

"I have class in—" Marsh broke off, glancing at the clock, and he swore, then turned bright red. "Sorry," he said toward

Greg's parents. "I mean, um, I have to run. To class. Now. Five minutes ago, really. But I'm done by six."

"Perfect," Greg's mom said. "Our reservations are at seven."

Her smile was entirely too eager, and Marsh had no idea what he was getting himself into. Greg kind of wanted to warn him, but this felt too good. Meeting the parents was serious. Agreeing to go to dinner with them was even more so.

And maybe this conversation they were going to have tonight would go the way Greg wanted it to after all.

Marsh looked to Greg, and Greg nodded. "Sure. I'd love to come." His voice was tight, but Greg beamed anyway.

"And Yulia?"

All heads turned to her, but she held up a hand. "Thanks, but I have plans. Plus, fifth wheel and all."

"Any friend of Greg's is a friend of ours," his mom insisted.

"Really, thank you, but I can't."

"Fair enough," Dad jumped in. "I'll call and add one to the reservation."

"We can pick you up?" Greg rubbed his thumb over Marsh's knuckles. "Your last class is over near Whitney Hall?"

"Yeah. Sounds good."

"Sounds great."

"So I should..." Marsh started to pull away, and Greg should let him, but he held fast for a second.

"Thanks again, for coming."

"Of course." Marsh flicked his gaze to the side and then back, and he leaned in closer, eyes searching all the while.

And they were in the middle of a lecture hall, standing in front of his parents, with his scientific idols watching on. Greg should have stopped him, but he couldn't. Not now. He accepted the kiss when it came, fleeting and chaste and the most public affection they'd shown each other, ever. "Later," Greg murmured against Marsh's lips.

"Yeah." Marsh smiled. This time, when he pulled away, Greg let him. He stood there, grinning like an idiot as Marsh bounded up the stairs, definitely not looking at the way his ass flexed in those slacks as he ran.

"Anyway," Greg's mom said pointedly.

Right. Greg coughed into his hand and dropped his gaze. "Um, I need to do a little bit of cleanup here. There's a coffee shop downstairs, if you don't mind killing a half hour or so?"

"Sounds perfect. Call us when you're done."

"Will do."

Greg's mom leaned in for one last peck on the cheek, grasping Greg's arm before she pulled away. "You did so well, sweetheart."

"Thanks, Mom."

"Right." His dad shuffled awkwardly. "Shall we?"

They took off, leaving Greg one of the last in the room. He nodded at Chu who was standing near the podium, talking to a couple of the visiting professors from another university. Chu gave a quick thumbs-up, and Greg had to stop himself from checking over his shoulder to see if Chu wasn't giving his approval to someone standing behind him. But no, the gesture was meant for him. It was the most validation he'd gotten from his advisor since he'd passed his qualifying exams.

If he'd had a better day in recent memory, he couldn't remember it.

So he was all the more shocked when he turned around to find Yulia standing behind him.

"Jesus Christ—" he started.

She silenced him with a single finger raised, stepping into his space. Leveling him with a stare that could have stripped paint off a wall, she said, simply, "He thinks you're using him."

"What?"

She raised one eyebrow. "This is your only warning."

"My—"

"Prove him wrong."

With that, she pivoted on her heel and strode away, taking with her any footing Greg had thought he'd gained.

Greg still felt a step behind a few hours later, sitting next to Marsh in a fancy restaurant. Across from his parents. He kept sneaking little glances at Marsh, trying to read his expression. A few days ago, Greg had scarcely dared to imagine there was anything between them but sex and the occasional bit of takeout, and now they were doing this.

He wished he'd thought to do it earlier—to take Marsh someplace nice as just the two of them. Kiss him in front of the world, call him his boyfriend. Prove beyond a shadow of a doubt that he wasn't *using* him.

Because that was still too much to even start to get his head around.

"So, Marsh," Greg's mom said, once their orders had been placed and the menus cleared away.

"Yes, ma'am." Marsh snapped to attention, focusing on her.

It wasn't something Greg would have necessarily anticipated, the kind of instinctive politeness that seemed to kick in every time one of Greg's parents addressed Marsh. He was usually so casual around the house and around Greg, but the *ma'am*s and *sir*s poured out of him so readily.

A lick of suspicion tickled in the back of Greg's mind. Someone had taught Marsh to act like that.

Something to think about more later. For now, Greg's mom had that gleam in her eye, and that took precedence.

"Be nice, Mom," Greg warned.

She gave him a scolding glance. "When am I ever not nice?"

"When you're talking to one of my boyfriends," he grumbled, not bothering to mince words. Marsh was here, after all. He'd agreed to this, and his hand was on Greg's knee beneath the table.

The whole thing made Greg pause, heart stuttering in a good way. It had been a long, long while since Greg had even had this much. Even longer since his folks had gotten the chance to quiz someone.

His mom waved away his concerns with a flick of her wrist. "Ignore my son. I'm very nice. Now tell us all about yourself."

"Um." Marsh visibly squirmed, and his fingers flexed against Greg's thigh. "Not sure what there is to tell."

"Well, you live with Greg."

"Yeah. Er, well, not like that. Not that I wouldn't, but..." Wow, Marsh was nervous. Too nervous. Greg put his hand over Marsh's and squeezed him tight.

"He was our last-minute addition to the house," Greg explained, because his parents were well aware of that whole mess.

Marsh nodded. "Right. I, uh, was supposed to rent a place with a couple of the guys from the team, but I couldn't afford it after—after some stuff that happened, this summer. These guys were looking for a housemate, and the price was right."

"Our boy's always been very frugal," Greg's dad said, and there was pride there.

And Greg had heard that lecture often enough, about the difference between being frugal and being cheap. London men knew value when they saw it. They didn't need to spend very much to be comfortable—forget that they didn't have much to begin with. But when it came to things that mattered, they did it right. They saved and they budgeted.

They spent what they'd saved on visits out to see their son, and nice dinners when something happened worth celebrating.

But Greg's mom picked up on other things. "Team?"

"Yeah," Marsh said. "Baseball."

"Ooh, an athlete." Mom's eyes went wide, and she put a hand over Greg's dad's.

Greg wanted to roll his eyes. "Dad played football back in high school."

"Oh. Um. I mean, it's not a big deal."

"Sure it is." Greg furrowed his brow. It was huge. "Greg said something about you having a scholarship, right?"

"Yeah, but that doesn't mean a lot."

Greg's dad interjected, "Not sure how we would've gotten Greg through undergrad if he hadn't pulled in some scholarships."

"Yeah," Marsh said, "but those were because he's so smart."

"We all have our talents," Greg's mom said.

Marsh shrugged and looked to the side. Greg didn't like the way his mouth turned down.

"Anyway." Greg slid his fingers between Marsh's, "Marsh is really good."

Marsh cocked his head, looking at Greg funny. "You ever seen me play?"

"Once or twice, last year. But you're the starting shortstop. You have to be good."

"I don't know."

"I do." Greg gave one more squeeze before letting Marsh's hand go, shifting to rest his forearm on the table, fidgeting with one of the forks in front of him.

Marsh didn't reply except to give a little grunt.

Greg's mom took a sip of her water, then asked, "So you're in undergrad?"

"Yeah. A senior, though."

"And you're majoring in..."

"History." Marsh withdrew his hand, twisting around in his seat. Picking up his butter knife, he gestured toward Greg with the blade. "I'm not like Greg."

"I don't know anyone who is," Greg's mom said conspiratorially.

Greg gave a little groan. "Which is why you've been saying I'm exactly like my father for twenty-five years now?"

"In temperament, sure," she admitted before refocusing on Marsh. "The things this boy used to say to me when he was a kid. He'd come home with these science books he got from the library, and I'd just sit there and nod and smile. Even when he was this high," she held her hand three feet off the ground, "he knew more than I did about that stuff."

"Hasn't changed much, huh?"

"Not a bit." She darted her gaze to the side, giving Greg a warm smile. "He's always outshone everyone. And he works so hard. Too hard." She gave Marsh a pointed look. "Which is why he needs people in his life who know how to have a good time and put the books down once in a while."

"That's me," Marsh said, chuckling, but the humor sounded forced.

It wasn't much of a tell, but it was the second or third thing he'd said tonight that made Greg frown. Because Marsh could be self-deprecating—he acted that way all time, but this ran deeper. Was uglier. And Greg didn't like it at all.

For a beat too long, no one said anything. Greg glanced at his father, who shifted forward in his chair. "Any idea what you're going to do next year?"

To Greg's surprise, Marsh laughed, and his grip was too tight on that knife. "Frankly, sir, I don't know what I'm doing next semester."

Okay, now Greg really didn't know what to think. He twisted around to face Marsh more fully. "What?"

"Nothing." Marsh waved him off, and everything about the gesture said not to press. That they'd talk about it later. Greg opened his mouth anyway, but Marsh talked over him, "Anyway, um, a history major isn't exactly very marketable right now. I guess there are office jobs. Maybe."

"Any interest in grad school?" Greg's mom asked.

"Ah, no." Marsh tapped the knife against the table in a twitchy, staccato rhythm. "School's not exactly my strong point."

"Can't blame you." Greg's dad smiled, and Greg had never appreciated him more than he did in that moment—been more aware of how he could diffuse things. "Was never mine either. We weren't kidding—" he pointed at Greg, "—we have no idea where this one came from when it comes to book smarts."

"Still," Greg's mom said. "Especially if you don't care for classes, you'll be a college graduate. That's saying a lot."

A dark expression passed over Marsh's face. "It would be. Yeah."

And Greg wanted to reach out and touch him, to *shake* him and make him explain what was going on, but for now all he could do was slip an arm around the back of his chair and run a thumb along his shoulder blade. "Marsh is pretty amazing," he said.

But he might have been the only one of the two of them who believed it.

"I'll pick you guys up at eight tomorrow? Quick breakfast before we head to the airport?"

"Perfect," Mom said, pulling him into a hug. "I just wish we could stay longer."

"Yeah, me, too." Greg wrapped his arms around her and held on.

A much quicker hug from his dad, and that was more or less that. He gestured behind himself. "Well, Marsh is waiting."

His mom gave a knowing smile. "He is a lovely boy. A little lost, but lovely."

"Glad you approve." The *lost* part echoed in Greg's thoughts the loudest, though.

"You have always made good choices."

Not always. Not when he stayed silent while everything in him was screaming at him to ask for more. Not when he was working himself to the bone. "I try," was all he could concede.

"And that's all we ask." She shooed him toward the door. "Go on. We'll see you tomorrow."

"Okay." Greg gave a parting wave and headed out.

Just like he had the night before, he paused outside the door to their motel room, but instead of looking at the sky, he stared at the parked car where Marsh was sitting in the passenger's seat, doing something on his phone. Greg hadn't been exaggerating back at dinner, when he'd told his parents Marsh was amazing. These past few days, Marsh had done more for Greg than he knew how to thank him for.

Damned if he wasn't going to try, though.

Greg inhaled deeply, then let it go. He strode the few steps across the parking lot and slipped into the driver's side door. Sliding the key in the ignition, he turned to look at Marsh.

"Home?" he asked.

And for the longest time, their eyes connected.

Until Marsh looked away, nodding jerkily as he gazed out the window. His voice was quiet as he echoed, "Home."

Chapter Twenty

"So."

Marsh flinched internally at the sound of Greg's voice, that one short syllable, uttered sharp and quick. They'd just made it through the door of the house, and now they were standing there in the entryway, the air crackling between them, and Marsh didn't know exactly what came next.

"So," Marsh echoed, turned away from Greg. The whole ride home, his nerves had been rising, because the signs had been good. Greg had slept in his bed last night. He'd taken his hand in front of all those people.

He hadn't been embarrassed of Marsh.

But Marsh had intruded in so many ways, first with Greg's schedule, and then by showing up uninvited to his talk and letting Greg's parents cajole him into going to dinner. He shouldn't be able to get away with all of that.

It felt like time for it to all come crashing down around him, these weeks of sex and growing intimacy and unspoken wanting. Every second when it didn't felt like borrowed time.

"So. Your room or mine?"

Well, no one had ever accused Greg of being anything other than efficient.

"Mine." It was the only bedroom on this floor, and from where Marsh was standing, it didn't look like anyone was hanging out in the living room or the kitchen. They'd have the least chance of being overheard here.

And if things went badly, Greg wouldn't have to kick Marsh out. He'd just be able to leave.

"All right." Greg headed in that direction, but Marsh needed a second.

"I'm just going to..." He pointed down the hall. "Get a drink. But, uh, go ahead."

Greg nodded sharply and started walking. The second he was out of view, Marsh ran a hand over his face, exhaling hard, shoulders sagging. He needed to chill out, or get a grip, or just...not freak out. Not freaking out would be awesome.

He headed to the kitchen, where he perused the fridge for a second just to feel the cool air and buy himself some time. A beer was tempting, but probably not the best idea. He picked a soda at random and popped the top, then took a big glug, draining half of it in one go. It felt good on his throat. Closing the fridge door, he leaned up against it for a few breaths.

All right. Time to face the music.

Leaving his soda on the counter, he headed back to his room, shoulders square and spine straight. Greg was standing at the foot of the bed, by the opposite wall. He'd loosened his tie, and the top two buttons of his shirt were undone, his hair sticking up a little on one side like he'd spent the last five minutes running his hands through it. He looked good. Amazing, really. And Marsh knew the shape of the body underneath those too-nice clothes. He knew this man. He just had to have some faith in him.

Marsh closed the door behind him and turned to put his back to it, bending one knee and kicking to brace his foot against the wood. At the sound, Greg looked up at him, and his face was open and honest—unguarded in a way he so rarely was, especially around Marsh.

Marsh *wanted* to know this man. All the little pieces of himself he kept hidden away.

Looking down, Marsh shoved his hands in his pockets, only he couldn't keep his eyes averted for long. Glancing up again, he settled his gaze on Greg's mouth.

"Hi," Marsh said, and it wasn't fair how breathy and tentative the word sounded on the air.

"Hi."

Marsh chuckled, fidgeting and sucking the inside of his lip between his teeth. "How're you?"

"Good. I guess." A momentary pause. "It's been a hell of a couple days."

"Tell me about it."

"Marsh, I—" And the earnestness in that tone took the molten pieces inside of Marsh and sent them coursing through his bloodstream, lodging them in his heart.

Because they'd talked about things a little yesterday, but it wasn't really settled. Marsh still didn't know where he stood, and everything felt too uncertain—Greg's easy acceptance of everything Marsh had done and his public affection all night long and just *everything.*

"I'm sorry," Marsh choked out.

All at once, Greg's face fell, his expression stricken. "I— You— You're...sorry."

Marsh's eyes felt too hot, his chest ready to fly apart. "Everything, these past couple of days. I didn't have any right."

"What—"

"I didn't mean to intrude or impose. First with your schedule, or—"

"No, that was—"

"But you were drowning, and when you were sick you looked like you needed someone to take care of you. And I wanted to be that person."

That declaration hung in the space between them for a moment that seemed to stretch out forever before Greg said, quiet, like a confession, "I wanted you to be, too."

Marsh had to look away this time. He *had* to focus on something other than the line of Greg's mouth or the jut of his chin. "I wasn't going to go today," he said, talking to the wall to his right. Greg said nothing, but the floorboards squeaked. Greg was coming closer, and Marsh had to get this out. "I didn't think you wanted me to. But it was open to anyone, and Yulia showed up with a flier, and I...I wanted to. I wanted to see you. Even though I was too dumb to understand any of it."

"Would you stop it?"

Marsh jerked his head back to center, and there Greg was, right in front of Marsh, only inches between them, his expression the weirdest cross between anger and pleading.

"What?"

"That's the sixth time tonight you've said something about you being stupid. If it were anyone else talking about you that way, I'd punch them."

And that was an image, wasn't it? "Seriously?"

"Like a heart attack. Nobody talks about my—about you like that. You act as if you're an idiot, or—"

"What else am I supposed to act like?" Marsh pushed off the wall, shoving past Greg, because he needed some air. He flung his arm out to the side when he could breathe again. "I'm not you, or any of your friends. When you guys talk, sometimes I feel like it's a different language."

"Then tell us to slow down."

Yeah, like that was ever going to happen. He didn't need to point out that he wasn't smart enough to keep up, when really he was happy they even let him listen to them talk at all. "It doesn't matter."

"Yes, it does. How long have you been feeling like this?"

Laughing, dark and ugly, Marsh dragged a hand over his face, muttering beneath his breath, "Since I was born?" Louder, he said, "I don't know. It's just how it is. If it weren't for baseball, I wouldn't be here at all. Not exactly college material, you know?"

Not even close. Just like his dad said, he didn't belong here.

"Bullshit."

"Right, listen—"

"No, you listen. Jesus." Greg had his hand in his hair again, and he was going to be bald on that side if he didn't let up soon. He crossed the room, reaching down to tug out one of Marsh's textbooks. "This stuff isn't easy. Athletic scholarship or no, you're doing stuff that's hard. I don't think I could do what you do."

"Sure."

"Seriously. Science? Math? Yeah, I've always had an okay time with those, but you should have seen my high school English papers. They were more red ink than black."

"But anyone can learn that."

"And anyone can learn math! If they work at it."

"I do work at it." A rage he never gave enough air to lit his lungs. "Even the history and the English and shit, I work my ass off and I barely pass. I needed tutoring for all my gen-ed classes. It's not just the scholarship. If the team didn't set us up with people to help us get through our classes, I'd be fucked."

"Marsh, we're at a really good school. Even if your academics aren't your strong point, or even if you need help, you're making it. You read these crazy things." He rattled off one of the titles from an article Marsh had tucked inside the book. "And you're into it. I've seen you studying, and you get totally lost in it. You have books everywhere, and maybe you're not a nerd, but you're good at it. All the history stuff. You like it."

"Well, it's interesting."

"And I think science is interesting!" Greg looked like he was ready to throw his hands up in the air. "We all gravitate toward what we like, and we make it happen because we care. And one thing isn't better than another, and if you put down the stuff you do one more time, I'm going to..."

"What?"

Greg drummed two fingers against his lips and shook his head. "I can't decide. Kiss you or hit you."

"I know which one I'd prefer."

"I know which one I would, too."

"Look," Marsh started after a couple of beats. And why was he trying to convince Greg he wasn't good enough, or wasn't smart enough? Why, when all he wanted was to be that good. That smart.

To be someone Greg could love.

But Greg was rounding on him now, striding closer again, though he stopped when there were still a few feet between them. He lifted a hand but let it fall to his side before it could connect. They hadn't touched since dinner. Greg flexed his fingers then curled them up into his palms.

"What did you mean?" he asked. "Before. At dinner."

"About?"

"About not knowing what you were doing after college? Or even next semester."

Oh, hell. Marsh had said that, hadn't he? He dragged a hand over his face. "It's a long story."

"And all we have to do tonight is talk."

"Look, it's..." Only he didn't know what it was.

Finally, Greg bit the bullet, shattering the space between them to run careful fingertips over Marsh's knuckles. The warmth of it burned through Marsh's skin. "What's going on? I mean, I knew I'd have to worry about what you'd do next year. If you'd want to go home, or go to school or travel or get a job. Somewhere else. But next semester?"

And Marsh...couldn't do this. Greg was laying all these expectations on his shoulders, and the weight of them all was suddenly too much. A dam cracked inside him, and he gave up, retreating over to his bed where he perched on the edge and dropped his head into his hands. "I'm broke." Why was that so hard to admit?

"Broke?"

"Like, I don't have any money. At all. Thank God my folks gave me what I needed for this semester in advance, or I'd be gone already. I think I have enough left for rent through December, but that's it."

"What—"

Finally, Marsh lifted his gaze. Looked right into Greg's wide eyes as he spat out, "My dad found out I was a fag this summer." He sucked in a deep breath and tasted bile. "He saw me with a guy. I wasn't careful, and he doesn't give a shit that I'm bi or whatever. He didn't think I was good enough for college, and he just, just stopped paying the bill. Didn't even say anything. And now I'm screwed."

"But the baseball scholarship..."

Marsh shook his head. "It's only partial, and it doesn't touch living expenses."

"But are there loans, or—"

"Right." Marsh swiped at his nose and he chuckled darkly, shoulders racking. "I mean, sure. I talked to the financial aid people, and I have options, but what's the point? I might just fail out anyway."

"In your last semester?"

"I've been on academic probation half the time I've been here. I fail anything and I won't graduate. And even if I do?" Marsh looked up at Greg. He was still standing right where Marsh had left him, near the wall, and his eyes were *huge*. Marsh's voice cracked again. "What the fuck am I going to do with a history degree? I can't sit in an office, and there's no way I could swing grad school. I might as well give up now." He sniffed and rubbed his eye. "Go get a job. My dad says factory work is stable, you know? Live somewhere cheap. Find some roommates."

"Your dad is an asshole."

"No shit—"

"Is he the one who keeps telling you you're not good enough for any of this?"

Marsh snorted. "Not like anyone really needed to tell me."

"Have you even talked to him? Since the money stopped coming?"

"No point, is there?"

"Jesus Christ." And yeah, that was a tone Marsh recognized. Exasperation. He knew that sound really well. "There are a lot of things I pegged you for, but never once did I think you were a quitter."

"I'm not." Marsh shrugged, and sure, he was a giant hypocrite, but whatever. "It's just stupid. Won't change anything."

"You have got to be kidding me," Greg muttered, and he turned away.

And it was just so instinctive. Marsh was braced, waiting for Greg to go. Maybe Greg had finally figured it out. It would be better if he had, really. Because he would, eventually, and Marsh didn't know how he was going to handle it when he did if this went on for too much longer.

But then Greg was *right there*, on his knees next to the bed, and his hands were on Marsh's shoulders. He gave Marsh one good shake, then waited until Marsh looked up and met his gaze. As Marsh tried to pull free, Greg let go, but he didn't give up any ground.

"You know," Greg said, voice gritty and harsh. "Ronnie asked me where you were today, before the session started. And I looked at him like he was crazy."

It took Marsh a second to catch up, because that was a wicked curveball as changes in topics went. But he caught up fast enough.

Right. Greg hadn't invited Marsh to his symposium, because Marsh didn't belong there. Of course Greg would be confused when he showed up. He closed his eyes.

"Marsh." Greg's voice was quieter now, and his fingertips brushed against Marsh's cheek, so light it hurt, so soft Marsh wanted nothing more than to turn into them and soak in that contact while he could. "Marsh, it never occurred to me to ask you because never, in a million years, did I imagine you'd want to be there."

"Of course I wanted to. You were there."

But Greg kept on going, vehement and intense. "Not because you weren't smart enough, or any of the, frankly, *bullshit* excuses you just spewed. I didn't even think to invite you, because...because it was boring. *I'm* boring." Greg's voice was just aching, something Marsh couldn't name buried there in those words. "The talk I was giving was nerdy and geeky, and why would you— You're cool and you're popular and you're on the fucking baseball team. People throw themselves at you. Why would you want to come listen to some *nerd* ramble on about engineering?"

"Because—" Marsh had to jerk his mouth shut, because those weren't safe words that wanted to come out of his mouth. They were too big, though, growing to fill his lungs, and he stared at Greg's lips. He stared and he wanted, and he couldn't keep it in. Quavering, barely more than a whisper, he confessed, "Because I love you."

Absolute silence, and Marsh was dangling, but then Greg threw his arms around Marsh's neck and reeled him in. He jammed his face against Marsh's, breath hot against his neck.

Greg spoke right into his ear, fierce and too loud, "And that's why I never even thought to imagine you were anything less than brilliant, and cool and amazing." He cut off, the bobbing of his throat a pressure against Marsh's own. He scrambled back, holding Marsh's head in his hands, and yes. That was the expression Marsh coveted and treasured and hoarded for his own. That openness and easiness, like Greg was his. Greg's mouth looked like it was set to crack wide open as he said, "Because I love you."

There wasn't enough air in the room.

The words *I love you* echoed in Marsh's brain, and all at once, everything felt like it snapped into place. Marsh couldn't get hold of Greg fast enough, searching for purchase with hands that needed skin, and he needed the taste of Greg's mouth like nothing else. When he finally got him close enough to kiss, it was a clashing thing, teeth hitting, and then Greg tipped his head, and Marsh parted his lips, and it was perfect. Too perfect. He pressed forward with his tongue and got Greg's shirt untucked so he could place hot palms to bare skin and dig his fingers in.

But Greg was tearing away, still grasping Marsh's face between his hands. "And if you ever, *ever* say anything that mean and untrue about the guy I love to me again, I'll..."

"What?" Marsh croaked. He couldn't stop smiling.

Greg's eyes went even softer. "Not like I can hit you now. Guess I'll have to kiss you until you believe me."

The bubble of feeling inside Marsh's chest felt ready to explode, because this was too much. This was everything he'd wanted but would never have expected. "I don't know." He sniffed, the corner of his lips twitching. "Might take a lot of kissing."

"I'm a very patient man."

And he was. He'd shown that plenty of times, and he showed it now, tumbling them into a kiss that was achingly slow. Deep and powerful, and so wet and raw Marsh felt it in his toes.

"We're not done talking about this," Greg said against his lips, but his fingers were working at the buttons of Marsh's shirt.

"Uh-huh, but we're going to talk about it after we get you inside me, right?"

Marsh had never said "I love you" to another person and meant it, not like this. He was pretty sure that was supposed to lead to sex. He hadn't gotten Greg naked in days. Fuck, he hoped that led to sex.

But Greg stiffened, hand stilling, and Marsh could cry.

"Actually," Greg said, and Marsh braced himself, ready to pull away. Then Greg lifted his gaze and met Marsh's eyes. "I was thinking." The shadow of his Adam's apple shifted as his throat bobbed. He took Marsh's hand in his, lifted it from his shoulder and set it firmly on his ass, fingers dangerously close to the crease. "If you want. I'd like."

Fuck. Oh, fuck, no way.

Marsh had no problem bottoming—he wasn't that guy or anything. He liked it. Loved it, even, when it was Greg on top. But he'd been thinking about getting up inside Greg for so long now, feeling that tightness all around him, being able to rear back and look Greg in the eyes as he pushed into him.

"Yeah?" Marsh asked, throat dry. He dared to edge his hand lower, fingertips drifting over Greg's hole through his pants.

Greg sucked in a breath and brushed his lips against Marsh's, eyes fluttering closed. When they opened again they were dark and hot.

"Yeah," he breathed. "Will you?" Another dry swallow before he seemed to find his nerve. "Will you fuck me?"

Chapter Twenty-One

Greg's skin felt hypersensitive, every inch of him aware and waiting. He was starved for oxygen and starved for touch and *starving* for a chance to let go.

Time and time again—not just tonight, not even just these past couple of days but the whole time they'd been doing this, Marsh had been putting himself out there. He'd made himself vulnerable. He'd asked for what he wanted and given so much more, and Greg had been holding everything back, too terrified to leave himself open like that.

He'd been so caught up in looking confident and powerful, because he'd felt anything but. Meanwhile, he'd left Marsh floundering, as uncertain as Greg had been.

He'd been such a fool.

The seconds passed, one after another as he knelt between Marsh's legs, finally asking for what he'd wanted all along. To let go and let someone else take him and possess him. To be vulnerable. Marsh stared at him, eyes wide with lust, grip barely on the right side of too tight. And Greg just blinked in return, scarcely breathing, waiting.

When Marsh's answer came it was a bitten-off groan, and for a moment Greg floundered, but then Marsh was reeling him in, lifting him and turning him, pushing him down until he was on his back on the bed. Marsh climbed over him, and yes. Yes, this was what he'd wanted, what he'd *needed*. How could he have pretended anything else? How could he have not let Marsh see the desperate parts, the ones just aching to be torn apart and pushed open and used?

All the air left Greg's body, and his bones turned to water as he spread his legs for it, pulling Marsh down into the cradle of his thighs. Marsh came willingly enough, mouth bruising against Greg's. He tugged at Greg's tie, and maybe one day he'd wrap the strip of fabric around Greg's wrists, tie him to his bedpost and take what he wanted. Someday. For now, the tie hit the floor, and Marsh tore at buttons even as Greg yanked Marsh's shirt from his waistband and wrestled with his belt. Greg paused just long enough to let Marsh push his dress shirt off his shoulders and shove his undershirt off. Sitting up straight, Marsh pulled at his own shirt while Greg got his pants open.

Then when Marsh dove at Greg it was all skin on skin and the brush of Marsh's chest against his nipples, coarse hair dragging, and it felt too good. Greg arched into it, and Marsh ground his hips down. Electricity sizzled at the press of Marsh's erection against his. Groaning, searching for Marsh's mouth, Greg pulled hard, digging his nails in to the meat of Marsh's back.

Marsh grabbed his wrists in a lunge, pinning them against his pillow to either side of his head, and oh God. "Yeah," Greg said, half groan and half breath and all of it melting.

Marsh bent to bite down hard on the side of Greg's throat, and Greg swallowed a scream. Breathing hot against Greg's ear, Marsh asked, "You know how long I've wanted you like this?"

"As long as I've wanted you to do it?" Greg asked, panting.

Swallowing a string of curses, Marsh attacked Greg's mouth again, nipping and sucking, and his tongue fucked forward the way Greg wanted him to with his cock. He struggled against Marsh's grip, swelling harder when he refused to let go.

Right up until he turned Greg over, rolling him and tugging at his hips until he was lying with his face buried in the pillows, his ass up in the air, thighs spread like the needy bottom he was, the one he ached to be when he was spinning out of control and wanted to just give in to it. He made a noise that was pure need. Marsh swore again as he fumbled beneath Greg's hips, but somehow or other he pulled Greg's belt free from its buckle. Got Greg's pants and underwear to his knees, and Greg lifted up so Marsh could tug them the rest of the way off.

Greg's cock hung heavy beneath him, dripping and painfully hard, and this was Marsh taking him apart. Marsh who he loved, and who loved him, too, and Greg all but sobbed into the sheets when Marsh stroked a dry fingertip over his hole.

"Please," Greg begged. "Need you—"

And Marsh pushed in, and it hurt and it was perfect, and Greg should have let him do this ages ago. The mattress shifted underneath him, and he heard Marsh digging in the pocket of his bag. Blunt fingers came back slick and cool and smearing around Greg's entrance, and he bit his lip so hard he thought he'd draw blood.

"Yes. That's." Greg was barely coherent as he mumbled, face pressed hard against the bedding. "Should have let you. Fuck, feels so good."

"You love this."

"Yes, yes, God yes."

"You *love* this."

And there wasn't any reply to that but to push back against the fingers that were working him open and swear, "Love *you.*"

Because he couldn't have done this, not if he didn't love Marsh. He spent too much of his life all buttoned up and under control, and it took too much to let anyone close enough to see this side of him.

He couldn't have trusted anyone else with both his body and his heart.

Marsh groaned and pressed his brow to the center of Greg's spine even as he eased another finger inside, thumb ducking down to tease along the stretched-open rim. And it was such a contrast, soft brushes of lips and the fluttering of eyelashes made all the sweeter for the rougher way Marsh worked Greg's ass, and Greg never wanted it to end.

Except that he did, because he wanted even more. Wanted everything. "I'm ready," he slurred, twisting, then clenching his jaw shut as Marsh thrust faster with his fingers. Words and prodding died on his tongue, everything but the painful-perfect pressure disappearing, until all he could manage was, "Please."

And Marsh took mercy. He pulled his fingers loose, and Greg gasped, clenching around an emptiness too slick and hot to bear, throbbing, and the skin of his spine felt cold without Marsh draped over it. He craned his neck just in time to watch Marsh tear the rest of his clothes away, and then Marsh was rolling on the condom and drizzling lube over the latex. Greg forced his shaking arms to hold him up and made motions at turning over. "Can I? Want to see you..."

"Yeah." Marsh put a wet hand to Greg's hip and helped him turn.

Settled on his back, Greg spread his legs and keened at the way Marsh loomed over him, at the brush of his hot length against his inner thigh. He scrabbled at Marsh's waist, trying to tug him closer, but instead of pushing in, Marsh hovered there on all fours, looking at Greg.

Suddenly, it wasn't just the sex. The needy ache inside and the heat prickling his skin faded away, taking second seat to the way Marsh was looking at him. Greg was stripped bare, more naked than he had ever been before, and it was so much more than sex. It was exactly what Greg had wanted and been too afraid to ask for.

"Greg." Marsh's pupils were blown, his voice husky, and he shifted to touch Greg's face. He leaned down, and then it was just the warmth and the taste of his mouth, the enormity of his kiss. It spoke things that were too big for words, even the ones they'd shared so far tonight.

When Marsh pulled away, Greg was thrumming, blood rushing, and he felt like his every cell was aglow. Like he was light and reeling. He reached for Marsh and urged him even closer, wrapping his legs around his hips. Their cocks slid against each other, and their mouths met, and Marsh was stuttered back. The latex skidded against Greg's abdomen and along the crease between his torso and his thigh. When the tip nudged against his hole, Greg gripped Marsh by the scruff and held on tight.

Marsh snuck a hand between them, positioning himself before pressing forward.

The first breaching was a shock, even after all of Marsh's prep. But Greg made himself be easy, made his body remember that he wanted it. He opened for the intrusion and let Marsh in, breathing through the sting of pain before Marsh was retreating, only to push back in, deeper and deeper until he was all the way inside. They breathed out as one, and Greg was swimming in it. In the pleasure and the relief. He grinned, sloppy and soft, and ran a hand through Marsh's hair. Marsh caught it, kissing the palm and closing his eyes. He took a gentle thrust, and Greg arched into it.

For all the intensity of being filled this way, the pain was gone, leaving only the stretch and the magnitude and the surrender. Greg entwined their fingers, holding on for just a moment.

Then they were moving. Marsh took him slowly at first, long strokes that had Greg bordering on the edge of madness, enough and not even close. Greg grabbed Marsh's hip, and everything sped up. When Marsh angled his hips just right, Greg threw his head to the side. Electricity sizzled up his spine, and his cock, untouched between them, hurt with the pressure and the need to come. "Touch me," he begged on a gasp, but Marsh shook his head and thrust harder.

And Greg could take himself in hand, could work to relieve this unrelenting ache, only he didn't want to. He let Marsh move how he wanted, pressing forward into his thrusts and making breathy little noises every time Marsh hit the place inside of him that set his nerves alight. He felt like he was babbling, an incoherent mess.

Until somehow he missed it, the sudden change in rhythm, the flexing of the muscles in Marsh's side. Greg's breath left him in a whoosh as they flipped, the mattress disappearing from underneath him. He barely had time to even start to ask, "What?" before Marsh landed on his back, and Greg cried out against the sharpness of being on top. Of gravity taking him that last inch, of Marsh being so deep inside him, there wasn't room for anything else. Not for reservations and not for fear.

Greg squeezed his eyes shut, because it felt so good. So full.

"That's it," Marsh murmured. His clean hand came up and cupped Greg's face, and he swiped his thumb over Greg's bottom lip.

Greg sucked, scraping teeth over the pad and laving his tongue across the nail.

Marsh groaned. "That's right." He pushed up with his hips and sent another jolt of electricity through the secret places in Greg's body, and Greg lifted only to set right back down, driving Marsh even farther into him. "That's it. Take what you need."

Greg shook his head, pleasure and protest all at once, because that's what he'd been doing all along. Taking what he needed, and only what he needed. Not what he wanted. Not giving Marsh what *he* wanted.

"Wanna give it to you," he breathed against Marsh's lips. He kissed him in soft brushes as he started to move. Watched the way Marsh's jaw flexed, the rush of desire in his eyes. And when he moved faster—yes, like that—Marsh's breathing sped. His hand clamped harder on Greg's hip. "Wanna watch you come," Greg said. He wanted to watch that over and over again, for as long as Marsh would let him.

For forever.

Marsh looked pained with the force of his restraint. “Waiting for you—”

Shaking his head more fiercely, Greg fucked himself down harder and faster, and stared as the pressure showed on Marsh’s face. The edge of climax was a hot ball inside Greg’s chest, every stroke against his gland pushing it higher. His thighs burned but he rode Marsh with every bit of the frenzy he felt in his heart.

Finally, Marsh clamped his eyes shut, and he jerked, hands seizing, and he yanked Greg down. Greg met his mouth in a kiss that was all tongue and lip, no finesse. He groaned, letting the need sweep him under. As Marsh pulsed inside him, Greg pushed himself to the edge.

And it was as easy as falling, to let himself go. To come untouched with Marsh so deep inside him.

As easy as falling in love.

Because with Marsh, Greg had never stood a chance of holding his ground.

It was later, much later, after they’d cleaned up and pulled their underwear on and climbed back into Marsh’s bed. Greg lay with Marsh’s chest pressed to his spine, their hands entwined. Marsh beat out a gentle rhythm of taps against Greg’s heart.

When Marsh spoke, his voice was a rush of air beside Greg’s ear, lips brushing the shell. His hand stilled. “You wouldn’t let me. Before.”

And it wasn’t any mystery what he was talking about. Greg shivered just thinking about it—about what he’d let himself have when he’d given in and gotten over himself and asked Marsh to press inside. Squeezing Marsh’s fingers, he said, “Wasn’t ready.”

"But." Marsh stilled. "You're...ready? Now?"

Greg's reply felt like it would choke him, because he was. Ready for sex, ready to feel all these things he felt for Marsh.

Ready to not be alone.

He kissed Marsh's knuckles and folded himself deeper against his body. "Yeah. I am."

Chapter Twenty-Two

Marsh drifted into consciousness slowly, rolling over and pressing his face into his pillow. He slid his hand forward only to find the sheets cold, and frowned.

He blinked his eyes open and levered himself up so he could look around. Sure enough, he was alone. Again. But this time, before he could get worried or sad about that, he checked beside his bed. He grabbed the folded piece of notebook paper sitting on top of his phone and took it with him as he shifted to lie on his back, frown easing into a grin.

Taking my parents to breakfast/the airport. Back before noon.

He glanced at the clock and saw it was not quite ten. Late, but not *too* late, though he'd probably missed Greg by an hour or two. That was going to take some getting used to, dating a morning person. His smile got even wider.

He was dating Greg. They were together, a couple. Greg loved him, and he loved Greg, and the world looked rosier than it had in a long, long while.

Setting the note aside, he reached for his phone. One message from Yulia, saying simply, *So?*

So I've got a boyfriend, he typed, and apparently he was a teenage girl now, but whatever.

A reply came seconds later. *Tell me something I didn't know.*

He considered answering with, *My boyfriend likes taking it up the ass*, but decided that might be too far over the line, even for her. Didn't stop him from going hot at just the thought, though, because damn. Sure, the sex had been good before, great even, but when they both let go—when Greg *really* let go...it was incredible. The best he'd ever had.

Another message came in before he could figure out how to say that in a way that wasn't too TMI. *You're happy, though? Really?*

Yeah, he replied. *Very.*

With that, he blanked the screen and set the phone down, stretching and yawning. Shoving the covers off, he stood, then rummaged around in the pile of discarded clothes from the night before until he came up with a shirt. He tugged it on and wandered blearily out into the house.

Muted voices were spilling out from the living room. Marsh ducked his head in and waved when he saw Ronnie sprawled out on the couch with a bowl of cereal in hand, papers strewn out around him, all covered in symbols and graphs. SpongeBob SquarePants was having some kind of manic freakout on the television, and Marsh raised an eyebrow.

"Classy, man," he said.

Ronnie took one quick glance up before smirking and looking down. "Almost as classy as stumbling out of bed wearing your boyfriend's shirt?"

Shit. Marsh looked down, and yup, this was Greg's. Oops. Oh, well, everyone knew, and anyone who didn't would find out soon enough. Still not quite awake enough to form a coherent argument, and too happy to bother defending himself, he flipped Ronnie off and turned to head into the kitchen. Somebody had already made coffee, thank God, so he poured a cup and doctored it up. Grabbing it and a protein bar, he shuffled to his room and sank down to sit on the edge of his bed.

For a few minutes, he just sat there, fueling up and staring at the wall. Finals were coming up soon, and he had a lot to do, but really all he wanted was for Greg to get home so he could drag him back to bed. He glanced toward his backpack and the pages spilling out of it. There was that big poli sci paper he had to write, and he should really get back to the gym and make up for the sessions he'd missed while Greg was having his nervous breakdown.

And there was that slip of yellow. The folded corner of an unpaid tuition bill.

Marsh gulped down the rest of his coffee, but when he looked again, the bill hadn't gone anywhere. In over a month of ignoring it, it had stayed right there.

Past results were not a predictor future outcomes, his ass.

Setting his mug down and pitching the wrapper for his breakfast into the trash, he lurched to his feet, snagging the bill as he went. He scanned it over for what had to be the hundredth time. The number at the bottom was staggering, and it was only the portion not covered by his scholarship. He rolled the paper up and tapped the edge of it against his chin.

There was still a part of him that said he should just let it be. He should spend the rest of his day hunting for a job, because who the hell cared if he passed his classes now?

Except...*Marsh* cared. He cared a whole fucking lot, and the easy defeat he'd been letting hitch a ride on his shoulders this whole semester was suddenly an unbearable weight. Sure, he wasn't the smartest guy, but he worked his ass off. He did his best, and he was so close.

And Greg. Greg cared, too, more than Marsh had ever dared to let himself believe.

It hadn't been the plan to spill his guts to Greg the way he had. The minute he'd started talking, though, it had all come pouring out, and it had been terrifying and freeing, speaking aloud things he'd put so much effort into keeping silent. He hadn't really expected Greg to agree with him when he'd said it was pointless to even try. But somewhere deep inside he'd been waiting for precisely that, and having Greg beside him, calling bullshit and telling him he was worth more than that...

Sure, he'd heard it from Yulia enough times before, but they'd been friends for so long now. She *had* to tell him he wasn't worthless. Greg wasn't under any such compulsion.

But Greg believed in him. Greg *loved* him. Marsh didn't know if he'd ever deserve it, but fuck if it wasn't about time to at least try.

Before he could stop himself, he crossed the room and grabbed his phone. As he brought the screen to life, the time flashed at him. Ten thirty on a Saturday morning...Marsh's dad wouldn't be at work, but odds were even that he'd be off doing something out of the apartment. Either way, Marsh couldn't put this off a minute longer.

He pulled up his parents' number and hit send, then grasped the front of his shirt and tugged it away from his throat.

This was stupid. This was a disaster—*Marsh* was a disaster, and they were just going to tell him exactly what he already knew.

But before he could scramble to hang up, the ringing cut off and his mother's voice said, "Hello?"

The sound of her cracked something inside of him. He tried to gather enough moisture in his mouth to speak, and for a moment the silence was deafening. Then, finally, he croaked out, "Mom?"

"Marshall?"

His heart fell at the way she lowered her voice. "Yeah, it's me. Sorry it's been so long, but..." *But I didn't know if you'd want to hear from me. But it's not like you called either.*

"Oh, that's fine. I know how busy you get."

"Yeah. Um. Schoolwork and practices and stuff."

"Of course."

Part of him wanted to ask her how she'd been and what had been going on at home, but he'd called for a reason. He had to get this out. "Mom." His fingers caught as he unfurled the bill, and he stumbled over his words. "I got a bill from the university. It's, uh, overdue."

There was a long pause. "Your father never talked to you?"

Fuck. "Er, no."

"Well, money's real tight right now, sweetheart."

"Right."

"And he was concerned that you weren't really serious about your, well, your future."

"My future."

"Yes. What you're going to do after college."

"I told you, back over the summer, I'm working on it."

"He's just—"

"Mom." He clenched his hand into a fist and squeezed his eyes shut. "*Mom.*" When she didn't say anything, he took a deep breath and opened his eyes to look at the wall in front of him. "Can we please cut the bullshit?"

"Language, Marshall."

"I call it like I see it." He knocked the knuckles of his fist against his brow. "And apparently Dad does too, right? I heard what he called me. That night."

She hesitated for long enough that he thought she might have hung up on him, but then her voice was back, quieter than ever. "We pray for you, sweetheart. Every night."

Oh, *wow.* They'd scarcely gone to church growing up, and she was pulling this card now? "So that's how it is, is it?"

"I wish things were different."

"You wish *I* was different."

"That's not what I said—"

"I heard you. Loud and clear." He fought to keep his voice level.

"We're not kicking you out or disowning you or anything."

No, they were just cutting him off, in his last damn semester. "Sure." He cleared his throat against the tightness there. "Well, have a nice life, Mom."

"Do you want to talk to your father? Or…?"

"Nah. I think I'll follow his shining example."

"Marshall. I know you're upset right now, but this is for the best."

The sick part was, his father had probably actually convinced her of that. "Whatever helps you sleep better at night."

"Don't be a stranger, okay?"

"I don't know." He shook his head, squeezing his hand into a fist until his knuckles turned white. "I think I already am." Maybe he had been for a very, very long time. "Bye, Ma."

"Goodbye, Marshall."

He hung up the phone before the bubble in the back of his throat could force its way through, before his voice could break. He pointedly did not throw his phone at the wall. It wasn't like he was going to be able to afford a replacement, possibly ever. The instant he set it down, though, his hand started shaking, and he curled his arm across his chest, digging his fingers into his shoulder to try to get the tremor to pass, or to hide it, at least from himself.

Amazing how, even when you expected absolutely nothing, you could still manage to end up disappointed.

Only, it wasn't just disappointment. It wasn't even just the bitter ache in his gut—the inadequacy. He'd fucked up plenty of things in his life, but this wasn't one of them. After all the things his daddy had stripped him down for, this wasn't even his fault.

He wasn't resigned. He was fucking angry.

And he really wanted a hug right now.

His eyes felt watery and hot, and he dug the heels of his hands into them hard before huffing out a sigh and lifting his head. And he just about choked to see Greg standing there, peering in through the gap of his door. "What the—"

Greg pushed the door a little wider. He had the good manners to look apologetic, ducking his head and scratching at the back of his neck. "I didn't mean to listen in." Glancing up, he made a little wincing face. "Was kind of hard not to, though."

"Don't care."

"About me listening, or about..."

Marsh shook his head. "Any of it. All of it. Just—" He cut himself off and launched himself forward a couple of feet. Maybe things between them were still new, but Greg was a good guy. Even if he was having any regrets, he'd heard what just went down. He wouldn't deny Marsh this.

Sure enough, Greg opened his arms the instant Marsh moved, and Marsh fell into them. Greg pulled Marsh in close, and it was perfect. A balm. The kind of thing that made all that terrifying laying-yourself-out and making-yourself-vulnerable stuff worth it. Because once someone saw you like that and decided they wanted you anyway, it opened the way for this. For hugs that felt like they could solve anything.

Greg stroked a hand up and down Marsh's spine, and Marsh shivered. Even if it wouldn't fix a thing, Marsh would stay here happily. Because really, it was at least worth a try.

"You wanna talk about it?" Greg asked after a long couple of minutes.

Marsh shrugged but didn't pull away. "Not much to tell. It's basically what I thought it was, but even worse."

Greg's hand stuttered at the nape of Marsh's neck. "Worse?"

"She was rationalizing, when really it's just that my dad's a bigot who never thought I was worth his time in the first place."

"That's not true."

Snorting, Marsh buried his face further against Greg's shoulder. "Right. Easy for you to say. Your parents like you."

"And I'm sure yours do, too. They'll come around eventually."

"Not likely. And definitely not in time."

Greg squeezed him tighter. "Do you know what you're going to do?"

Marsh shook his head, eyes clenched shut. "No clue."

But there were options. A lot of them. He'd been telling himself he didn't have any choice for a long time now, but he'd been wrong. He'd been wrong about a lot of things he'd thought he couldn't have.

He pressed his face against warm, nice-smelling skin and breathed in deep. "But it's about time I make up my mind."

Chapter Twenty-Three

It would have been funny, if it hadn't been so close to breaking Greg's heart. Back in the beginning, he'd had so many reasons in his head for why this thing between him and Marsh could never work out. Marsh was exciting. He was cool and self-possessed, and Greg was anything but.

He'd always assumed that when the school year was over, Marsh would be going places, while Greg would still be here, plugging away at a boring degree in a boring field, working steadily toward a stable career that made people yawn just hearing about it.

Greg's heart gave a little squeeze, and he rubbed a hand up and down Marsh's spine. Because here they were, standing in Marsh's bedroom, together, and the whole damn time, Marsh had been sitting on this secret—this fear that he was the one not going anywhere.

Turning his neck to press a kiss to Marsh's hair, Greg asked, "Would it help to talk about it?"

Marsh sighed and pulled away. "Maybe?" He crossed the couple of feet to flop on his bed, then grabbed a pillow and dropped it on top of his head.

And Greg could be patient. Taking care not to crowd Marsh, he settled on the edge of the mattress beside him. For a minute, he just watched the steady rise and fall of Marsh's ribcage as he breathed.

Greg pushed off to sit up straighter, flexing his fingers as he went back and forth in his mind. Reach out or don't reach out? Finally, he brushed his hand against Marsh's knee and asked, "What do you *want*?"

"Hmm?" Marsh's grunt was muffled from behind the pillow. Greg wanted to snatch it away so he could look Marsh in the eye, but if Marsh wanted to hide right now...well, he was exposed in lots of other ways.

"Don't think. Just answer. If you could do anything with yourself, with your life, where would you be?"

Marsh shifted the pillow a little higher so it didn't block his mouth. "Depends? You know any Major League scouts in need of a new shortstop?"

Greg swatted at his knee. "If I did, you think I'd be here slogging along at grad-student wages?"

At long last, Marsh threw the pillow away entirely. He shifted, rising up onto his elbows, and gazed at Greg with a look of confusion Greg couldn't quite place. "Um. Yeah. Of course you would."

"Hey." Greg put a hand to his own chest in mock offense. "I had a two hundred batting average in Little League, you know."

Sitting up, Marsh shook his head. "No. That's not what I meant. Not that that's not impressive." The tilt of his eyebrows said he was underplaying just how *not* impressive that really was. "But it doesn't matter. You would. Still be here, I mean."

"I don't know. I wouldn't mind a million-dollar contract for few seasons of sitting on a bench."

"You would, though," Marsh insisted, his forehead furrowing, and there was a fervency to his expression. An earnestness. Then the light in his eyes faded, his features falling. "You don't get it, do you?"

What?

The confusion must have been written all over Greg's face, because Marsh chuckled, lifting his shoulders and then setting them down. "You're just—you're so lucky." Now that was really confusing. But before Greg could say anything, Marsh continued, "You know what you want to do, and you're *good* at it. All that science stuff. I mean, I saw you yesterday, talking about what you do. It was amazing. I just." He twisted his neck, looking off to the side. "I wish I could do that."

"Marsh. I sit in a lab all day, and then I come home and look at graphs on my computer. I don't have a life. I'm not—" *Cool.*

"Shut up." Marsh waved his hand, all dismissal, but his tone was laughing, not biting. He looked to Greg again, and his eyes were so damn deep. "You do things almost no one else in the world can even begin to understand, and you're incredible at it, and you love it. Don't you get how lucky that is?"

And for just one second, one glorious, lingering moment, Greg did.

Greg softened his stance and his voice and his smile. He reached out, taking Marsh's hand in his own. "You're right. I am lucky." Lucky to be sitting here, next to the guy he loved, the one he'd thought was so far out of his league, but who wasn't. Not really. The one who was just a guy, twenty-something and scared, and yeah. Greg knew what that felt like. Quietly, he asked, simply, "What do you love?"

"Besides you?"

Was Greg ever going to get tired of hearing that? He lifted Marsh's hand to his lips and kissed his knuckles. "Besides me."

"Baseball."

"Okay."

"I..." Marsh hesitated. "I like history."

"Mhmm."

"And..." Another long breath. "I don't know."

"Yeah, you do."

Greg *knew* Marsh did, because the instant Greg asked, Marsh turned his head, looking to the corner of his closet. Toward the box where he kept those letters from the kids he'd taught over the summer. But he didn't say anything.

When Greg couldn't take it anymore, he put a hand to the side of Marsh's face, nudging gently until Marsh twisted to look at him. "You know what I think?" Greg asked.

"No. But I'd really, really like to."

"I think you're lucky. And amazing. And if you just trusted in that enough, you could do anything you wanted to."

But Marsh was already shaking his head, fighting the loose grip Greg had on his jaw. "I'm not. I'm—"

"You love kids, and you love history, and you love baseball. Forget all that bullshit from yesterday about going and getting a factory job." Because it was obvious, wasn't it?

"I don't know..."

"You'd be an awesome teacher, Marsh."

"No," Marsh said, pulling farther away, but Greg grabbed his wrist, keeping him close.

"You would. And I bet you'd love it, too."

And Greg's chest *hurt*, it ached to see the way Marsh's gaze burned. To see the doubt there. "I'm not smart enough."

"You keep saying that." Greg couldn't keep the frustration from his voice now. "And I don't know why."

"Try looking at my transcript. It's not that hard to figure out."

"Having a hard time with your classes when you're at one of the best colleges in the country is nothing to be ashamed of. You'll still walk out of here with the same degree as anybody else."

"I'm only here because of baseball."

"You're here because you deserve to be. And sure, maybe you had a leg up because you're good at sports, but you made it anyway. You are making it. You can do this."

Marsh's eyes were shuttered, his whole posture closed in, and he was picking at his fingernails. "I'd—It'd be an extra semester. I looked into it once before. I'd have to cram in another course in the spring, and then stay another term to do student teaching."

"So stay another term. You were the one who was so worried about what you'd be qualified for once you got out of here with this degree. If you know there's something you'd like, and you're just one semester from being able to do it, why wouldn't you?"

Marsh's expression was still twisted with hesitance and denial, though, and he was right. Greg *didn't* get it. He couldn't begin to imagine what this was like, because, yeah, he had been lucky. He'd known what he wanted to be since he was a kid, so there'd never been this doubt. He'd decided what he was going to be, and he'd gone for it.

He didn't know why Marsh wouldn't want to do the same. Not when he was so good, and when his future held so much promise, if he'd just stick with it and see this thing through.

"It's so much money," Marsh said.

"It is." There wasn't any denying that. "But if you only end up with one year's worth of student loans, you're still doing better than I did."

That made Marsh's head snap up. "You have student loans?"

"Four years' worth of them. I got scholarships to cover a lot of it, but you met my folks. You know where I come from. We couldn't afford tuition."

Marsh's gaze searched Greg's with a wildness, but for the first time, there was something hopeful there, too. "How'd you know? That it would be worth it?"

"I didn't." Still didn't, honestly, because he would be paying those loans back for years once he was out of grad school. "But I knew what I wanted. So I took the risk."

His parents had always taught him to shoot for the stars and never to settle. He'd taken those lessons to heart. Most of the time.

He still couldn't believe he'd settled for so little from Marsh for so long, when he could have had it all. When he could have had *this*.

A warm, sly smile cracked Greg's lips, and he put a hand on Marsh's shoulder. "At least think about it?"

"Yeah. I will. Coach has been keeping them off my back while I figure out what to do, but the financial-aid people have been bugging me to set up an appointment for next week. I figured it was going to end up being when I let them know I wasn't coming back next semester, but..."

Hope leapt faintly in Greg's throat. "But it could be for something else."

"Yeah. It could be." Marsh snapped his mouth closed, but there were words still hanging on his lips. Something that needed to be said. He glanced up, eyes open and wide, a vulnerability ringing the edges that made Greg's heart feel like it was being stretched right out of his chest.

"Marsh?" he asked.

"Do you think I can do it? Seriously?"

And Greg couldn't help himself. He leaned in and closed his eyes and pressed a hard, closed-mouth kiss to those perfect lips. Shifting his palm to press against the warm expanse of skin over Marsh's pulse, Greg said, as earnest as he could make himself. "If you want to...I think you can do *anything.*"

"Well, Mr. Sulkowski, I'm so glad we finally managed to get a hold of you."

"Yeah." Marsh tugged at the collar of his shirt. Greg had told him to wear a tie, that when you were dealing with people about money you should always wear a tie, but he couldn't bring himself to do it. There'd be time enough for that, someday, but for now Marsh was going into this dressed as nothing but himself. He forced the one corner of his mouth to twitch up, affecting the kind of smile that usually got people to do what he wanted them to. "Thanks for being so patient with me."

The woman across the desk from him smirked and opened up a file full of pink notices—pieces of paper that matched the pile he'd been amassing quite the collection of himself. "Coach Hartman may have put in a good word or three for you." She pushed the unpaid bills aside, riffling through to produce two stacks of paper. She lay them out in front of him, rotating them so he was looking at them right-side-up.

The words stared back at him. The two paths from which he had to choose. A stack of loans that would follow him for years, or a statement of intention to withdraw. He sucked in a deep breath as he stared them down.

"So," she said. "Have you decided how you'd like to proceed?"

Greg's words echoed in his mind.

What do you *want*?

Marsh's dad had told him what he thought he was good for, his coaches what he was good at, and his teachers, more often than not, what he wasn't. But it had been a long, long time since someone had asked him what he wanted.

Before Greg had shown up, he hadn't really let himself want much of anything. Even then, he'd scarcely dared to believe that he could have it.

Squaring his shoulders, Marsh fixed the woman with a steady gaze. "I believe I have."

Her fingers twitched against the pieces of paper. "Well?"

For the second time in a handful of days, he stood on the precipice between one vision of his future and the next. And he stepped forward, shifting his weight out onto nothing but faith.

"Hey, Greg."

Greg started at the sound of knocking at his door, his heart racing right up until he recognized Ronnie's voice and spotted his head peeking around the corner.

"Hey." He adjusted his glasses and absently hit save on his computer, glancing at the time as he did so. It was getting late. Marsh should be back any minute now.

Fidgeting, he cracked his knuckles and swiveled in his chair toward the door. He'd been twitchy as hell all afternoon, waiting. He didn't know how long Marsh's appointment was going to take, but this seemed to be dragging on forever.

But that was okay. It was a good sign, really. Withdrawal forms probably took less time to fill out than promissory notes. Greg drummed his fingers against his knee. Sure, Marsh had seemed to be leaning the right way whenever they'd touched on the subject over the past few days, but doubt had lingered in his eyes, like he still didn't know if he could do it, or if he was worth it.

Greg wanted to *shake* him.

Ronnie stepped a little farther into the room, crossing his arms over his chest and leaning his shoulder against the wall. He shifted his gaze pointedly between Greg's twitchy fingers and his face.

Greg forced his hand to still and breathed out a long, deep sigh. "What's up?"

"Not much." Ronnie angled his head toward the hall. "Meeting up with some of the other guys for a burger. Maybe some drinks after. You in?"

"Nah." He gestured toward his computer instinctively, preparing to make an excuse about work, but then he stopped himself. That wasn't what this was really about—not this time. "I'm waiting for Marsh to get home," he admitted.

Ronnie *tutt*ed at him, but it wasn't a serious rebuke. "First you ditch us for your data, now for your boyfriend. You ever gonna get your priorities straight?"

"I don't know." He couldn't help the grin that stole across his face. "Think they're pretty well sorted as it is." Much better than they had been a couple of weeks ago, in any case.

"Yeah, yeah, whatever. Give me a call if you change your mind."

"Will do."

With that, Ronnie pushed off, giving Greg a decidedly non-regulation salute and then disappearing down the hall. Greg let his shoulders slump as he turned toward his desk.

All the finagling Marsh had done with Greg's schedule last week had bought him some breathing room. He'd gone back to work at his part-time job, but only in a limited capacity—no more extra shifts. Ronnie had stopped asking him for so much shit, and he'd finally been able to put some quality time in at the lab. If he could just sift through this last set of data, he'd probably even be able to give Chu those results he needed.

He shoved his glasses up his nose, because he was going to concentrate, goddammit. Marsh would be home when he was home, and until that time, Greg still had work to do.

Who was he kidding?

A torturous, painfully unproductive twenty minutes crawled along before the sound of the front door opening and closing rang out, following by a moment's silence and then the pounding of footsteps on the stairs. Greg's heart leapt up into his throat, but he held his ground. This might just be Ronnie remembering something he'd forgotten, or Jason coming home.

Or it could be Marsh, shoving through Greg's door without knocking, looking fit to burst, all his efforts to suppress his smile a miserable failure, and Christ. Greg loved seeing him like this, eyes wild and happy, face flushed, like he'd just run a marathon. Or like he'd just faced down a giant pile of fears and told them in no uncertain terms to fuck off.

Greg just loved *him*.

"You're staying," he said, before Marsh could get out a word, before he could even get three feet into the room. Because the hope was bubbling up inside him to the point of pain.

Marsh would stay. He wouldn't run off into some unknown future where he didn't want Greg following, or into some self-imposed exile because he didn't think he was good enough. Marsh had to stay, because he deserved to.

Because Greg had not had even close to enough.

Marsh's step faltered for half a beat, but then he found his footing again. He crossed the last few feet, not bothering to hide his grin now as he launched himself into Greg's chair, making it wobble alarmingly. Greg caught them, though, getting a hand on the corner of his desk to stop them rolling backward and bracing himself with a foot against the floor.

And then his arms were full of Marsh, Marsh's thighs straddling his hips, and his face was right there, so close and perfect and handsome and his.

"How did you know?" Marsh asked.

"You're smiling." Beaming almost as hard as Greg had to be right now. "If you're smiling, you're staying."

The curve of Marsh's lips only deepened, his eyes melting into an expression so soft it seared right through to Greg's heart. "I'm staying."

"Thank God," Greg managed. The hot press of Marsh's mouth cut him off before he could say any more, chased by the slick glide of his tongue. His brow pressed against Greg's, and Greg felt surrounded—held in a way he never would have imagined, even though Marsh was the one sitting on his lap, Greg technically the one supporting Marsh.

Even though, really, it was hard to tell who was supporting whom, and Greg didn't think he'd ever want it any other way.

Greg pulled back from the kiss, grasping the sides of Marsh's face in his hands. "I'm so proud of you."

"I know you are." Marsh's smile got a little less wide, a little more raw but no less real. He reached up and touched the frame of Greg's glasses and then his cheek. "Made all the difference, you know. Having someone believe in me."

Grinning, Greg kissed him again. "I know exactly what you mean."

With a little shake of his head, Marsh hopped up off Greg's lap, bounding backward a couple of steps. His gaze went to the pile of notebooks and printouts strewn all over Greg's desk. "You busy?"

And Greg could hear the caution there. It was well-placed, really. Greg had a ton to do, but he would *always* have a ton to do, and there were more important things than work. Better ways to spend his time that shouldering the world and going it alone.

Because everything was easier when there was someone to share your burdens with you. And it was a hell of a lot more fun.

Greg stood, straightening his shirt and adjusting himself inside his jeans. He pushed his chair under his desk and turned his monitor off. Waving at all the work covering his desk, he said, "It can wait." He closed the space between himself and Marsh, setting eager hands on Marsh's hips. With their lips just inches apart, Greg intoned, "And even if it couldn't. I hear we have something worth celebrating."

Marsh curled his arms around Greg's neck, pulling him in. "Yeah, we do. A lot of things."

All thoughts of graphs and data left Greg's mind as Marsh pressed their bodies together, kissing him nice and deep and slow.

A handful of weeks ago, his work had been all he needed. All the other things he wanted—they hadn't been meant for someone like him.

But that had been before. Greg opened his mouth to Marsh's kiss and threaded his fingers through his hair. He was still the same man he had always been. Still a nerd and still decidedly uncool. But Marsh loved him anyway.

By opening himself up to it, Greg had gotten so much more than just what he needed. He'd gotten everything he wanted.

And he was never, ever going to let it go.

About the Author

Jeanette Grey started out with degrees in physics and painting, which she dutifully applied to stunted careers in teaching, technical support and advertising. When none of that panned out, she started writing.

In her spare time, Jeanette enjoys making pottery, playing board games and spending time with her husband and her pet frog. She lives, loves and writes in upstate New York. You can find Jeanette online at www.jeanettegrey.com, on Twitter at @jeanettelgrey, or on Facebook. She is also a regular blogger at Bad Girlz Write.

Sometimes good boys do bad things.

Nothing but Smoke

© 2014 *Daisy Harris*

Fire and Rain, Book 3

Michael Larson considers himself one of the good guys. He recycles, eats mostly vegan, and volunteers. But one night, while on a jog through a Seattle park, he encounters a sexy man on a motorcycle he wants to be bad with.

Firefighter Nicky O'Brian barely has time to even think about a sex life. Between his job and caring for his critically ill mother, his only pleasures involve a few racy videos and occasional nighttime forays to find men willing to help him forget his troubles.

It was supposed to be a one-time, anonymous hookup—until fate intervenes and their mutual attraction blossoms into a furtive affair. Michael doesn't date closeted guys, but for the haunted, lonely Nicky he makes an exception.

When Nicky's mother takes a turn for the worse, Michael is forced to make a choice between idealism and compassion. And as Nicky's needs spiral out of control, Michael realizes that a new set of ideals could be exactly what he needs to keep love in his life—for good.

Warning: Contains sex in the trees, sex in parked cars and sex in other uncomfortable places. Tissues are required, because the ending will make you cry—and maybe make you want to call your mom.

Love doesn't come with a syllabus.

Love Lessons

© 2013 Heidi Cullinan

Kelly Davidson has waited what seems like forever to graduate high school and get out of his small-minded, small town. But when he arrives at Hope University, he quickly realizes finding his Prince Charming isn't so easy. Everyone here is already out. In fact, Kelly could be the only virgin on campus.

Worst of all, he's landed the charming, handsome, gay campus Casanova as a roommate, whose bed might as well be equipped with a revolving door.

Walter Lucas doesn't believe in storybook love. Everyone is better off having as much fun as possible with as many people as possible...except his shy, sad little sack of a roommate is seriously screwing up his world view.

As Walter sets out to lure Kelly out of his shell, staying just friends is harder than he anticipated. He discovers love is a crash course in determination. To make the grade, he'll have to finally show up for class...and overcome his own private fear that love was never meant to last.

Warning: This story contains lingering glances, milder than usual sexual content for this author, and a steamy dance-floor kiss. Story has no dairy or egg content, but may contain almonds.

CPSIA information can be obtained at www.ICGtesting.com
Printed in the USA
BVOW08s1814211015

423550BV00002B/64/P

9 781619 226036